CW01431674

Seventy Six Sunsets

By Rose Wood

For my family and friends - the tides that keep me anchored and the waves that lift me higher.

You complete me.

CHAPTER ONE

His chubby finger prods my knee, snapping me awake. "That Shrek 2?" he asks, licking his lips.

I nod awkwardly, making a point of putting my headphones back on. That's the issue with long haul flights. If you're sat next to a weirdo there's no escape, not till the doors open. Or the plane crashes. Luckily I'm on the aisle, so I've managed to angle myself away from the large red faced man sat next to me. He's shovelled down three large packets of Quavers, a cheesy musk lingering about him. If he makes it four I'll go for the emergency exit. Or my wrists with the plastic butter knife. He makes a point to scroll on his little TV, sausage finger picking out Shrek 2, leaving greasy prints on the screen. He's done this with every movie I've watched. Every. Movie. As if watching La La Land and Shrek 2 at the same time as me are his ticket to join the mile high club. I neck the rest of my wine and shut my eyes, praying the sound of Mike Myers and Eddie Murphy bickering will lull me back to sleep. I hear yet another crisp packet pop open next to me and grimace.

The warm air envelops my aching body as I step off the plane, the rich scent of earth and plane fuel a welcome relief from Quaver man. He tried to help me with my bag as I left, cheesy orange fingers grasping for the handle. I've never moved so quickly in my life. It's evening, and the sounds of crickets and traffic floods my ears.

"Bye, thank you!" I nod to the teeny blonde flight attendant who sneaked me an extra Sauvignon Blanc. Despite the three units of liquid courage I've consumed over the last three hours, the butterflies in my tummy haven't subsided. I exhale deeply and gingerly make my way down the rickety plane steps, gripping tightly to the cool metal banister which paints my palm with crimson dust.

Passport control and customs are a blur. I've only ever flown for the odd European city break - there were never this many armed guards. As I exit the airport, wheeling my cumbersome neon purple case behind me (how did past me not realise why it was so cheap?!), I'm greeted by a sea of name placards, their owners' eyes darting from passenger to passenger trying to decipher who's theirs. The longer I search for my name, the quicker they all seem to blur into one. Maybe I shouldn't have had that third drink. Then I see it, a bright yellow sign held up high by little arms, a lifeline. 'Maddie Wilson'. That's me. I make my way to the sign, and lock eyes with the small man holding it. He beams back at me "Ms. Wilson?"

"Maddie, please!" I reach my hand out, and he grips it firmly. I feel my body slump a little as relief washes over me, knowing I'm not alone - at least for now. He has kind, brown eyes, is missing one front tooth, and his hands are scattered with calluses that tickle my clammy palm as he clasps it. "Lovely to meet you...?"

"Ishmael!" he responds quickly. "How was your flight?" he says, taking the purple monstrosity from me and leading me away from the crowd, like a shepherd herding a lost lamb. Ishmael helps me into a minivan, ensuring I don't bang my head on the roof (a habit I seem to have no matter the size of the vehicle), and then carefully loads my bags. "Your first time in Kenya?"

"Yes! I'm here for two weeks." I say, the van whirring to life as he pulls onto the main road, illuminated orange by warm streetlights.

"Ahhh, you'll love it. Are you here in Nairobi the whole time?"

"Uh, no actually. I'm heading to the Maasai Mara tomorrow for most of the trip."

"Oh nice! You're a big animal person then?" I think. I have a bunny - does that count? "Anything petting zoo friendly. The bigger ones scare me a bit!"

Ishmael laughs. "Well, you're a very brave girl then! Going on your own to the land of lions!"

I wince a little. "Are there… lots?"

"Yes, many! A long time ago, some friends and I…"

I purposely zone out from Ishmael's tales of lions and road trips to prevent my anxiety rocketing any further, and focus instead on the glimmering city lights dotted along the streets like constellations. Is this crazy? I've always wanted to travel but - this is an intense first solo trip. When Maria got Covid and asked me to fill in for her on this job I thought it was the opportunity of a lifetime. Now I'm infuriated at how naive I was. What if my photos aren't good enough? I break the equipment? Embarrass myself? Get myself fired? Am eaten by zebras?

Ishmael passes my bag over to the bellboy at the hotel, and waves goodbye as he clambers back into the van. "See you tomorrow, lion girl!"

I force a smile - an attempt to fool myself as well as him. The hotel is nice, modern, sterile. The lift smells like cherry air freshener. I'm grateful the bellboy doesn't make any attempt at conversation, instead we watch the numbers on the lift increase - 1, 2, 3, 4. My room is directly opposite the lift, and the bellboy swipes my key and ushers me in. Like the opposite of the plane, the door whooshes open to a chilled breeze of dry air conditioning that makes my throat tickle as I fumble with my purse for his tip. Flustered, I hand him 500 shillings, still unsure of the exchange rate. He bows his head in appreciation, quickly making his way back downstairs before I have time to work out the maths. That was probably too generous for an elevator ride. I guess I can expense it?

My worries subside as I lay my eyes on the bed, beckoning to me with its crisp, ivory sheets. I force myself into the shower before I dive into them, aware of the musky plane scent that's been following me. The cascading hot water soothes my muscles, and I scrub myself till I'm pink with the small bar of complimentary hotel soap. Cardamom. Not my favourite but better than the mix of airplane Mac n' Cheese and sweat, badly masked with Dove that's been lingering on me.

As I brush my teeth, I can't help but study myself. I used to hate my body, but when I hit 25, I swore I wouldn't waste time with those thoughts anymore. It's just a vessel to help me function, I should be grateful, blah blah blah. Times like these, when I'm nervous, or tired, or in a room full of people I don't know, the bad thoughts get harder to bat away. I try focus on the positives. I love my collarbone. I've grown to love my hips and thighs, my main cause of grief before. I'm proud of my tummy, and the baby abs that have started to grow since I started jogging again. I hated my auburn hair as a child but have noticed since being an adult it seems to award me intelligence points - people assume I'm good with numbers. Ha. I run my hand along my arm, inspecting my skin. Red hair does mean I bake in the sun like a little piglet on a spit roast. I need to remember suncream tomorrow.

I spit out the frothy mint, and watch it swirl down the drain, grateful I'm finally able to collapse into bed. I leave the curtains open, so I fall asleep to the twinkling city lights. Motorbikes splutter. Street vendors sell. People laugh. The soundtrack of Nairobi lulls my eyes shut, and I doze off into a deep dreamless slumber.

Despite Ishmael being a total motor mouth again on our way to the airport, I can't silence the anxiety whirring around my mind about the journey I've yet to travel. I made the mistake of Googling the plane I'm flying on this morning. A seven-seater. I'm bricking it. As the van slows my eyes widen, taking in the scale of the airport - I've seen Starbucks bigger. I'm guessing to match the size of the planes that fly in and out of it. Ishmael swings open the door, a grin plastered on his face. I clamber out, gripping the sides of the van and feel my head scuff against the roof. Ow. Not a good omen.

Ishmael wheels over my purple bag, and I grip the handle tightly, my knuckles white. I have half a mind to beg him to take me back to the hotel, I could say I forgot something, or maybe just be honest with him, tell him that I've made a mistake, that I–

"Safe travels, lion girl. Don't get eaten!" he firmly grips my clammy palm for our final handshake. I grimace, biting my cheek. Too late for escape.

"Thanks for everything!" I hope he didn't think I was rude today. "Sorry I've been so quiet– I've been–"

"Preparing your hunting strategies, no worries," he laughs, a big rumbling one from his belly. I feel mine cramp with nerves.

Check in, security, coffee. I go for an iced Americano since they've run out of oat milk. Will they have any at the camp? Maybe I should've brought some. I'm here early - I wasn't expecting it to be so small. I don't really know what to do with myself. To absolve myself from time wasted, I fish my laptop out my satchel and decide to look over the emails from Maria. I've been her PA for two years and am still to this day surprised I have a job I enjoy. Maria is a photographer, who made a name for herself back in the noughties with a coffee table book of the world's most beautiful hotels. Now any hotel worth anything wants her to revamp their brand with her artistic vision. I like her style, though my preference is portraiture. I love capturing moving, living faces. The wrinkles and moles and scars that map someone's life story. Perfect imperfections. I still shoot when I can, and actually got paid a couple months ago to photograph some up and coming LA DJ. Granted, he was about 15 and had parents who threw money at his numerous ventures rather than have to listen to him talk about them, but hey, a job's a job. I find the emails about our Kenya client, and skim over them for the hundredth time. New owner just renovated a safari camp he inherited. Needs to rebrand website. Wants to tap into wealthy Nairobi millennials as opposed to old rich white Kenyans. Should be simple enough. They want photos of the camp, the different experiences and safaris they offer, and their work giving back to the community. I scoff, knowing all too well fancy hotels "donate" either to claim tax back on charity work or improve their reputation. If they're lucky, both.

"Flight 187 to Maasai Mara, please go to gate." Crap.

I squeeze my eyes shut the whole of take-off. There are five other people on the plane. A Kenyan family, mother, father, son. The child looks out the window the whole time, every bump and dip making him giggle. Great. An eight-year-old is braver than me. The other pair are an older white couple decked out in khaki, binoculars and cameras at the ready. I'm guessing this is the market we're trying to avoid. Once the initial fear subsides, I force myself to look out the window, down, down to the savannah below. Its expanse is mind boggling. Beige terrain as far as you can see, dotted with acacia trees and boulders.

"Zebras!" The child exclaims. I lean further, and to my surprise spy little black and white blobs below.

"Please don't eat me." I whisper, a smile creeping across my face. I'm aware of my anxiety mellowing, being replaced by cautious excitement.

CHAPTER 2

The first thing I notice when I step off the dinky steps of the plane is the rich, earthy smell, tenfold the one from when I landed in Nairobi. There are three cars waiting next to the airstrip, one van with big open windows, and two Land Rovers with no sides or roofs. I've never seen anything like it. The Kenyan family excitedly wave at the driver of one of the roofless Land Rovers; obviously not their first rodeo. The driver strides over, hugs them all and helps with their bags. The older couple and I exchange a glance, sizing up the last topless car. I hope it's theirs. A Maasai man hops out the vehicle and waves towards us, his colourful beads tinkling as he moves. He wears a red and black chequered shuka, his hair plaited in little braids the ends of which are adorned with beads of yellows, blues, reds and greens. As he walks closer I notice his hair is coloured deep red, the clayish dye turning his head matte against the bright sun.

"Ms. Wilson?"

"Heya– uh– Jambo?!" I respond awkwardly. The man laughs and makes his way towards us. The older woman gives her husband a sour look, clearly unhappy with his booking choice.

"I'm William!" the Maasai man says, as he shakes my hand and leads me to the topless car. "How was your flight?" he asks. I think.

"Definitely… memorable."

"Welcome to the Mara!"

When we slowly pull into camp my hair is matted and my face dusty. I wasn't expecting an open top, let alone an open side car and my hair grip is at the bottom of my case. I didn't want to ask William to pull over so I could grab it, especially as we drove past two different herds of zebras. I peer at myself in the wing mirror, reconsidering every aesthetic choice I made from the comfort of my air-conditioned hotel room. I'm wearing a white linen shirt, professional but light. Good choice, aside from my sweat rendering it more sheer than usual, my black lace bra now glaring through the delicate stitching. I should've worn my flesh coloured one but was so sleepy getting dressed this morning I didn't stop to analyse the potential faults in the mirror or add on 10 degrees and the inevitable nervous sweats. I'm wearing the one pair of denim shorts I've owned since second year of Uni, bought for a girls trip to Zante. I pick at the frayed bottoms. Are they too short? It is 31 degrees, does professional attire still apply in this heat? In a holiday camp? On my feet are my beaten-up white Air Force Ones. I've wanted another pair for ages but can't seem to bring myself to replace them. Near the dirty rubber soles are little doodles my best friend Anya drew. Shit, I forgot to text her that I'd landed last night, she's probably going nuts. I'm sure they'll have WiFi here?

"Here is the camp! Welcome to Tukio!" William says, as he opens my door for me. The level of service makes me feel awkward, and I try show him as much gratitude as possible.

"Thank you so much!"

Another man dressed in a white polo and khaki trousers greets me with a glass of something bubbling and a tea towel that radiates warmth and the scent of tea tree. I gladly wipe my neck and face free from the itchy layer of dust and reach for the cold flute. "Thank you, this looks amazing!"

"No worries. We'll take your bags to your room. Daniel will be out shortly to greet you himself," says the man with a smile.

"Amazing, thanks so much!" I say, welcoming a sip of the ice cold amber bubbles. I've never been much of a wine person, but I can tell it's champagne. Maybe

Prosecco. It is definitely fizzing and alcoholic. As quickly as my welcome party materialised, I'm now alone once again. I lift my head up to take in the camp. I'm standing on a vast wooden platform, encapsulating some of the surrounding trees, the oak planks carved into circles around their powerful trunks letting them grow as they please. The camp is built on top of a large hill, making the view immense, stretching plains as far as the eye can see. To my left a large canvas gazebo hangs above the floorboards, sheltering a cozy yet open living area. Inside it I can spy a bar, a pool table, and two soft cream sofas mirroring each other either side of a towering granite fireplace. I walk past the large circular oak table surrounded by seven canvas chairs in front of me, to the very edge of the balcony. Below I see a lower level with a rock pool, sun loungers and a rustic wooden bar, and far below that a racing river dotted with boulders. Wait - moving boulders? Hippos!? I clutch the wooden railing, steadying myself. Two weeks ago, I was in my dinky studio flat, and now I'm stood drinking champagne in Africa, hippo watching. Who would've thought?

"Enjoying the view?" A deep, well pronounced voice purrs from behind me, snapping me back to reality. I turn to see a tall, dark man wearing a grey linen shirt and khaki trousers. A slim silver chain dangles around his neck, and he wears a moonstone pinky ring on his right hand. His eyes are the colour of caramel and he smells like a mix of sweat and sandalwood. I feel my cheeks get hot, I'm not sure why. Maybe I should put on more suncream. Ginger idiot. "I've never seen anything like it!" I muster the words, my mouth suddenly dry. He smiles warmly at me.

"Hopefully in a good way. I'm guessing you're one of Gia's entourage? Just arrived?"

"Partly correct. I'm not Gia's entourage, but I have just arrived. I'm here for work actually" I say, sheepishly looking at my bubbles. His brow furrows.

"Ms. Wilson? Maria's associate?" he grimaces.

"Uh, yes, Maddie!"

"Daniel Kimani." He holds out his palm, and I fumble to juggle my drink to my other hand so I can shake it. Shit. I see him look me up and down, moulding his first impression. I suddenly feel exposed, aware of my short shorts and thin linen. I should've worn something else. Ginger idiot.

"It's so lovely to meet you, your camp is incredible. I'm sure we'll create some beautiful work." I scramble. His frown hasn't subsided.

"I thought you'd be older." he says bluntly, any warmth now vanished. I'm totally thrown off.

"Uh, well, what I lack in age I make up for with naive optimism!" His face remains blank. I continue, "Sorry. Bad joke. I know I may be different to what you expected when you booked a rebrand with Maria Brookes, but I've worked alongside her on countless projects over the last two years, and as you were keen to launch the site before the end of November this was the only option. She'll be reviewing all the content I take, giving feedback and notes and available for consults at all times. Think of me as a bit of machinery being operated by her."

I can feel my upper lip slowly bead with sweat. I try wipe it away nonchalantly. His blank expression doesn't flicker, his eyes still studying my face.

"Alright. Get settled in this evening. Please organise a call with Maria for tomorrow breakfast. We can all sit down and go over the plans for the week."

"Yes, of course. Sounds great. Anything you need just say!"

"As you with me." He gestures over to the man who greeted me with the bubbles. "Ben will show you to your room. If you'd like dinner, it'll be at 8. We meet at this table."

"Amazing, thanks again! I look forward to working with you!" Daniel forces a smile in response, before dismissing himself to a large tent about fifteen feet from the living area. Once his tall frame has disappeared into the creamy canvas I down the rest of my bubbles, so quickly I feel some rise up my nose. I cringe, remembering Ben's presence a few feet away. He smiles at me, unfazed.

"This way ma'am."

My bags are already waiting for me in my tent. It's the most beautiful space, the epitome of glamping. The floor is the same wooden beams as the main area, with a plush sherpa rug underneath a big four poster bed made up with fresh cream sheets. Each side of the bed has a little oak table, one which holds a sprig of Frangipani and a glass pitcher of water, and the other a large honeycomb candle. There's a small desk in the corner, detailed with ornate floral carvings. There are two doors, one made of mesh where the bed faces which leads to an outdoor patio area, with a view of the river below. On it sits a large cream sofa, the floorboards draped in two more sherpa rugs guarded by a wooden coffee table. The tent is a little lower down on the hill than the main area, making the pool and river seem ever so slightly larger. And the hippos, to my dismay. The other door inside the bedroom is canvas and leads to the bathroom. Its walls are complete mesh facing the view, with a smooth butter coloured bath set deep in the ground. For the more adventurous, there's an outdoor shower through an even smaller mesh door.

I plonk on the bed, my mouth tangy from the bubbles and head sore from the sun. This is the most heat I've had since a family holiday to Spain when I was seven. I got heatstroke. I reach for the glass bottle of water next to the frangipani, and chug down as much as my stomach can take. I can't afford a repeat. I lay on the cool sheets for a couple moments, until my belly feels a little less slushy. Then I slowly rise and pad across the soft, cool, beams into the bathroom. Above the smooth limestone sink, there is a large mirror lined with stained glass and teeny indigo evil eyes. My reflection stares back at me, dusty and tired. My hair looks unkempt, and the sticky sweat on my torso has made my shirt even more opaque, sticking to the curvature of my breasts beneath the black lace. A concoction of embarrassment and failure washes over me. This was my big break, my first opportunity to take pictures and get paid handsomely. And Daniel thinks I'm a complete moron.

I decide to brave the outdoor shower, the idea of wind and cold water against my sticky grainy body a welcome concept. I grab one of the eggshell towels off the rail and spend a good thirty seconds running my fingers over it. I've never felt anything so soft. Would it be weird to ask Ben what softener they use? I gingerly clamber out the small mesh opening, careful to shut it behind me to stop any bugs getting in. I kick my slides off and step onto the square slate tiles, twisting on the cold tap, water jetting out the bronze shower head immediately. Usually, I have to hype myself up to get in a cold shower, but this time I'm under the cascading droplets without a second thought. The icy water sends a shock through my body, pricking up every single hair on the back of my neck. I watch as little droplets of red dirt descend from my skin and swirl onto the grey slate below. When I turn to look at the view, it almost makes me a jump. For a moment I'd been so focused on the sensation of the water, I'd forgotten where I was. Now outside, the view down the hill across the valley is even better, and I have to quickly grip onto the faucets to fight the rising vertigo.

I spend a few more moments enjoying the cold before I remember dinner, and my plans to dress professionally for it. Task for the evening; impress Daniel. I quickly shut off the tap and spend a couple seconds feeling the gentle breeze tickle every inch of my being, as the water becomes one with the air again. Suddenly my body realises how cold it is, and I swiftly reach for the towel wrapping it around me. I definitely need to ask him what softener they use. I slip on my slides and go to open the zip.... to open the zip. It doesn't open. Is it... it's stuck? I wiggle it, first cautiously, then frantically. Still nothing.

"Shit!" I exclaim, visions of hippos and zebras whirling around my mind. I look fearfully towards the bushes and surrounding land. Two options. Wait for dinner, they notice I'm not there, send someone to my tent. Drawback: they may think I'm skipping dinner as I'm jet lagged, tired, not hungry. Then I'm left outside to sleep with the lions and man-eating zebras. Whether they find me or leave me, it ensures Daniel will think I'm even more incapable than he already does. Option two. I follow the vague, dirt path that leads away from my tent and hope for the best. I guess I can always turn back? I'm sure it's there for a reason, it'll lead somewhere… right?

I hold tight for five minutes, hoping to hear someone walk by. No luck. There's a large rustle from a bush below me, which jolts me into action. I try grip my damp toes to my slides like little monkey feet to prevent them falling off, as I desperately make my way over the red dust. The path gets smaller, and I'm just about to turn back to familiar unsafety, when I see a khaki roof peak through the bushes. I breathe a sigh of relief. The path widens, revealing another canvas tent - even bigger than mine. It has a large wooden balcony, stretching out a couple feet off the ground. On it is a hammock, a large sofa atop a plush sherpa rug, a small hardwood bar and a couple sun loungers.

"Uh, hello?" I call out hopefully. As I get closer, I see a slender, female silhouette lying on one of the loungers. She props herself up on her elbows, peering around trying to locate the sound.

"Hi, sorry, down here!" I yell, trying not to be too loud and alert Daniel to my predicament. She raises a hand to her forehead shielding her eyes from the evening sun, which is now trickling over the savannah hills in golden tendrils, and peers down at me through large tortoiseshell Gucci frames.

"Room service?" She laughs down at me. I know that voice. Holy shit.

CHAPTER 3

As if the today couldn't get any more humiliating, I'm stood in front of Gia Tucci, wearing nothing but my towel and Sports Direct slides. She's an absolute vision leant against the balcony rails, her long raven hair in skinny braids running down her back like a cloak. She's wearing a slinky green bikini, with a forest-coloured silk sarong wrapped effortlessly round her hips. Just above the sarong her mocha waist is adorned with a gold belly chain dotted with little green garnets. I never knew she had so many tiny tattoos, decorating her slender arms and waist with the most intricate, fine illustrations and words. They must cover them up in films. She crouches to the ground, gently setting her misty cocktail on the wooden beams whilst reaching her other hand towards me.

"Outdoor shower?" she questions, the corners of her mouth spreading into a large smile.

"Please tell me you did the same?!" I exhale, feeling some of my anxiety trickle away.

"I actually did when I arrived. Daniel had to rescue me!"

We both laugh as I grab hold of her soft hand, helping me clamber onto the deck without flashing any hyenas.

"Ben is still training and doesn't normally do the welcome speech. He keeps forgetting to tell us about the safety features." Gia continues while I gain my balance, letting go of her hand and walking towards her tent door. She's taller than I imagined, but knowing Hollywood I wouldn't be surprised if they stuck some of her male counterparts on top of boxes.

"See, if you shut it from the inside, you can't open it from the outside, so when you're asleep you're completely safe. If you're gonna be in and out there are these velcro bits instead of the zip." she explains, flicking one of the velcro tabs playfully with her ballet slipper nail.

"That actually makes a lot of sense."

She looks up at me, the smile still on her face, rosy lips slightly parted.

"Sorry, this is so weird. I'm not trying to be annoying or intrusive, I can go now you've rescued me!" I spurt, cutting through the silence. She laughs as she slinks past me to grab her cocktail, some of the yellow liquid lapping over the sides of the martini glass. She smells of smoky jasmine.

"No, please! Stay! Have a drink!"

"Are you sure?"

"Yes! Honestly I've been bored out my skull this afternoon. A few girlfriends were meant to be meeting me down here but one of the fuckers got Covid and now they're all isolating."

"Oh shit, is she OK?"

Gia snorts into her cocktail. "Please, I've seen her take two tabs of acid at Burning Man. This'll be light work." She sets her cocktail down on the coffee table and makes her way over to the bar. "Margarita OK?" she asks, holding up a bottle of El Patron.

"My favourite!" I go to join her, and suddenly remember my attire.

"Maybe I should go back and get changed quickly first?"

Her green eyes look me up and down. They're almost the same colour as the little garnets decorating her waist, but with teeny flecks of gold and brown. I feel the hairs on the back of my neck stand up again, I must be getting chilly after my icy shower. "If you want." she shrugs "Be careful not to flash Daniel on your way!"

Her eyes flicker playfully as she delicately squeezes a lemon into the metal cocktail shaker, its silver outside beaded with sparkling drops of condensation. I feel my stomach tighten.

"Is there a chance he'd see me?"

She shrugs again. "Maybe. He's like a little Whac-A-Mole, always popping up where you least expect him." She laughs, a radiant, warm laugh. I bite my lip, embarrassed to tell her my predicament.

"See, the thing is, I'm technically here for work. My boss is a photographer, and she actually got Covid too. Daniel needed the shots by November, so I'm here filling in. I already think he hates me, or at least thinks I'm incompetent. I'm scared if he sees me bumbling around like this it'll piss him off even more."

Gia leans on the bar, brushing a slender finger across her lips in thought. "Why do you think he hates you?"

"I don't know. When he saw me, he just seemed, disappointed?"

At this Gia smirks. "I've known Daniel for a while, I wouldn't sweat it. He's weird. Hard to read. I'm sure he doesn't hate you - but to set your mind at ease here's what we'll do. You're gonna borrow something of mine, sit on this balcony with me and drink at least two margaritas before dinner."

She's so nice? And wants to hang out with me? I guess she doesn't really have a choice... But I still feel some butterflies take flight my belly. I'm not technically working tonight, that starts tomorrow. Tonight, I can allow myself fun.

"Ok. Sold."

Gia leads me into her lavish tent towards a large closet, overflowing with sequins and silks. "Don't worry, I'm not this organised. Ben unpacked my case, I told him not to, but he insisted after the shower debacle." She takes a sip from her drink, nearly finished, licking the salt crystals from her lips. "Pick whatever you want, I'm not very possessive of them."

"They're all incredible. Are dinners here... fancy?"

"If you want them to be! I'll leave you to it. Don't be too long, your margarita will get warm!" She says, prancing out the tent.

I run my fingers over the the collection of garments, feeling the prickly sequins, cool silk, soft velvet. I'm touching Gia Tucci's clothes. Wait till Anya hears about this. My fingers stop on a turquoise slip dress. I pull it out and hold it up to my body gazing into the mahogany mirror to my left. Not too fancy. Not too casual. Not too expensive looking? We have a winner!

I sheepishly emerge from the tent to find Gia leaning on the wooden railing, admiring the view whilst sipping her refreshed drink. She spots me and immediately screams. "Ahhhhh you went for the Bob Mackey! It's perfect!"

I feel my cheeks flush. Shit. "Oh God, sorry! It didn't have a label! I thought it was one of the - uh - lower end ones?" Shit shit. Wrong word choice. Gia furrows her brow and squints at me.

"Bob Mackey? Low end?"

"Fuck, no - I didn't mean it li-"

Gia's cheeks puff up, trying to stifle a grin.

"You bitch!" I rasp.

A laugh bursts out her cheeks in a joyous roar. "The label was itchy! Don't worry, girl, enjoy it! Blue isn't really my colour anyway." She delicately passes me my ice-cold margarita, our fingers brushing for a second during the exchange. Her forest eyes lock mine. "It's definitely yours though."

We lie on Gia's sun loungers, gossiping and laughing as the butterball sun slowly dips past the horizon, painting the savannah a deep orange, wisps of pink and purple splattered on the wispy clouds. I try steer clear of all the questions buzzing around my head like wasps to a glass of cola on a hot day - celebrity drama, scandals, Hollywood. I learn her father is Kenyan, and her mother Italian. Daniel and she met when they were young, her father and his mother moving in the same circles. She lived in Nairobi until she was 5, then her parents moved to the Big Apple. She still lives in New York, but is currently looking at a bungalow in Carmel, yearning to be by the white sandy beaches. The more I find out, the less she looks like Gia Tucci, and becomes just Gia. My lips are starting to tingle from all the margaritas, the lime juice and salt crystals singing despite how much I lick them. As I watch the last pools of orange light disappear from the valley, I realise I'm more tipsy than I intended on being. I look over to Gia, who's tracing little shapes in the mist of her glass with a pearly pink nail. I notice her dark eyelashes blink slowly. Good. At least she's drunk too. I've never met a celebrity before. And now I'm sipping margaritas in Kenya with one.

"You're so pretty." I say, slurring slightly. Gia laughs, twisting her body towards me in her chair.

"Are you coming onto me?"

"Oh no! God, no! Noooo, I'm not… you know."

Gia holds my gaze for a beat, before rising up.

"Water?" She asks, looking down at me.

"Please!" I get up too and we make our way to the bar.

"I may have been a bit heavy handed with the last one!" Gia says, as the water jug she's pouring wobbles precariously over the glasses, puddles sloshing over the sides.

"Fuck it. We're on holiday. Ish."

We both chug our waters while staring at the first baby stars, little milky dots peppering the sky. A bell tinkles, snapping me back to reality. I look at Gia with confusion, and she meets my gaze with a cheeky grin.

"Diiiiinnnneerrr!" she squeals, as she grabs my hand skipping us out the tent.

The lounge area is dotted with glass lanterns, making little shadows dance around the canvas tents and tall trees. The dinner table is now draped in a silky white tablecloth, with three hardwood placemats inlaid with teeny flowers made from mother of pearl. Each wooden placemat is lined by multiple different sizes of silver cutlery. Great, another way to prove my incompetence in front of Daniel. In the centre of each placemat sits a round porcelain dish, containing a leafy salad, glazed baby carrots of purple and orange, and a large roasted courgette steak dusted with pepper and chilli flakes. It looks incredible, but nowhere near hearty enough to soak up the amount of tequila that's pulsing through my veins. An older man stands next to the table, wearing a chef's jacket and dark trousers.

"Ladies, your starter. Slow roasted courgette on a bed of mixed garden salad, all grown and harvested here at Tukio." He speaks with a voice warm as treacle, bowing his head before leaving us to eat.

"Thanks Mustafa, looks insane as always!" Gia calls after him, as she takes a seat. Good. This is just the starter. I pray the main will be a juicy burger and mountain of fries. She pats her hand on the khaki seat next to her and looks at me expectantly.

As I sit, I notice how the candle in the middle of the table makes the shadow of her eyelashes look cartoonishly big. Ben approaches the table and smiles.

"Any drinks to start off with?"

"Um, just water is great thanks—" I start.

"Two Merlots please." Gia says, winking as she delicately unfolds her napkin and places it on her lap. I follow suit, just as a dark figure emerges from the tent next to us. I watch his large hands slowly zip up the tent behind him, his fingers now adorned with two more silver rings as well as the little moonstone one. I feel my stomach tighten, my mouth hot from the alcohol. I don't know whether to reach for my water or my wine. Daniel smiles at Gia, and nods towards me.

"Evening."

I smile at him and nod back.

"Did I miss the dress-code?" He purrs, looking down at me as he pours himself a hefty glass of the Merlot. My cheeks flush, feeling his eyes survey my dress as he sits down. I try force a smile.

"Uh, it's a long stor–"

"I heard her arrive earlier, and I've been so insanely lonely I held her hostage and we had a couple drinks. I thought she was too gorgeous to not wear something like this to her first dinner."

"Ah. It's yours. That makes more sense." He says, lifting the glass of red to his full lips.

"You've been raiding my alcohol stock then have you?"

"Well, I thought since I'm doing you this favour I was owed some kind of compensation!" Gia responds playfully.

"What favour?" I ask. Daniel sets his glass down.

"I hosted Gia's partner's—"

"Ex!"

"Sorry, ex-partner's birthday event here last year. Free of charge, for old times' sake. So, she kindly offered to bring some friends down and model for the rebrand shoot. She's got some pull, you know."

"Some pull?" I scoff. "You'll be batting people off with sticks when they see her draped over one of your sun loungers!"

Daniel smiles. "Yes, it's very kind of her to have another complimentary trip here and have a professional photographer document the whole thing ready for Instagram." He smirks. I feel my cheeks go hot again. Is he making fun of me? Gia swats him with her napkin.

"Don't be rude! If you don't want me here, I'll leave!" She dramatically rises from her chair. No wonder she's an actress. Daniel brushes his thumb over his lips as he laughs, maybe the first genuine emotion I've seen from him all day.

"Sit down, you plonker." he says, topping up Gia's wine, but not mine. Gia falls back to her seat, and as the laughs fizzle out, we sit in silence for a beat.

"I'm sorry to hear it didn't work out wi—" Daniel starts.

"Don't be. Cheated. I'm over it." Gia says quickly.

"How could you have this?" I gesture to Gia "And want to cheat!? There's no hope for us mere mortals clearly. He must have been a total twat." I exclaim, taking a large sip of the dry red. Gia smiles at me warmly and squeezes my hand.

"Thank you. She is."

"She?" I repeat out loud, confused. I clasp my hand over my mouth in embarrassment. May the ground swallow me now. "Oh, she! Sorry, I'm so jet lagged my brain isn't functioning at full capacity."

Daniel smirks at me across the table. "Or maybe it's the numerous margaritas," he digs. I try laugh, embarrassed, but Gia smiles at me again.

"Don't worry, you weren't to know. I like to keep my private life, private."

I smile back at her, the hunk of courgette I've eaten stuck in a lump at the back of my throat.

34

"Are you ready for your main?" Mustafa's deep voice rumbles as he approaches. Gia smiles at him and takes his hand.

"Always! What is it?" she asks, slurring slightly.

"Sautéed beetroot and goats cheese parcels, on a nest of baby spinach and fresh rocket salad."

Gia claps her hands excitedly. I reach for my water and chug it down, accepting the certain hangover that'll arrive tomorrow. Why did I finish all my snacks on the plane?

CHAPTER 7

The glass in my hand is half full, each time I gently tap the rim the water ripples, dispersing little sun rays across the table. It's 10am but feels like 4am. After dinner I passed out in my tent still wearing Gia's Bob Mackey; luckily I didn't dribble on it in my sleep. I don't want to know how much her dry cleaning costs. When my alarm blared me awake, I could barely muster the strength to shower, let alone put on a fresh face of makeup. So now I'm sat next to Daniel, barefaced and freckled on a zoom call with Maria trying not to vomit my brains out onto Daniel's laptop.

"Right, Maddie?" Maria asks, both her and Daniel waiting for my response.

"Um, yes. Definitely." I gamble, snapping back from my thoughts. Daniel nods, consoled. I exhale, relieved with my choice of words.

"Good luck darlings, I'm excited to see the results!" Maria coos before hanging up. I gulp down the rest of my water, trying to cool my hangover sweats. Daniel shuts his laptop and looks at me. I can feel the redness in my cheeks, as his eyes flicker across my face, inspecting it.

"OK. Shall we meet back here in thirty minutes with your equipment?"

"Uh, yes. Sounds good!"

I make sure to be back in the lounge area in twenty minutes instead of thirty and sit waiting for Daniel glass of water in hand. I'm feeling better thanks to the amount of it I downed this morning and had time to slap on some concealer so hopefully look better too. Daniel calls over to me from the green Land Rover I'd arrived in, William sat in the front. I grab my equipment bag and head over to the car, wobbling a little with its weight. Daniel smirks and gently takes the bag from me, placing it in the backseat.

"Thanks!"

"No worries."

We clamber into the backseat, my camera bag a welcome blockade between us. I quickly remember to tie up my hair with the cream scrunchie on my arm, avoiding the birds nest the wind styled for me yesterday. The car sputters to life, and as we drive the red dust swirls in clouds around us.

"So, this afternoon we'll focus on getting some good animal shots, and then the sunset meal setup. Gia will meet us for that."

"Great. Do we have a location for the sunset setup?" Daniel's brow furrows, and I immediately regret asking. I'm sure we spoke about it on the Zoom this morning, the Zoom I was incapable of paying any attention to because of my pounding headache.

"Yes... a small cliff that overlooks the river, about twenty minutes from camp."

"Amazing!"

Daniel's eyes linger on mine, before peeling away to look out at the view. "Are you excited to see the lions, Ms. Wilson?" William calls out from the front. I can sense Daniel watching me, waiting for my response.

"Uh, yes! Ecstatic! I love the Lion King!"

Daniel snickers. "Hakuna Matata," he says dryly. Prick.

We drive around for a couple hours, each moment a struggle to stay in work mode. I've only ever gone to the zoo as a child for school trips - seeing real wild animals is something I can barely wrap my head around. The first we saw was a giraffe, elegantly strolling across the amber plains. I was struck by how slow and graceful her movements were, as if she were walking a runway in Milan. I was also struck by her sheer size, I had to stand on the backseat, head poking out the top of the car to get a good shot. We saw lots of deer like creatures, whose names I can't remember but gentle eyes I certainly do. The zebras were like something out of a cartoon, their contrasting stripes the most unlikely camouflage ever.

I'm busy flicking through my photos, savouring every image as William slows the car for a break. I barely notice we've stopped until he reaches over handing me a warm silver flask.

"Refreshments?"

"Wow, thank you!" I smile at him in thanks whilst unscrewing the lid, giving it a sniff. Rich, warm cocoa fills my nostrils, taking me by surprise. "A very rogue drink choice for a thirty-degree day in Kenya!"

I laugh, as I pour the frothy brown milk into a paper cup from the seat pocket in front of me, watching all the little creamy bubbles slowly settle. Once I'm finished pouring, Daniel takes the flask from me, our fingers grazing.

"I know." He admits. "We have other soft drinks in the cooler at the back if you want. It's a guilty pleasure of mine. I always request it for drives."

"I'll give it a go. Doubt it'll beat my Mum's though." I say, raising the cup to my lips, its flimsy paper exterior softened by the hot liquid. Warmth fills my mouth, the sweet cocoa making my taste buds tingle, along with another fragrant spice I can't quite put my finger on.

"What is that?"

"Cinnamon." Daniel says, a small smile creeping across his lips. "My grandmother's secret - so don't tell anyone, or I'll have to kill you."

I laugh, and feel my stomach tighten. He's actually being nice to me? Cracking jokes?

"Sir, can I use your binoculars?" William asks from the front.

"Of course!" Daniel says, passing them over. Despite the sweat I feel forming on my upper lip from the hot drink, I can't stop sipping. William hands back the binoculars to Daniel, a darkness in his eyes. In a hushed tone they speak in Swahili, and I see the darkness leak into Daniels too.

"What's happening?" I ask, feeling more sweat seep out of me now from panic. Daniel ignores me and keeps talking to William, who starts the car and starts driving. "Daniel? What's wrong?" He looks at me, his eyes sullen, unsure of what to say.

"William–William thinks there might be something by that tree. Something dead."

As we get closer, I see the small grey lump lying motionless underneath the lone acacia tree, flies buzzing around it. William slows, him and Daniel alertly scanning the surrounding area.

"What are you looking for?"

William looks at me and then to Daniel, who nods at him without removing the binoculars from his eyes.

"It's a baby elephant. Elephant families are very close, so even if the baby is dead, sometimes the Mama will stay close by mourning her child. We are just making sure she isn't near so it's safe to get out and take a closer look."

I feel a lump form in my throat, looking at the sad grey form, lying still and alone under the beating white sun.

"I don't see her." Daniel says firmly, urging William to drive closer. He does, and as we approach the grey blob takes form of a teeny elephant, I see its little legs, flappy ears, fuzzy skin. Like a little grey peach. William stops, and he and Daniel hop out the car to inspect it further.

"You can stay here, we just need to confirm that it's dead before we inform the rangers." Daniel says before he follows William towards the tree. I shut my eyes and try remember the breathing exercises my Anya taught me to stop panic attacks, 6 seconds breathe in, hold breath for 7, 8 seconds breathing out. 6 in, hold 7, 8 out. 6 in, hold 7, 8 ou–

The front door of the vehicle opens fiercely, and William speaks urgent Swahili into the radio. Daniel rushes over to my window.

"Water!" he orders, pointing to the cool box. I scramble quickly to open the lid and pass him a bottle of Evian.

"More," he says, looking back nervously at the baby.

"Everything OK?" I panic, handing him two more.

"She's alive."

Daniel and I kneel by her little head, as William speaks to the rescue team from the car. Daniel relentlessly tries giving her water, tipping it first by her trunk and then over her mouth. I stroke her back, little flakes of dirt falling off with every touch.

"She's so tiny." Daniel says, his eyebrows knitted together with worry. "She was probably still on milk. Water won't do her much good."

"It's the best we've got." I say softly, surprised I'm the one consoling him. He looks bereft. I keep stroking her, running my hand across her back, then her little belly, and then her legs. I feel something wet and warm and quickly recoil, raising my hand to see deep crimson dripping from my fingers. My mouth feels like sandpaper, and Daniels eyes widen.

"What's that?"

"I don't know. I was stroking her leg!"

Daniel quickly leans over me to look, the scent of musky sweat and sandalwood wafting after him.

"Shit." he says, unbuttoning his shirt. I watch in confusion as he takes it off and leans over the wound, rinsing it with the water and wrapping it in his shirt. I watch the concentration in his eyes, their deep mahogany colour intent on nothing but the task at hand. His lips, pressed together in concentration. His torso, toned and glistening with sweat as his chests moves up and down with each deep breath.

William calls out "They'll be here to collect her in 45 minutes!"

"Thank you!" Daniel calls back, not looking up from the calf. We silently watch as his crisp linen is slowly painted deep red, the blood travelling through the stitching of the fabric like veins. Fuck it. In one sudden motion, I rip off my T shirt and press it on top of Daniel's, the red cloaked by white once again. Daniel looks at me in shock, and I suddenly remember I'm wearing my sheer lace bra. He clears his throat and quickly looks away, as if reading my mind. We sit together, our pinkies touching as we press the fabric into the wrinkly grey leg, trying to ignore the pounding sun on the back of our necks.

In the hour we spend waiting with her, she opens her eyes three times and flaps her ears once. With each movement Daniel and I are reinvigorated with energy to keep pressing, reinvigorated with hope. The sun has started to creep down towards the horizon, transitioning from a ball of white heat to one of golden beauty. The light transforms Daniel's eyes to marbled pools of rich honey. The sky is fading from bright blue to pale orange, making the silhouettes of the dotted acacia trees look like a painting. A large van slowly appears in the distance, leaving a streamline of dust in its wake. Daniel and I lift our weary heads waving to the van, as it approaches and halts next to our Land Rover. Three men and one woman wearing long green jackets, armed with large bottles of milk and a stretcher quickly run towards us.

"Mr. Daniel, thank you for staying with her!" one of the men exclaims, as he urgently strides towards us. Daniel and I stand to give him space to examine her, my head aching from the sun. I sway slightly as I rise, hardly noticing a firm hand on my shoulder, steadying me. Daniel's hand. He offers me the remaining bottle of water, which I take gratefully, savouring every gulp despite its warmth. As I drink, his hand releases my shoulder and drops back into his pocket. The man approaches us smiling and pats Daniel gently on the back. "She has a good chance."

"And she'll be at the shelter?" Daniel asks.

"Yes. We'll keep you updated. Please get in the shade, you don't want to get sick. Thank you again!" He says, hurrying off to help the rest of his team with the large stretcher. We stand in silence for a moment, until Daniel squats back down to the elephant, gently picking up her trunk holding it towards me. Confused, I kneel and I take it, soft and warm and fuzzy. She feebly wraps her trunk around my hand, as if trying to hold it. My heart melts.

"Blow in it. Then she'll always remember you."

"Really?" I slowly lean down and blow gently, I'm sure I see her ears twitch. I hand it back to Daniel, who does the same.

"Thank you." I rasp, touched by the sentiment.

The rescue team smile at us, and we wearily make our way back to the car. William has put the canvas roof up, and I welcome the shade as we sit and watch them feed her, wrap her, and load her into the vehicle. We rest and sluggishly watch the van drive off and dissolve into the horizon, its only trace the dancing cloud of red earth trailing behind it.

"Shit!" Daniel suddenly scrambles for his radio.

"Hello Mustafa, I'm so sorry. We had an emergency, I don't think we'll make it in time for the right light. Yes, dinner at camp please." Daniel rubs his forehead wearily.

"Do we have an update of when Gia's friends arrive? It could be a blessing in disguise, the pictures of the dinner would really cater to a larger group."

"Um, yeah. I think the day after tomorrow."

"Ok great. We'll do the dinner setup then."

Daniel nods solemnly.

"Back home?" William asks from the front.

"Please." Daniel sighs.

We drive in silence, the only sounds the jiggling of the car and gentle chirping of the cicadas. Lifting my eyes from the savannah, I look to Daniel, and almost jump to find him still topless, muscular arms sheen with sweat. My stomach curdles as I remember I am too, and look down to see every bump and jolt the car makes over the rocky terrain my chest following suit. I cross my arms in embarrassment and try distract myself by glaring out to the evening star. I jolt as I feel something nudge my lap and turn to find Daniel offering me a fleece jacket. "I always keep a spare in the car."

"Are you sure you don't–"

"No, no. Please. You didn't have to do that. Did you burn?"

I snort. "I burn when the TV is on too bright!"

He releases an amused huff of air, much to my surprise.

"William makes a great cream, I've got some in my room. I'll give it to you when we're back."

"Thank you. That's very kind."

CHAPTER 8

We arrive back at camp, Ben waiting for us with iced lemonade which we both gulp down ravenously.

"How was the drive?" Ben asks.

As Daniel tells him the story, I walk over by the wooden railing to admire the view. It's just after sunset, the sky splattered with deep oranges, violets and pinks. The pool below reflecting all the colours, a literal Monet painting you could dive into. Daniel approaches, still topless, and joins me.

"The pool looks beautiful."

"This is my favourite time of day. I always think the light looks like a painting."

"I was just thinking that! A Monet. I've never seen sunsets like these ones."

Daniel looks at me. "This one's particularly special."

We watch it for a moment, the ripples in the pool making the colours marble and dance.

"If you're up for it, we could go down and get a couple pictures of the pool, that way we free up Thursday to focus on the dinner setup?"

"Sounds great. I'll have Ben bring us some snacks and refreshments."

Daniel sits on one of the sun loungers, watching me watch the light. I'm kneeling on the floor, trying to get a low angle shot of the pool with the view and sunset in the background. I'm awkwardly aware that my ass is stuck up in his direction, and once again I'm wearing my shorts that are too short. I clearly didn't learn. It may look strange but for a low angle it's the position I always take, I'd explained to him. He'd merely shrugged in response and turned his head out to the evening sky. Once I'm pleased with what I've got, I join Daniel on the sun lounger to show him. He looks content, but not happy. He wears the same expression as a mother whose toddler I once photographed. The child had a non-stop tantrum, so even in the pictures where he wasn't screaming he still had watery red eyes or little trickle of snot. Content, but not happy.

"What don't you like?"

"What, no, they're great!"

I tilt my head to one side, telling him I'm not buying it. He sighs. "It's just... I think they'd look better with someone in them. So people can really imagine what it feels like to be here. But Gia's busy, and her friends aren't here so… it is what it is."

"I guess. Unless you got in." I respond playfully.

Daniel sits deep in thought for a moment. I bite my lip. Bad joke. "Fuck it," he says, starting to unlace his boots. He looks nervously to the sunset, a deep violet now overpowering the pinks and oranges. "How long have we got? Light-wise?"

I look to the sky, and then my gold Casio watch Anya gave me as a good luck present for the trip. She'll be pleased I'm actually using it. "Um, I'd say about 15 minutes. But darker dusk shots are fine too, I can always edit them in post."

"Ok," he says. His socks and shoes are off, and he's now stood over me undoing his brown leather belt. I shift in my seat to look away, unsure what to do with myself, so keep my eyes focused on the sunset until I hear a loud SPLASH. I turn to see Daniel in the pool, in nothing but his blue boxers and silver chain. I grab my camera and head to the edge of the pool, raising the viewfinder to my eye. He jokingly puts a hand behind his head and pops a hip, which makes me laugh. I splash some water at him with my bare foot. "Stop! We don't have time!" I say, gesturing to the sun.

"Oi missy, don't you know not to splash a man in a pool while you're holding an expensive camera?"

"Fuck off!" I giggle, as I start snapping. It's funny, through the lens it looks like a perfume ad. A tall, chiselled man looking out into the sunset, water trickling down his muscled back. I take my time composing the photos, letting my eyes linger on the way his wet skin reflects the gold light, the shadows of his abs, the little drops of water on his lips. "I think we got it!" I yell to him, just as Ben makes his way gingerly down the stone steps with a tray containing two drinks and an assortment of snacks. I thank Ben, and sit on a lounger snacking on crisps, though I can't help peek at Daniel as he hoists himself out the pool, his biceps flexed. In my defence, it's been over a year since my last date, I'd probably get turned on by a Ken doll. He pads over to me and grabs a towel from the lounger to my right.

"They look good?" he asks, gesturing to the camera.

"Great." I say, reaching for one of the drinks and bringing it to my lips. Before I take a sip Daniel reaches out, holding his hand above my glass.

"What are you doing?"

"Uh, drinking?"

51

He laughs, and sits next to me, grabbing the other drink. "This is Dawa, a traditional Kenyan cocktail. It's vodka, lime and honey. You see this?" he says pointing to a wooden pestle in the drink. I nod.

"You have to crush the lime at the bottom, so it properly infuses with the honey and vodka."

I raise an eyebrow at him, skeptical.

"I know it sounds pretentious, just try it."

"Ok capt'n!" I say, saluting him with the pestle. It flicks a little liquid onto this arm. "Shit. Sorry!"

He laughs and leans to lick it off. "Just try it."

I squish the lime with the wood, watching the little bits of flesh float around the drink, mixing with the golden honey into a little tornado. I take a sip, and my eyes widen. First you get the kick of the vodka, then the tang of the lime, and finally the sweetness of the honey. I look up to see Daniel watching me expectantly whilst crushing his own lime.

"OK. I get it."

He laughs and takes a long sip. I look out to the pool, the only colours painted on it now a deep purple dappled with fuchsia splodges. The sky is navy, speckled with the first stars of the night, with a strip of violet-pink leaking over the horizon. "Was the water nice? It looks so beautiful."

"Have a dip, if you fancy." Daniel says, taking another sip. I consider.

"Fuck it." I say, standing up and unzipping the fleece. Daniel looks surprised but doesn't avert his eyes the way I had as he'd undressed. I look back at him, and jump in. The water is colder than I expected, and I feel every hair on my body prick up in defence. I stay under the water, admiring the way the surface looks, puddles of deep blue with rays of pink light bursting through, marbling together like an abstract painting. I feel my hair weightless around me. I used to always think I was a mermaid as a child and would hold my breath and play in the water for hours. That was when we lived in Cornwall. I was sixteen when we moved to London to be closer to Mum's doctors. I stopped swimming unless we went on holiday. A loud crash rips through the peace, sending the colours into frantic swirls. I feel something large grab my waist, yanking me up to the surface. Disorientated, I start panting and spluttering water.

"You're OK!" I hear Daniel yell and realise it's his arms wrapped around me. I quickly squirm out of them and grip the side of the pool.

"What the fuck?!"

"What? I thought– were you not drowning?"

"No! I can swim!"

"Oh! Shit! Sorry! You were down for so long I thought you hit your head!" he says, embarrassed, an emotion I wasn't aware he had in his repertoire. A laugh bursts out of me and I splash him in retort.

"Dickhead! Just cause I'm from London doesn't mean I can't swim."

"Apologies. How can I make it up to you?"

I eye the drinks on the table, and before I say anything Daniel heaves himself out the pool in one swift motion to retrieve our drinks. I lean back, looking at the stars letting the water lap around my ears. Every time I look up it's like they've multiplied. I hear a clink in front of me and see Daniel setting our drinks on the edge before he slinks back into the water. I reach for mine and take a big gulp, not able to taste the vodka anymore. I feel the heat radiate off Daniels body next to me, as we both look up to the stars. "I can't believe it's November and I'm in an outdoor pool."

"Perks of the equator, I guess."

We float by the edge of the pool, sipping our drinks and comparing knowledge of constellations. The more time passes, the closer our bodies draw together. Daniel points out Orion's Belt, but my focus flicks from the twinkling stars to his large, strong hands, up his muscular arm dotted with shiny aqua beads, across his wide shoulders, up his neck, past his full lips, the way they move as he talks, to his deep expressive eyes. He turns to me, and I see surprise ripple across his face to find me looking at him. My cheeks go hot, but I don't look away. Neither does he. I feel our bodies pulling closer, I brace myself for a kiss, shutting my eyes. I can feel his face near mine, his breath hot on my lips. I hear a loud gush of water and open my eyes to find Daniel out of the pool, by the loungers flinging a towel over his shoulder. He chucks the other one towards me. "Have a nice evening. I'll see you tomorrow, I have some work to finish up."

I can barely keep my jaw shut, utterly frozen with shock and embarrassment.

I was so sure we were going to kiss, I could see the hunger in his eyes, the way they gazed into mine and glided up and down my body. As soon as my tent's in view I thank the watchman who escorted me back and quickly make my way inside, flopping onto the bed. My whole body feels like jelly. I look to my bedside table and see the leftover glass of red from last night and reach out for it lazily. My fingers just find it, nearly tipping it onto the sherpa as I guide it to my mouth. Despite my wet hair and soggy underwear my body feels like it's on fire. I strip off my sodden bra and panties, feeling the patches of duvet beneath them now damp, and lie in the candlelight nude. All I can hear are the soft chirps of the crickets, and odd grunt of a hippo. I look to the zip of my tent and imagine those big hands carefully unzipping it. Him walking in, unbuttoning his linen the way he had earlier. Making his way over to the bed. The smell of his sweat and cologne and the coconut oil on his hair, all swirling into one. His body towering over mine, him kneeling on the bed between my thighs. He lowers his head, our lips crashing together with lust, his tongue caressing mine. He draws away, breathing heavy, his tongue now making its way from my mouth, down my chin to my neck. I feel his teeth graze me, now by my nipple, and then lower, lower. I keep imagining for another twenty minutes, my hand between my legs pretending it's him. I haven't slept so well in months.

CHAPTER 9

I stand examining my reflection in the mirror, the morning light streaming into the tent. No matter how embarrassed I feel, I have to look incredible. Show him who he turned down. What he's missing. I'm wearing one of the three dresses I brought, long and flowy with a Bardot top, and a slit up my mid right thigh. It's white with forest green flowers that contrast nicely with my hair. I'm wearing my favourite silver hoops that Mum gave me for Christmas last year. I touch them gently, their metal soothingly cool against my warm hands. My hair is down, unfortunately I didn't bring my curlers with me but I scrunched it non-stop after my shower so it has some volume. I've put effort into my makeup, and it shows. It's the type of makeup that a straight man would consider *natural,* when in reality I spent fifteen minutes alone perfecting my contour. Happy with the finished result, I make my way back to the bedroom, grabbing my planner off the bedside table and flopping onto the bed. I have two full days left at Tukio. This morning is easy, just pictures and videos of camp. This afternoon I'm unsure of, Daniel's been pretty aloof with the details but I think we're heading to a nearby village. I'm guessing where some of the fresh produce comes from? And tomorrow - my last day is all food and drink based, ending with the sunset dinner and a disco.

I grab my camera off charge and make my way out the tent, along the little path lined with stones and lanterns to the lounge. Today will be great. I'll be sexy, coy, quietly make my way around camp getting the content I need. If Daniel sees me, he'll see me looking good and working hard. I step onto the decking of the lounge, feeling the breeze caress my face. I take a deep breath. The air here is completely different to what my lungs are used to. Crisp, clean, and earthy; in comparison to London which smells like smoke, smog, and if you're under a bridge or in an alley, then piss. I whip out my camera and start snapping shots of the lounge. The morning light compliments it well, everything looks bright and welcoming. Ben obviously knew this is what I'd be up to today, as I note there isn't a glass unpolished or a rug off centre. A large green eye suddenly appears in the viewfinder, making me jump and almost drop the camera. "Jesus Christ!" I yell, hearing that familiar tinkly laugh.

"Shhhh, don't tell Daniel I'm distracting you!" Gia hisses playfully.

"You muppet, I nearly dropped the camera."

"That was my intention! Then you wouldn't have to work and could hang out with meeee!" She sings, picking up a slice of watermelon from the breakfast table and taking a large bite. The pink juice runs down her plump lips dripping onto her collar bone. She wipes her chin with her forefinger, licking off the juice. "Watcha doing today?"

"Ummm, just taking photos of the camp, and then heading somewhere with Daniel."

"Ooh nice. Where?" She grabs another slice of watermelon before plonking herself down on the curved sofa that overlooks the view, patting the space next to her. I consider, I should really keep working, but surely five minutes won't hurt.

"I think a nearby village? I'm guessing for produce?" As I sit the slit in my dress falls to the side revealing the top of my thigh. I notice Gia's eyes linger on it for a beat, before looking back up.

"Sounds fun!"

"Yeah… it should be." I bite my lip, unsure if I should confide in Gia. I know she's friends with Daniel but can feel the words rising up my throat trying to burst through my mouth. "Actually. About Daniel…" My tone grows hushed, and Gia leans in closer, eyes gleaming. I can smell her Tom Ford perfume, it's always the one I spritz myself with at Duty Free but can never afford to buy. Tobacco Vanille. "Last night we were in the pool, and I think we nearly-"

"Ms. Wilson?"

A voice comes from behind, piercing the intimate bubble making both of us jump. I turn to see Ben stood behind us, smiling awkwardly. "Hi Ben!" Gia says cheerily.

"Good morning Ms. Tucci." He looks back to me. "Ms. Wilson, if you are free now there has been a slight change of plan. Mr. Daniel would like to move the trip from this afternoon to the morning."

"Oh! Yes, that should be fine!"

"Great. He is waiting by the car when you're ready."

"Amazing, thanks Ben!"

He nods goodbye to both of us before walking away. I rise, grabbing my camera and suede satchel. I think I have everything I need. "I'll tell you later." I say to Gia, who pulls a sour face.

"Fine. You better be here for dinner!"

Daniel is leant against the car flicking through the contents of a leather briefcase when I arrive. He nods hello, but no words are spoken. I do at least see his eyes gaze up and down my dress quickly. Instead of sitting in the back like yesterday, he clambers into the front next to William, who smiles and greets me warmly. As we set off, I root through my satchel, looking for a hair tie. Shit. Ends up that's what I forgot. I guess I'll be rocking the bird's nest again today. As the car goes faster the more my hair whips and tangles, and I awkwardly try to hold it down, fighting against the wind's strong talons. I clock Daniels eyes watching me in the rear-view mirror, and feel my cheeks grow hot again. Maybe this outfit was mistake, I was expecting a relaxed morning at camp, not being hurled around the car again. Daniel reaches into the dashboard, and pulls out a green scrunchie, offering it to me. I take it gratefully, somehow managing to wrangle my rogue locks into a messy bun. "Do you always carry a spare scrunchie?" I ask playfully. He looks at me blankly before turning back to the front.

"We usually keep spares in the cars for… unprepared guests."

I watch him in the mirror and notice his eyes flicker as he speaks. I'm not sure if I buy it. No more is said, and with each jolt of the car and warm ray of sun that hits my body, I feel my eyes grow weary with every blink.

CHAPTER 10

I'm woken by the loud slam of the car door, which jolts me to my senses. The right corner of my mouth is slimy, and I quickly wipe away any dribble with the back of my hand. William smiles at me as he swings open my door. "I'm so sorry, how long was I asleep for?"

"Don't apologise ma'am, only 20 minutes. It's a short journey."

I clamber out the car, grabbing my camera as I shield my eyes from the sun, everything blindingly bright after my impromptu nap. I take a couple big blinks and the white haze softens, finally able to take in my surroundings. We're in a village, as I expected. Terracotta brick buildings with colourful hand painted signs: 'Hairdressers', 'Butchers', 'Restaurant', and dotted huts with thatched roofs. I look for Daniel and spy him being swarmed by a group of children as he hands out letters from his briefcase. "What's he doing?" I ask William, who's watching too.

"He is a sponsor of the village, about 40% of profits from Tukio come here. He's helped make the school bigger and writes to the children to practice their English. It's been invaluable this year because of the weather, the crops haven't been growing well because it's so dry."

I'm in shock. 40%?! I look at Daniel, who's smiling and laughing with the children, and feel my heart flutter. Thanking William, I gingerly make my way over to him. The children all stare at me, and Daniel smiles. "They don't see many of your type here."

"No. It's so fine. Hi!"

I awkwardly wave at them, unsure of which set of smiling eyes to look at. I reach for my camera, about to snap some photos of Daniel and the children but he shakes his head. "Just the buildings," he says sternly.

"Are you sure? I feel like this would be more personal–"

"Just the buildings, Maddie."

"Can I show you around?" William asks from behind me. I can tell it's him from the jingle of his Maasai jewellery as he speaks.

"Thanks, that'd be great."

We leave Daniel laughing and talking with the children and make our way around the buildings. I can sense more eyes on me, this time from the village adults. "Everyone is friendly, they just don't see many *mzungus* so you're something different" William says. His reassurance makes me smile.

"Mazoongoos?"

"White people." he says.

"Ahhh. I see. That makes sense."

William stops by a brick building in front of us, the outside decorated with abstract murals. "This is the new school building. The children painted all of these." He says, stroking the whirling waves of colour. I get out my camera and snap some shots. The murals are beautiful, their childish simplicity adding to their charm. "You see here, this is the hills, and the acacia tree, and the cattle." William says, using his finger to trace the shapes.

"Ohhh, I do see!"

He steps inside and I follow him, immediately struck by the temperature change indoors, making the hairs on my arms prickle. "It's the clay and brick we use, keeps it well insulated."

"It's incredible!" I say, as I snap more pictures of the inside. There are three long tables with seats dotted around them, and big boxes in the middle of the tables overflowing with markers and crayons. At the other end of the room is a large whiteboard, on its right side a bookcase containing a mix of English and Swahili books. "Daniel did all this?" I ask William, impressed by the amount of learning provisions stashed in the small room.

"He provided the money and gave some ideas. The school teacher, Mercy designed most of it." He says, gesturing to a slim woman with kind eyes and beautiful bone structure, sat at a wooden desk in the corner reading some papers. She could be a prima ballerina. I jump at the sight of her, having been so enthralled with the building I'd been completely oblivious to any other humans in the room. She laughs at this, standing up to shake my hand.

"Lovely to meet you!" she exclaims, her handshake warm and friendly.

"You too! You've done an incredible job here!"

Mercy clasps her hands to her chest in thanks.

"Would you mind if I got a couple pictures of the children's drawings?" I ask, gesturing to the wall behind her, a mini gallery showcasing artworks ranging from little stick figures to expertly shaded drawings.

"Of course!" she says, talking me through each little masterpiece and the stories of the children who created them.

Once I'm happy with the material I've got of the school, as well as the new houses and cattle pens William showed me, we make our way back to the car. Daniel is now sat on the floor playing what looks like a version of

Duck Duck Goose in the red dust. I quickly turn my camera back on, snapping some photos. I smile as I look through the viewfinder, at the cheeky little girl who sassily walks around the group, fake tapping people on the head. All the genuine smiles, the way Daniel watches her proudly. Her excited scream when she decides to tag Daniel, and he stands up, his 6 foot 5 self towering over her as she runs round the circle, the little pink beads in her braids dancing behind her in the air. I see their little eyes turn to look at us, and I quickly put the camera away. As we walk by, they wave to us, yelling something Swahili. "They want us all to play before we go." William translates.

"OK!" I say, quickly running to the car to put my camera away before joining the group.

"Do you want to start?" Daniel says to me. His eye contact makes my skin tingle.

"Sure." I say, rising to my feet. I walk around the circle, the children giggling nervously unsure if they'll have to spring to their feet and run.

"Duck, duck, duck…" Once I reach the tiny head with those pink coloured beads, I rest my hand on it for a beat longer. "Goose!"

The little girl shrieks with delight and quickly jumps up, chasing me round the circle. I slow my pace, enough for her to catch me if she works for it. I can see the white hem of my dress has turned a bright orange from the dust, but don't care. I feel a light tug at it and turn to see her mischievous face, eyes glimmering. She yells something at me, and the group roars with laughter. "She says you're slower than her grandmother!" William calls up from where he's sat.

"Tell her she's too fast - ready for the Olympics!" I say, wiping fake sweat from my brow. I glimpse down, and see Daniel watching me, the corners of his mouth curved into a smile. My heart thumps faster.

Daniel sits next to me on the drive back to camp, eager to look through the pictures. I've chugged one bottle of water and am halfway through a Coke as he looks, I hadn't realised how dehydrated I'd got in the midday sun. I swirl the cola round my mouth, appreciating how it cools down every crevice, every tooth. At this moment I don't care about cavities, all that matters are the sweet icy bubbles fizzing around my mouth. While I've been chugging, I've made sure to sneak peaks at Daniel, who looks pleased with the photos. I think I did a good job with my composition; architecture has never been my strong suit but I'm proud of what I took today. Suddenly I notice his face darken, and he tilts the camera towards me. "What's this?" he demands, gesturing to a picture of himself, laughing deeply next to some giggling children while a little blob runs behind him, too fast for the camera to capture. I quickly swallow my mouthful of bubbles, so fast I feel them nearly emerging through my nose.

"Sorry. I know you said just buildings, I didn't take them for the website, I thought you might like them, for you."

He thinks for a few seconds, brown eyes scanning my face for any deceit. Content with the answer he continues to look scroll through the photos.

"You don't have to answer if you don't want to, but how come you don't want any pictures of the people? I think they're really gorgeous, and more personab–"

"I don't want to."

"I know, I just don't understand why–"

"Because I don't want to be one of those companies that exploits people, especially children, for their own marketing."

"Yeah, but you're genuinely helping them. So, I don't think it's necessarily exploiting them."

Daniel shakes his head. "The target market for the website is rich younger Kenyans, yes, but we're also expecting to cater to rich millennials from all over the world. When people think of Africa, most think about those adverts on TV that show emaciated children with no water. It ruins people's perceptions of the continent, and I don't want to play a part in it. These people aren't helpless, sure, the money and medicine and clothes that are donated are a help, but the West presents them as if without our interference and charity they'd cease to exist. I don't want to have any hand in perpetuating that stereotype. I'm fine showing some of the buildings, as we did help build them, but I refuse to use any of those three-dimensional beings to be presented as two-dimensional ideas."

I silently sip on my coke, unsure what to say, the taste now sickly sweet. I'm both impressed and disgusted at the same time. Impressed by Daniel's conviction, the way he worded his thoughts with such poignance and ease. And disgusted with myself, knowing I'm guilty, maybe even when we first arrived at the village today of the very preconceptions he spoke about.

"You're right," is all I can muster.

He gently places a hand on my knee, and I feel the tingles shoot around my body like electrical currents.

"I'm sorry. The pictures are beautiful, and I will cherish them myself. But I don't want to profit off them. I didn't mean to come across harsh, I'm just passionate about this. My grandfather was from a village like that, and I want to do right by him and all my other ancestors."

I gaze into his eyes, studying the way the sun makes all the different shades of brown pop, like intertwined tendrils of tree roots, some deep mahogany, others golden. The sombreness in them. The vulnerability. He gazes back into mine for two seconds, and then quickly recoils his hand from my thigh, clearing his throat. As his hand leaves, so does the electricity that's been coursing through my veins. He could feel it too, I'm sure of it.

It's sunset as the car pulls into camp, and we are greeted by shrieks of laughter roaring from the lounge. Daniel quickly exits the vehicle, heading straight to his tent.

"Cheers for today, Maddie. Good work!" he says, waving a hand at me without turning back.

"No worries, see you at dinner!" I call after him. He doesn't respond, maybe he didn't hear me. As I walk towards the lounge, my trainers making the little stones crackle beneath their worn rubber soles, I peek through the branches concealing my view of the living area. I can make out Gia, splayed on the sofa like a Greek goddess. Surrounding her are three other girls – I'm guessing her friends have finally escaped quarantine. I take a big gulp. There's something about a group of girls my age laughing, if I don't know the joke for some reason, I immediately think it's about me. The crackle turns to a creak as my soles step onto the deck, all four heads snapping in my direction.

"Yaaaaay!" Gia shrieks, rising up and hugging me, her Tom Ford enveloping me in the scent of safety.

CHAPTER 11

The five of us sit at the dinner table, a sixth place laid in front of an empty chair. Maybe he's running late with work? To my right is Gia, wearing a brown silk cowl neck dress, showing off her collarbone which she's lightly dusted with gold glitter. Her braids are loosely held off her face with a tortoiseshell claw grip, gold hoop earrings peeking through the plaits. She has little dabs of the same shimmery gold as her collarbone on the inner corners of her eyes, and her lips shimmer with gloss. Ethereal is the only word to describe her. To my left is Cassie, who reminds me of a Latin Aphrodite, curvaceous and golden with slick dark hair running down her back. She's about 5'3, so makes Gia seem like a giant when they stand next to each other. She's wearing a gorgeous red kimono dress, which she's matched perfectly with her crimson lips. She looks like the type of woman I'd normally be terrified of but radiates warmth as soon as she looks at you. I'm grateful she's sat next to me, as opposed to Mandy. Mandy sits on the other side of Gia and gives me PTSD from school days. She's tiny, even skinnier than Gia, has tanned skin and a perfect blonde bob which she runs her long fingers through every thirty seconds. She's wearing hardly any makeup but somehow looks the most put together at the table, her button nose dotted with little constellations of freckles which compliment her hazel eyes perfectly. She's wearing a dinky white tube top, the outline of her nipples so prominent you can nearly see their rosy pink shade. She's matched it with a silk baby blue skirt that's down to her ankles. Where Cassie radiates warmth, Mandy radiates ice. Next to Mandy is Daniel's empty chair, and on Cassie's left is Brielle, Gia's old roommate from New York. She looks like a young Naomi Campbell if she had a part time job at an artsy bookstore, wearing black linen dungarees with no bra, chunky butterfly locks tied up with a Dior headscarf. It's safe to say I've never felt like such a toad in my life. Maybe it's a good Daniel isn't here, to see me in a lineup of more attractive women he could probably get – excluding Gia for obvious reasons.

Mustafa has served our starter, olive tapenade on crostini with goat's cheese. I never know how you're meant to eat crusty bread things in a formal setting. I attempt to pin it in place with the pressure from my fork and cut through it with my butter knife but I can't pierce the hard crust. I change tactic and try stabbing down the centre of the bread with my knife, exerting a good amount of pressure. Suddenly it splits in two, one half remaining on my gold rimmed plate and the other pinging across the table. Towards Mandy. And her white tube top. The conversation hushes, as Mandy flicks off a blob of tapenade from her chest.

"Shit! I'm so sorry!" I hold my breath, until the silence is broken by Gia's roaring laughter, snorting into her champagne flute. As soon as the sound leaves her mouth, everyone else joins in. Mandy smiles at me, her eyes cold, delicately placing the toast back on my plate.

"Don't worry, queen. I look good in purple too."

I smile back at her warmly, trying to muster some kind of rapport. I come up blank.

"It's very avant garde. Yeezy season 7?!" Brielle jokes, and everyone laughs more. I catch Gia's eye, and she nods to her crostini, which she's holding in her hand and eating like pizza. I smile back at her, grateful for the tip. That's the last time I try impress with unfamiliar dishes.

The main is filet mignon for Gia, Mandy and I, and a chunky grilled aubergine for the veggies; Cassie and Brielle. As the drinks flow, we talk more, and my scared inner schoolgirl who ate her lunches in the toilet, goes to bed. I keep looking towards Daniel's tent, expecting to see him emerge in his evening wear, a smile plastered on his face whilst apologising for his tardiness, but no such luck. When I see Ben carrying a plate of French fries past the dining table towards his tent, my heart sinks entirely. I guess he decided to order in. Dessert is gooseberry crumble, which is one of the most delectable things I've ever eaten. Sour berries, mixed with crunchy sweet buttery topping, and fresh cream – a crescendo of flavours dancing in my mouth. I lay back in my chair, hand on my belly in defeat as Ben comes to clear the plates.

"Any *digestifs* ladies?"

"Do you have Limoncello?" Mandy asks, her accent turning Italian as she says the drink's name. I roll my eyes internally.

"Apologies Ma'am, we don't"

"They have Kahlua!" Gia chimes happily. "5 of those please Ben, thank you."

Ben smiles and nods, leaving us. Brielle's been tapping away on her phone incessantly for the whole of dessert, and quickly looks up at Gia.

"I have to get my piece sent off tonight as they want it live tomorrow afternoon, are you still ok to read it over?"

"Yeah of course! You wanna do it now?"

"Please? That way I can actually sleep!"

"Of course!"

"We will be back… maybe…"

Gia says as they both rise. As she walks past Ben, she grabs her and Brielle's Kahluas from his tray. Looks like that might be goodnight then. We sit in silence at the table, unsure of what to say. I take a big glug of my remaining champagne, as Ben sets our shots down in front of us. I watch Mandy take a small sip, tousle her hair, cross her arms and lean into the table. I really never thought hazel eyes could be cold.

"Sooo. Is Daniel around?" she asks, running her a French tip around the rim of her shot glass.

"Uhh yeah. I was with him today for a shoot."

Mandy smiles sweetly and tilts her dainty neck back to down the shot. I imagine slashing it with my butterknife. Jesus, where'd that come from?!

"You know…" she continues, using that same French tip to dab the corners of her pink lips. "Last time I saw him he was looking real cute. He like that now?"

"Like what?"

"Cute."

I stab my tongue into my cheek. Why is this triggering me? I don't even know if he likes me. Or if I like him.

"I guess, I hadn't really noticed."

Mandy tilts her head back again, this time to release a small cackle.

"Miss girl, you must have a pussy like the Sahara to not feel anything when that man walks into a room."

I see Cassie awkwardly sip her liquor, aware of the dig.

"The stars here are crazy" she says, looking up trying to change the subject. It's appreciated.

"I know! Daniel and I were in the pool together the other night and he showed me the big dipper, see those little three there!" I say, looking straight at Mandy for a second before pointing it out to Cassie. "We were down there for ages, just the two of us." She stares daggers back at me. "I didn't know pools could be that steamy in November! Maybe it's heated." I finish my Kahlua in one swift gulp and make my exit, feeling like the baddest bitch in Kenya.

As soon as I reach my tent, I start rifling through my satchel to retrieve my phone. I have to tell Anya everything. I need her level- headed advice to help with this… Lust? Jealousy? Confusion? I suddenly remember plugging it in by the bar in the lounge, and my heart sinks. Shit. I can't go back now, not after my grand exit. But I can't not have my phone, most importantly for my alarm tomorrow. I planned on getting up earlier than needed to make myself look gorgeous. Shit shit shit! I decide to read my book in an attempt to stay awake. I fight every slow blink, the alcohol in me a warm, gentle fuzz and the crickets outside singing their twinkly lullaby. I feel my eyelids grow heavier by the moment as if made of lead, and can't resist sinking into a deep slumber.

I peel my eyes open, scanning round the tent. I have no clue how long I was out. Double shit. I drag myself across the room, now shivering in the cold. I pull my dress off over my head - nearly toppling over and throw on my stripy linen pyjama bottoms and 2019 leavers hoodie. I plod to the canvas door and flick my lantern on and off a few times. An *askari* makes his way over, holding a large stick and a flashlight. We smile at each other, and he starts to guide me towards the lounge.

"What time is it?" I ask wearily, hoping I was asleep for a few hours as opposed to thirty minutes. Mainly so I don't have to see Mandy and her fuck ass bob again.

"4am ma'am" he responds.

Thank God. As we approach the lounge, I can see it's already clean and empty, breakfast table set for tomorrow. I exhale a deep sigh of relief and make my way inside the candlelit interior. I stop in my tracks at the sight of him, wearing blue plaid pyjama trousers, a white vest, and his silver chain. He's stood by the pool table, one hand holding a cue stick, the other a little crystal glass of amber liquid. I watch as his long fingers stroke the cue stick, pondering his next move as he lifts the tumbler to his lips, taking a sip. I try creep in slowly to retrieve my phone without disturbing him, but on my third step the floorboards betray me and release a loud creak. He turns to face me, leaning his hip on the table. He looks at me, eyeing my pyjamas, but doesn't say anything.

"Evening." I break the silence.

"Morning." He responds.

I keep on my path, making a bee line for the charging port where my phone sleeps.

"Fancy a game?" he continues, nodding towards the pool table. I feel the butterflies in my belly take flight.

"I don't actually know how to." I respond, yanking my phone off charge and slipping it into my hoodie pocket.

"I can teach you," he says, filling another crystal glass with whiskey, holding it out to me.

"Alright."

I take the drink, our fingers grazing for a second. I feel that same static shock rush through them. We both take a sip, holding eye contact as the fiery liquid trickles down my throat. He sets his down on the edge of the green felt and lowers his body down to the table. He shuts one eye lining up the cue with the balls, and in one quick shot sends a yellow ball flying down into one of the sinkholes.

"Nice. I have no clue if that was good. Looked cool though."

He laughs. "Your go."

"OK. Don't be insecure though, I'm really good."

He smirks into his whisky as he takes another sip and watches me as I try figure out how to line up the cue.

"Need some help?"

I peer back at him, a small lock of hair falling between my eyes. "Sure."

He walks behind me, the scent of sandalwood and whisky wafting in the air making my insides do somersaults.

"Firstly, your stance is wrong. You need to get your body lower, so you can see the billiards properly." He places his hand on my shoulder pushing me down, gently but firmly. The tingling's now relocated to between my legs. He's stood behind me, his tall form leaning over my body. I can feel his breath on my ear as he speaks, smell the drink on his lips, maybe that's why he's got the confidence to act like this – or the unprofessionalism.

"Bring the cue to the table, and line it up to the ball you're aiming for," he purrs into my ear as he takes hold of my right arm where I hold the cue, stretching it out on the pool table. I feel my breath grow heavier, feeling the press of his body against mine. I try keep my focus on his instructions, but my body doesn't feel connected to my mind anymore. I feel his lips brush against my ear, and then onto my neck. Oh my god. I clench my fingernails into my fist till it hurts, testing if I'm dreaming. His lips start kissing my neck, his body rubbing against me, his breathing now as heavy as my own. He runs his hand along my arm, still stretched out holding the cue, all the way down to my waist. I feel them creep under my hoodie, their warmth caressing my torso, finding their way to my bare breasts.

The tingling between my legs has now developed into an aching for his touch. As if sensing this, his right hand leaves my breast and slowly moves down my belly, teasing me, stroking everywhere but where the yearning stems from. Suddenly he uses his legs to force mine completely open, making the air feel cold against my wetness. He then touches me, a loud moan escaping my mouth. I hear him chuckle softly in response, his lips still on my neck. The electrical current returns, stronger than ever, starting between my thighs and shooting manically around my body. Another moan leaves my mouth, and he firmly places his left hand over my lips, pressing down to stifle the sounds as his right hand caresses me. I let my body melt into his, giving him all of me. I feel my heartbeat grow faster, and then suddenly the electricity stops, like someone pulled the plug. He's recoiled from me nearly as quickly as he'd touched me. He reaches for the rest of his drink and downs it, I watch still bent over the table, my mind hazy.

"We should get to bed. Big day tomorrow," he says.

"Uh, what?" I say, running my hand through my hair, trying to reconnect my body and mind to become a functioning human again. He's already out of the lounge, heading in the direction of his tent. I prop myself up on the table, in shock of what just transpired from the simple task of retrieving my phone.

CHAPTER 12

"That's it?"

"Yep."

"What the fuck?!"

"Yep." I shovel another loaded spoonful of yogurt and granola into my mouth in despair. I'm sat cross legged on my bed; my phone propped up on a pillow whilst I FaceTime Anya. She works remotely as a writer for the up-and-coming Gen Z version of Buzzfeed; Blabber. Today is obviously a day with meetings, as her blonde hair is slicked back into a low bun and she wears a white and black polka dot shirt, but she's sat cross legged in her chair so I can see her grey joggers just peek into frame.

"Had there been... this sort of energy before this?" she asks, chewing on a pen. I shovel another heaped spoonful into my mouth and shrug. Before waddling back to my tent last night, I'd left a note for Ben requesting breakfast in my tent. I needed time to compose myself before seeing Daniel again.

"Maybe, I guess? But I thought it was just me, he's been so hot and cold, I actually wasn't even sure he liked me... like as a person."

"That's always the way with the ones that really fancy you. I guess maybe he just wants to stay professional? When do you finish?"

"Tonight basically. I fly home tomorrow evening."

"Ok. Great from a selfish basis, I've missed you lots. But also great from a Daniel basis. You wrap the project tonight, so if it's professionalism holding him back that should all disintegrate as soon as you take the last shot."

I shrug, massaging a chunk of granola with my tongue. "Maybe. But the actual job won't be done for another couple weeks, Maria will be building the website and editing the pictures in London."

"True. But you'll be done with it. You'll be back to picking up her dry-cleaning and answering her emails."

I check the time in the corner of my screen, shit, nearly 11. "Ughhhhhhh I gotta go soon, I'm meant to be starting at 11."

"OK. You look fit. Don't stress. I'm sure he fancies you; he just doesn't want to seem unprofessional. He came into control of the business recently, you said. He's probably still trying to find his feet."

"True true. You're very wise. I'll see you Thursday. Love you."

"Love you more!"

Anya waves goodbye, her gold bangles jangling before her face disappears, and I'm left staring at my own reflection in the black of my screen. I got up early, as planned, and look nice today. I made sure to wear extra concealer on my cheeks, to prevent any blushing at eye contact with Daniel. I'm wearing a white vest and blue jeans, that hug my ass nicely but have a baggier fit at the bottom. The vest shows just enough cleavage to be enticing but not immodest. I spoon the dregs of my granola into my mouth, throw my linen shirt over my vest and grab my camera and satchel. Just before I'm out the tent, I quickly retrace my steps and spritz on a heap of perfume. Ok. Ready.

Waiting for me by the lounge is Mustafa, dressed in full chef whites standing with his hands clasped in front of him. Behind him to his left, I see a long pair of toned caramel legs dangling over the arm of a sofa, their toenails painted a shimmery lilac.

"Are you ready for some fun?" Mustafa says, his deep voice rumbling out of him like soft treacle.

"Yes, of course!"

"Please…" he says, gesturing towards a white thatched hut I'd never entered, but had noticed smoke trickling out of most evenings. Gia pokes her head over the sofa, revealing the owner of the purple toes.

"Watcha doing?"

"I'm not sure, I think I'm going to take some photos of the kitchen?"

Mustafa nods and smiles. "You'll get a free cooking lesson too. I'm going to make lunch for everyone."

Gia jumps up, slamming the script she's reading on the coffee table. "Can I help?"

Mustafa smiles "Are you a good cook?"

"Nope!" Gia responds, following us towards the hut.

I help tie Gia's apron around her small waist, she's about four inches taller than me so it's an easy job. Her braids are down today, reaching just past her waist. They smell like almonds and vanilla, and I can't help leaning a little closer as I tie the flannel in a bow. The hut is small, a squeeze with three people. Mustafa works on his own in the kitchen, I have no clue how.

"I thought there would be at least two sous-chefs." I say to myself, admiring the racks of dried spices that line the white stone walls. Mustafa smiles and holds out his hands gesturing to me and Gia.

"They are right here!"

We all laugh, and then turn our attention to Mustafa's demonstration. He's making spaghetti meatballs from scratch and gives an in-depth tutorial for his pasta recipe. I snap pictures of each step, making sure to get his warm face in each one. The snowy well of flour he sculpts on the oak countertops, the bright orange egg yolk he expertly cracks into it, delicately separating it from the opaque egg whites and plopping it in the centre. Gia follows along with her own mini version next to him, clumsily breaking the yolk as she attempts the transfer. The orange goo runs down her long fingers to her wrists, and Mustafa points her to the sink. She sheepishly rinses them as Mustafa tends to the rich tomato sauce, simmering away on the stove.

"I must confess, I cheated. I made the meatballs yesterday to save time, but see, they are still fresh." He says, opening the fridge and removing a large plate containing a spiral of large meatballs, dotted with onions and fresh herbs.

"See the four in the middle, how they are greener in colour?" Gia and I nod. "These are the vegetable ones, made with a spinach base." I snap a photo.

"They look insane!" Gia says, leaning her chin on my shoulder "This was a bad idea, it's just making me really hungry!"

Mustafa next shows us how to thinly roll the pasta dough and slice it into tagliatelle. I jump at hearing Daniel's voice, "Hello Mustafa, can you meet me in my tent to discuss dinner. Thanks."

I feel my hackles go down realising it just blared out from the radio in the corner. Mustafa answers, and heads for the door.

"Can you girls please hang the pasta, like that?" He points to long tendrils of tagliatelle dangling off beams on the ceiling "I'll be back in 5 minutes."

"Sure!" we say in unison, and then we're alone.

Gia dips a pinky in the tomato sauce and rolls her eyes back in pleasure as she licks it off.

"You have to try this!" she says, and I reach for a spoon. "Don't be silly, we'll have to wash that up!" she hisses, dipping her ring finger in the sauce and holding it out to me. A large glob slides to the bottom of her finger, ready to fall. "Quickly!" she giggles, and I do as she says, wrapping my lips around the end of her finger, my mouth singing with all the different flavours. She gently pulls her finger from my lips and licks off the residue sauce. I knew she was beautiful, but I don't think I'd realised how beautiful till now. She's wearing no makeup, but her long dark lashes easily reach her feathery eyebrows when she looks up. Her nose is spattered with teeny freckles, and she has a larger mole on her right cheekbone. It gives her the quality of an old-Hollywood movie star. I notice I've been staring at her silently for longer than is socially acceptable, and I think she does too. She flicks a handful of flour at me, making me jump.

"Bitch!"

"Quit staring, creep!" she giggles at me, biting her lip. My cheeks get hot, and I'm grateful for the extra concealer - just surprised who triggered the need for it.

"You're gonna regret that!" I say setting down my camera.

"Ohh shit!" Gia giggles more, trying to duck behind the work bench. I reach for the first thing I see, an egg, and grab it. "Oh no. You wouldn't!" she says, crouching below me.

"Oh really?" I tease.

"Oh fuck, Mustafa's back!" Gia says, springing to her feet. I turn around, to see the doorway empty, but feel a cold goo trickle down my scalp. I turn slowly back to

Gia, my mouth agape in shock. She stands grinning, holding a crushed eggshell in her hand.

"I wasn't actually gonna do it!" I say, still in disbelief.

"Well, you're a pussy then!" she says, darting out the way as I try fling more flour at her. I abandon the egg and dip a large spoon into the steamy crimson sauce. Gia holds up both her hands, as if under arrest while wiggling her nose trying to get rid of the flour dusting it.

"No! Truce - I just got this top!"

"Oh really?!" I say taunting her with the spoon. "I just washed my hair!"

"Ok I'm sorry the egg was too far. It was the only thing in reach. I'm sorry. I'll buy you dinner, a drink, a dress! Please! I love this top!" she pleads, getting onto her knees clasping her hands together below me.

"Fine." I say, rolling my eyes as we both laugh.

"What are you doing?" Mustafa's deep voice makes both of us jump, and we watch as the sauce bounces off the spoon, slowly towards Gia's chest, and then SPLAT! Onto her top.

I vigorously massage shampoo into my hair, making sure no strand is left untouched, the icy water shooting down my body. Gia warned me not to have a hot shower, otherwise it would cook the egg. She learned the hard way from a DIY hair mask she'd tried. Once I'm confident I've gotten rid of it all, I switch the water to hot, my body relaxing in relief. So much for the makeup I'd worked so hard on this morning. I take one last look at the view and exit the shower, wrapping the plush towel around me. I undo the velcro Gia had made sure I saw before leaving me to shower and enter the bathroom. Gia's stood topless, just in her denim shorts, aggressively scrubbing her stained top with a bar of soap. Her breasts are small and perky, and I can't help my eyes graze across them. She catches me and raises her eyebrows. "Was this your plan all along? Get me nude and scrubbing in your bathroom?"

"Yeah totally. I have huge mummy issues." I joke, and Gia laughs as she wrings out her top. "I am really sorr–"

"Don't! Not your fault, I've already said."

I exhale in relief, standing next to her in the mirror, removing the remnants of my earlier masterpiece, now just panda eyes.

"You look cute with no makeup." she says, not looking away from her sopping top. I crinkle my nose at the statement.

"I don't agree, but thanks."

She stops scrubbing, gazing at me with her big eyes. "You should."

I smile, and walk away, unsure why the fluttery pests are flying around my belly. I enter the bedroom, and frantically try slapping on my face again, extra concealer like before. If Gia, my new platonic friend is making me blush I hate to think how red I'll go in front of Daniel. Probably the same colour as my hair. I guess her fame must still be throwing me off. Gia emerges from the bathroom wearing her wet, now pastel pink top. "I'm gonna go grab some clothes from my tent, how long will you be?"

"Um. Maybe 25?"

"Ok. I'll meet you back here!"

Gia's back in 15 minutes, I'm just finishing up my base makeup and moving onto eyeliner.

"Oooh fancy!" I hear her exclaim behind me.

"Yeah. I thought since it's my last night may as well go all out." I say, turning to face her. She's cradling a bottle of red in her right arm and holds two crystal wine glasses in her left. Behind her is Ben, trying to avert his eyes from me, still clad in my towel. He holds a tray with two silver cloches and cutlery.

"What's this?" I say confused.

"Lunch!" Gia says, setting the bottle on the tray as she takes it from Ben, smiling in thanks. She walks past me to the patio area, and precariously places the tray down on the coffee table.

"Finish that later, let's eat while it's hot!"

I set my eyeliner down, despite having already started on my left eye. I join her on the sofa, and she triumphantly lifts the cloches to reveal the meatballs and tagliatelle we worked on this morning.

"Oh my god! They actually look really good?!"

Gia smirks as she fills our wine glasses.

"Ha! I may have told Mustafa to give everyone else the pasta we made and give us his."

I raise my wine glass to her as she flops onto the sofa next to me "Cunning. I like it."

She's wearing grey baggy basketball shorts and a black bandeau. She sees me looking and nods her head toward a bag she must've brought with her.

"Comfies for while we eat. I brought my clothes for tonight with me. Thought we could get ready together!"

"I mean, I'm super down but... How come you don't wanna have lunch and get ready with your friends?" I say, as I prong a meatball with my fork. Gia shrugs as she does the same, hers skidding across her plate as she misses.

"I dunno. I can see them anytime. I don't know when I'll see you again. And I like you."

I try hush the butterflies in my belly so I can swallow my big bite of meatball, which now feels stuck in my mouth. I reach for my wine and take a big swig to wash it down.

CHAPTER 13

Gia and I jiggle up and down as the car drives over the savannah terrain, both struggling to hang onto the deck of Top Trumps in our hands after finishing off the bottle of Rioja. We're running a touch late for dinner, losing track of time dancing to my 00's playlist whilst doing our makeup. Brielle, Mandy and Cassie left for dinner half an hour ago. Gia's tied her braids up in a low bun, which is tinted gold by the rays of the setting sun. She wears baggy mom jeans, a black corset top and slinky black heels. I stupidly forgot we were dining in the bush, not shielded by the luxury of the tent and am wearing a black halter neck maxi dress, that hugs my curves nicely. I never had the confidence to wear it in London so I don't know what made me pack it and choose to wear it tonight. I'll wear my hair down for dinner but have a claw grip in it for the car ride. Gia braided me two little plaits either side of my face, which swing across my vision as the car moves.

"Agility 84" Gia says, raising an eyebrow as she peeks over her fan of cards.

"Fuck. 47." I say, handing over my Seahorse. It had been one of my favourites. I look past Gia's golden bun and to the view. I feel a pang of sadness, knowing it's my last night. I haven't been here long, but it truly feels like it's altered my brain chemistry. And now I'm nearly done. The sunset has just started, orange trickling into the hazy blue as the sun's strength weakens. When the acacia trees block it, you can look straight into the golden light peeking through the branches. The car slows as we arrive on a small cliff overlooking a river below, I'm guessing the spot Daniel described. William hops out the front, his jewellery singing and opens Gia's door. I see him make his way over to do mine, and I quickly fling it open myself, grabbing my camera and satchel. I feel so awkward being waited on, having been a waitress until working with Maria. I smile at him warmly, trying to show my appreciation. He leads us into a little clearing shielded by bushes, and Gia links my arm as our heels hobble over the rocks.

"Why didn't we wear trainers?" She hisses at me.

"Rioja courage." I respond, and see her smile grow. As we emerge from the bushy path, I stop in my tracks in awe of the set up. There's a round table draped with a white tablecloth, surrounded by six khaki camping chairs. The same glass lanterns as camp are dotted around, and there's a large fallen tree that's been sanded down flat and turned into a makeshift bar. Concealed by the bush branches I can make out a small campfire, laughter and conversation radiating off it. Sat on suede poofs around the fire are three figures, I'm guessing Brielle, Mandy and Cassie. I grip onto my satchel, my fingers turning white. Maybe I shouldn't have left it so frosty with Mandy last night. William pushes the last overhanging branches out the way, revealing the fire pit. My heart drops into my stomach. Daniel is here, sat on a brown poof. He's wearing his classic wardrobe, white linen shirt, top two buttons undone, khaki trousers and brown boots. It's not so much Daniel's presence that is unnerving me, but more so the pair of toned legs draped over his, sitting next to him on the poof. Sharing it with him. She's wearing white linen trousers and a tight white backless top, clinging to her body so well you could trace the outline of her abs. And once again, her nipples. Maybe I should donate the bitch a bra. One arm is around Daniel, the other outstretched holding a mojito.

"Hey queens!" Gia exclaims, and they all coo hello back. I watch as some of Mandy's mojito sloshes over the crystal rim as she waves at us. I can barely drag my eyes from them to greet Brielle and Cassie. I smile at them, my eyes darting back to him immediately. I can't feel if Gia's still holding my arm. I can't feel anything but a mix of embarrassment and rage.

"We should take some pictures while the sunset's still here." I say curtly.

"She's all business tonight!" Gia laughs, accepting a mojito from Ben. He holds out the silver tray to me, with one slim glass of clear icy liquid speckled with mint left. I shake my head and smile. I think if I drink anything I might end up pushing him off the cliff. Or her.

I grit my teeth behind the camera for nearly all the pictures. Even when Mandy was eating, her mouth open, full of food, of course she still looked sexy. The firepit ones look great, Daniel stood up, refusing to be in them which helped. He'd got up quickly and smiled at me "I think I've done enough modelling for a lifetime."

Was that meant to be a joke? The girls had posed by the firepit, chatting, laughing, drinking. I got some photos of the empty table, and then when it was time to eat some of them enjoying the starter and main, Daniel again squirming out of frame every time the camera clicked. I'd made sure I was sat between Brielle and Gia, not wanting to have to smell him. Smell her on him.

I take the first sip of my mojito, now diluted from the molten ice, when dessert is served. It's a pea flower poached pear, the outside bright purple, and the flesh light cream. It sits on a dollop of crème fraîche , speckled with little black dots - vanilla bean I'm guessing. I snap a photo before I take a bite, and then take a large gulp to wash it down. At least the night is nearly over. Mid-swig I look around, to find Daniel's eyes locked on me. I nearly splutter out the lukewarm contents of my mouth in shock.

"Excuse me." I say, getting up from the table with my camera and satchel. I'm aware of Mandy's eyes burning into the back of my head but I ignore them, and rest myself on a poof by the fire, my back to the table. I start reviewing the pictures, making note of the best ones in my little moleskine diary. I don't need to do this now; I was planning on doing it back home or on the plane. But there's no service out here so I can't fake a phone call or scroll Instagram, so this is the best social armour I have. I see Ben start clearing the plates and offer a bottle of armagnac to everyone. Hopefully this'll be wrapping up soon. Everyone accepts a small glass, aside from Daniel. Without looking at him I can feel his gaze still locked on me.

I snap a couple photos of Mustafa as he packs up, he smells of smoke from the portable outdoor stove and spices from the Moroccan lamb he'd grilled on it. I can hear the girls laughing and shrieking as they decide who's riding in which car. I stay and admire the now empty cliff, not caring who I ride with. As long as it's not Daniel. But I expect he'll go back in the staff car, not wanting to be around Gia's rowdy entourage and the girl he toyed with and humiliated for sport.

All that's left in the firepit are glowing amber embers, that still radiate waves of heat rippling through the air. I walk past it, near the edge of the cliff and look up. It's like a spatter of tiny rhinestones on rich black velvet. I wish I could see the stars in London. My flat has a view of the off-licence opposite, and to look up I'd have to literally hang out my window. When I'm out, I realise I never look up. Everyone in London seems to look down, avoiding eye contact, making sure they don't trip or step in dog poo. I need to remember to do that when I'm home. Look up. Maybe it's just as beautiful, but I've never seen it. I inhale deeply, filling my lungs with the rich smokey air.

"Sorry ma'am, the car is ready to leave." Ben says from behind me.

"Thanks Ben." I say, peeling my eyes from the view.

For fuck's sake. Is it an option to walk? I think I'd rather be zebra food than endure this drive. Sat in the back of the car is Daniel… and Mandy… who is currently playing with the chain around his neck, twirling its silver links around her finger like a cat playing with its dinner.

"Hey." I say dryly, clambering into a seat in front of them. At least the vans are 4 seaters, so I don't have to sit next to them. Or in-between them.

"What were you doing?" Daniel asks from behind me.

"Just looking at the view." I respond stonily.

I hear Mandy's schoolgirl giggles from the backseat, and Daniel whispering "Stop!" Quietly. I feel my stomach somersault in knots with each jolt of the car. I need some water. I rifle through the cool box, continually pulling out ginger beer or cola. Daniel's hand reaches between my seat and the one next to me, offering a bottle of Evian, half drunk.

"I got the last one, if this is what you're looking for." I take it from him.

"Thanks." I chug down its contents, my teeth clanking on the top three times as the car moves. I don't care. I try block out the giggling, Daniel's hushed deep whispers, focus on the stars that I may never see this well again. Fifteen minutes go by, they feel like fifty.

"STOP THE CAR!" Daniel suddenly booms from the back, making me nearly jump out my skin. The driver, one of the *askaris* - I can't remember his name, comes to a halt quickly. I whip around to face the two of them, and see Mandy clumsily hauling her tiny body over the open side. I look at Daniel in confusion, and notice his face looks weary. I hear a loud retching, and then a splatter from the side of the car. Ah. Is it bad her discomfort gives me a slither of joy? Mandy wipes her mouth on the back of her arm, her white top now dotted with tiny speckles of orange.

"You should sit in front next to Joseph." Daniel says. Joseph! That was it. "You'll feel less sick there."

Mandy nods and hobbles her way to the front of the car, flinging open the door. The car starts up again, and the dusty air flies. At least I don't have to listen to their giggles anymore. I feel Daniel's hand on my shoulder and turn to face him coldly.

"What?"

He pats the seat next to him. "Come here."

"Why?"

"Just come here."

I don't know why I obey, but I gingerly squirm between the seats to reach the back. As I do the car goes over a large bump, making me fly up to the ceiling and bang my head. "Ow!"

"Shit." Daniel reaches forward to the cool box, retrieving a frosty ginger ale and pressing it against my forehead. "Better?"

I shrug. We sit quietly, the throbbing in my head slowly giving in to the cool glass.

"Did you enjoy dinner?" he finally breaks the silence.

"Yep." I say, biting the inside of my cheek.

"Are you happy with the photos?"

"Yep."

"Are you going to answer every question with yep?"

I glare at him, turning to look at the stars. "Yep."

"Why have you been so frosty with me tonight?"

"I didn't know I had been."

"Don't. Just be honest."

I scoff. "Me just be honest? You're the one who's not been honest. Acting like you hate, then oh, you like me, then you hate me, then we nearly have sex, then you suddenly have another girl stuck to you like a parasite all evening right in front of me!" I hiss, glancing at Mandy in the front who's thankfully nearly passed out.

Daniel shakes his head, rubbing his hand over his chin. "It's not like that."

"Look. I'm actually over it. I'm leaving tomorrow so you'll never have to be in my presence again." I say, chucking the ginger ale onto the seat in front and reaching to climb back to my original spot. He pulls me back by my waist, making me fall back much too close to him for my liking.

"Listen. I'm sorry. It's just complicated. Firstly, on the subject of…" he glances towards the front of the car. "Her family have been very generous with the camp, so I have to keep her happy. If that means letting her think that there's some connection between us, so be it."

"So now you're a prostitute?"

"No! I've never done anything with her. And am never planning on it. But if she wants to rest her legs on me I won't object."

"Ok…"

"Ok?"

I bite my lip. "That's only half of it. You either act like you just want to sleep with me, or like I'm a piece of rubbish you can't wait to have removed from your property."

He's silent, hand still on his chin in thought. The car slows, pulling into the familiar trees of camp.

"Thank God." I say, reaching my hand to open the door. Daniel clasps my other one and I look back to him, his eyes weary and... sad? He cups my face with his large hand and presses his soft lips against mine. Then he pulls away, mutters "I'm sorry" and swiftly exits the van heading to his tent. I'm left alone and in shock, my heart pounding, as Mandy clambers out the front, catching her flowy trousers on the door nearly tripping.

Carley Rae Jepsen blasts from the little speakers in the lounge, and Gia grabs my hand spinning me round, round, round.

"Ben, my angel, more limes please!" slurs Cassie, sloppily filling up our shot glasses with El Patron. I stop spinning, and dizzily flop on the sofa. I got all my work done. The trip is over. Daniel kissed me. The words dart around my brain, and I quickly take another tequila shot, trying to silence them.

"Damn, she's not waiting on that lime!" Brielle laughs next to me, my face scrunching at the taste. It's nearly 3 in the morning, and I'm leaving for my flight back to Nairobi at 11am. After taking photos of the dance party, I partly stayed because it was fun – and probably the last chance I'll get for free top-shelf booze in a while – but also because I was hoping Daniel might join. I can see a sliver of turquoise peak out just below the balcony and think back to that night in the pool with him.

"Can we play beer pong on this? Or is that disrespectful?" Mandy slurs, draped on the pool table. I can't help but release a little laugh, the knowledge of her crush on Daniel, and the memory of what him and I did there. She squints her eyes at me and opens her mouth to speak, but doesn't say anything.

When 4am hits, I accept that Daniel won't be joining us. I stand up from the sofa, giddy with alcohol and serotonin. I should get to bed - I haven't even packed.

"I'm going to sleep–"

"Nooooooo!" Everyone echoes. Mandy even joins in, to my surprise.

"I know. My flight's early." I say helplessly, slipping my purple heels back on, which I'd thrown off while we were making up choreography to Christina Aguilera. Gia downs the rest of her G&T and stands up.

"I'm gonna go too. I'm making the executive decision to try start the hangover prevention for tomorrow."

"It's absolutely too late for that!" Cassie laughs.

"It was lovely meeting you all, maybe see you again someday!" I say, leaning over to hug Brielle, who gives me a warm squeeze back.

"I'm sure we will. I hope the pictures turn out well!" Brielle says as she releases me.

"Don't be ridiculous!" Cassie says as I reach down to hug her. "We'll get up tomorrow to say bye!"

"That's sweet. But just in case you're too tired!"

She kisses my cheek as I hug her, and I feel some of her signature red lip stain my face. I go to hug Mandy, who plasters a larger than necessary smile on her face.

"Sooo lovely to meet you." She says, her arms barely touching me. Gia locks her hand in mine and waves over to the *askari* who's been sat in the corner playing Candy Crush for the last three hours waiting to walk us back. The night air is cold, especially on my bare arms. I feel all my little hairs prick up; I hate to imagine how cold I'd be if I wasn't this drunk. Or how cold London will feel when I get back. Gia's tent is before mine, and she pulls me in for a massive bear hug.

"You have my number. Stay in touch. To be honest you're a massive breath of fresh air."

"Stop, they're all great." I say gesturing back to the lounge, Britney Spears quietly thumping.

"I know. But so are you."

"Love you. Sleep well."

"You too! If I'm not up to say bye wake me!" She says, wobbling into her tent.

CHAPTER 14

I'm astounded when my alarm blares snapping me awake, impressed I actually remembered to plug my phone in. My mouth tastes hot and sticky, I'm guessing I passed out before brushing my teeth and removing my makeup, seeing as I'm still in my black dress.

I'm being driven to the airstrip in an hour, just enough time to pack and eat breakfast. I sit up, the motion too much for my fragile body and feel the contents of my stomach rising. I tumble out of bed and reach the toilet just in time. I don't know why I stayed up so late and drank so much. I mean I do. It's probably a good thing he didn't show up, I hate to imagine what I could've said or done in my drunken state if he'd joined us. I splash my face with cold water, trying to soothe my puffy cheeks. I glance at the limestone bath longingly, knowing it would soothe my aching body. I'm guessing I toppled over a couple times during our "Dirrty" choreography, as I now have a large purple splodge forming on my hip. I tap my phone to check the time. 10.05. I could have a quick one.

Running the bath makes me feel like a child playing with my mother's toiletries again, making a potion. I tip in everything in sight, lavender bath salts, a vanilla bath bomb, rosehip oil. I like the temperature just hot enough to make my skin turn lobster pink. I dive in, hair and all. It feels counterproductive to wash this well before a day of travelling, but it feels too good to resist. I admire the savannah view, trying to really appreciate every tree, every rock, knowing I'll probably never see them again. Unless…unless something happened with Daniel. I imagine him surprising me outside my London flat, a handful of purple peonies. A bottle of Sauvignon Blanc. My right-hand creeps down my belly, towards the area that yearns to be touched – be touched by him. I imagine my hands are his, my toes curling. I imagine us in my dinky London bed, the way it would creak with every powerful thrust. Us lying together, sweaty, and tired and content. Ordering a Chinese after. What would he get? Chow mein? Szechuan? Sweet and sour?

No surprise that I'm the only person in the lounge; I shovel down as much toast and scrambled eggs as I can to try counteract the nausea. Gia said to wake her, but as I'd walked past her tent I'd heard tiny snores, the kind you'd hear from a baby pug. It made me smile, and I decided to leave her. I'd text her sorry when I got to

Nairobi airport, and probably send her a pug gif. I can imagine her laughing at it, showing the girls. I expected Daniel to be up as he had an early night, but he's nowhere to be seen. I consider going to his tent, seeing if he's there. No. If he wanted to, he would. That's the best bit of advice Anya ever gave me. If they wanted to, they would.

I watch William load my purple case into the car. I guess it's nearly time. I check my watch, 10.55. I'm wearing my travel comfies, a cropped white t-shirt and forest green baggy joggers. My hair is still wet from the bath, I decided not to wash it as it'll just get dirty on the plane. Instead, I let it soak up the lavender and vanilla water and tied it in a French braid down my back. I was sure Daniel would come and see me, so even did base makeup, which I'd never normally do before travelling. I'm such an messy sleeper I always end up smearing half of it off on the plane pillow. It had seemed worth it though, for him. I feel the eggy toast churn, unsure if it's from the six tequila shots I did or the thought of Daniel not bothering to say goodbye. Maybe the kiss was just an easy way out; another lie. Why wouldn't it work if he liked me? It's not like he doesn't have the money to travel? Or a fucking phone he can message me on?

"Ms. Wilson!" I see William waving at me from the car. I down the rest of my apple juice and grab my satchel making my way over. Lined up by the car are Ben and Mustafa. They reach out to shake my hand, but I make sure to hug them both.

"Thank you so much. It was unforgettable." I say, biting my lip. "Is Daniel around?" I see Ben and Mustafa glance at each other.

"Uh, no. He is working."

"Working. Alright." I say, clambering into the car. Ben and Mustafa wave as the car pulls out the drive. As we turn, I get a better view of Daniel's tent, and see him sat on his patio watching the car leave, drinking an espresso. It takes all my strength to keep my jaw from hitting the floor. Prick.

I'm nude, sprawled out on a large bed, the city view twinkling against the night sky through the large windows. I dig my fingers into the cold ivory sheets, the pleasure from between my legs intensifying. I look down to see Daniel, his fingers inside me while he slowly kisses where I yearn for him most. I can smell smokey cinnamon wafting over from an incense burner next to me and hear a warm fireplace crackling on my right. My back arches as I climax, staring at the crystal chandelier as the ripples of pleasure echo through every bone in body. I look down panting, to my shock finding Gia looking back up at me.

"Mmm, you liked that?" she says, kissing her way up from between my legs to my belly to my breasts. She gently strokes between my legs, its sensitivity nearly painful from the release, as she kisses my neck. She stops, and looks deep in my eyes, our lips grazing. "Any drinks?" she moans.

"What?" I mumble.

"Any drinks?" the flight attendant asks impatiently. I suddenly snap awake, the loud blare of the plane engine accosting my ears, ripping me from my dream.

"Uh, water please." I say, chugging down the mini bottle as soon as it enters my hand. That was weird. I check the flight time, three hours left to London.

I take a break from lugging my suitcase up the stairs one flight from my door. That's the problem with small old flats near central. No lifts. I sink to the carpet panting and vigorously rub my eyes. I don't care about my makeup smudging, seeing that I'm fifteen seconds from my apartment. It's 12.30am, and the only thing that gets me up the last few steps is knowing my bed awaits me. I fumble in my satchel for my keys, finding them amongst the half-eaten bags of snacks I bought for the plane. As I push them into the lock the door swings open, revealing Anya stood on the other side. Her hair is slicked back in a ponytail, and she wears her favourite baby blue Juicy Couture tracksuit. She pulls me in for a big hug.

"My baby's home!"

"You're still here?!"

"Yeah, I came to change his litter earlier and thought I may as well see you in!" She says, gesturing towards Sprout's green litter tray in the corner.

"I don't deserve you." I say, plonking myself down on the sofa. My apartment may be central, but it's tiny. When you walk through the door my dinky kitchen area is to your right, the counters also acting as a dining table with bar stools on the opposite side. I actually like it, as you can sit and talk to the person cooking, usually Anya. A couple feet from the counter is my blue velvet sofa, Anya and I found it abandoned in Clapham Junction and carried it all the way here on the Northern Line a couple years ago. I'd just moved in and had no furniture, save an old blow-up mattress I was sleeping on. We'd gone bar hopping in Clapham and were stood outside *Tonight*

Josephine as Anya took long, savouring drags from a Marlboro Light when we spied it abandoned on the other side of the road. It must've been liquid strength that granted us the ability to lift it, let alone carry it, pissing ourselves laughing the whole way. It was a bitch to clean, but I smile every time I look at it. My sofa faces my TV, which is in front of a large bay window that looks down to the street. I'm on the fourth floor. Most nights I don't bother turning it on, instead choosing to people watch out the large glass panes. Living in Central London is like having a front row seat to a never-ending soap opera if you really take the time to look. Hen parties staggering about with colourful sashes and vomit-stained dresses, arguing couples leaving a date night gone wrong, first dates leaving a date night gone right, a family of tourists trying to appease their snarky teenagers. The TV sits on a wooden table that Sprout incessantly chewed when he was a baby, so the bottom is dotted with tiny bite marks. For some reason they make me love it more, adding character to the bland Ikea piece. I have a loft bed at the back of my studio, my desk underneath, and the bathroom on the right. The loft bed is surprisingly comfy, and I've decorated the wooden railings with vines and fairy lights, giving the room a warm, glowing ambience. I have various cacti dotted on every free surface - an addiction of mine to buy a new one every time I see a different prickly fella if I have £3 to spare. Ever since being employed with Maria, that's been most times.

Sprout launches onto the sofa next to me, and I bury my face in his soft brown fur. I got him one year ago, just after my Mum passed, finding it hard to get out of bed most days. Sprout forced me out whether I liked it or not, he had to eat and have his litter changed. He saved me. It was actually Anya's idea, after I'd gone on a drunken rant about how cute bunnies were and pulled up his dodgy listing on Gumtree. He was a tiny baby, smaller than your hand and listed for £25. The same amount as a Domino's pizza. Anya had showed up at mine the day after, carrying a wriggling cardboard box and a shopping bag full of bunny supplies. He's the size of a large kitten now, with chocolate brown fur and a white belly. His eyes are deep brown, and his soft ears flop by the sides of his face, one slightly more than the other.

"How was he?"

"The best boy. I checked in on him every day and had snuggles."

I clasp Anya's hand as she sits next to me.

"Thank you."

"How was it all?"

I shake my head and put my finger to her lips. She laughs. "Ok. Understood. Get some sleep. When am I seeing you?"

I massage my temples, now that I'm not moving, the remnants of my hangover are creeping back. "Um. I'm back at work from tomorrow, so probably weekend?"

"Ok. Ooh, I need to go to Ikea on Friday afternoon, you wanna come?"

I groan at the thought.

"I'll buy you a cactus!"

"A big one."

"The biggest."

"Ok. Let's do it."

Anya rises and grabs her tote bag from one of the barstools and pauses before drumming her long fingernails on a box of tupperware on the counter. My eyes widen.

"Bun House?!"

"Yep. Fresh today. If you don't want it now just put it in the fridge before you pass out, please."

"I love you!"

"Love you too! Night!" she chimes, letting herself out. I know I need to put the takeout away, but the familiar smell of home, the rain tinkling against the window, Sprouts warmth on my lap - I'm out like a light.

CHAPTER 15

It's Thursday, and I've been back in the office for two long days. Going from being the one taking the photos to the one answering emails and watering succulents is a change that hasn't quite sunk in. Maria seems happy with the pictures; I made sure I shot them in her style as opposed to my own. I poke my fingers under my glasses to massage my eyes. They're meant to prevent blue light and help migraines, but they're yet to prove their worth. I've been trawling through Maria's inbox the last 48 hours; I don't think she checked it once while I was gone. My phone pings, and I look down to see a gif from Gia. A kitten falling into a bowl of yogurt. She's captioned it: "You entering Maria's inbox".

I laugh, still in disbelief that Gia Tucci actively wants to talk to me. I've checked off the steamy dream on the plane to being hungover, dehydrated, and tired. I once had a sex dream about Jonah Hill - before he got fit. It means nothing. I'd spent my first day back in the office scrolling through Gia's social media and Wikipedia, the level of her fame unfathomable. She has 13.2 million Instagram followers, and she posted a picture where my hand is visible. 13.2 million people have seen my hand.

I wish the girls from school knew it was mine. I nearly asked her to tag me in it but realised that might come across like I'm using her. Her most recent role was in an HBO spin-off of Westworld, where she played a killer robot. I binged it all over the last two nights, excited every time she came on screen. Is this stalking? I don't think so. I haven't heard anything from Daniel, but to be fair I don't think he has any of my contacts. I've tried to put him out my mind, turning back to the multiple dating apps I open when I need an ego boost, with zero intent on ever actually meeting any of them. Anya calls them my "Nintendogs". If he wanted to, he would. I googled Daniel as well and came up pretty dry - the opposite of Gia. There's a LinkedIn profile, an interview with Architectural Digest, the link to his hotel chain - currently un-viewable due to our renovations, and that's it. No Facebook. No Instagram. Nothing. I bite my cheek and find my fingers typing his name into the email search bar. There had been minimal contact from him when I'd got back, but I'd studied the email multiple times.

"Hi Maria,

I hope you're feeling better. Many thanks for making it work and sending your assistant, she did a good job. I look forward to seeing the website on its completion.

Best,

Daniel Kimani"

"She did a good job." At what, being fingered on his pool table? Dickhead. I look through his initial emails with Maria – ie me, talking about the type of design he wants, the costs, the dates. Then I see it, at the bottom one of his first emails:

"Emails sometimes take a while to reach me when I'm at Tukio; if it's urgent feel free to contact me on +254 708 661819."

I feel my tummy tighten. Should I? No. If he wanted to, he would. But what if he wanted to, but just didn't have the means to? He didn't have my number after all, and couldn't send my boss an email asking for it. I chew my cheek more, starting to taste blood, the metallic twang tickling my tongue. I take a large gulp of the San Pellegrino next to me (the only water allowed in the office), and pop in a stick of peppermint gum to try save my cheek from any further abuse. I add his number to my WhatsApp and start composing:

"Hey Daniel, it's Maddie. Just wanted to say thanks for the hospitality - I had a great time. I hope the website turns out how you want it."

Is that ok? I might've sent him that even if there hadn't been anything between us, just to say thanks. But is it weird because there was stuff between us? I massage the gum on the roof of my mouth, pressing it into all the ridges. Should I put an "x"? An emoji? He doesn't strike me as an emoji man. I test out adding an "x" at the end, unsure.

"Anything interesting?" Maria booms behind me, making me jump and drop my phone. She's 67, and incredibly stylish - but also incredibly in denial about her ageing body. She's been prescribed a hearing aid that she refuses to wear which means she talks about three octaves louder than necessary.

"Um, not really. Just the usual enquiries." I say, reaching down to grab my phone from the shiny oak floorboards. The office is a small space, my desk is in the reception area, which contains a mini-fridge, coffee machine and a mammoth green velvet sofa. Through a white door behind my desk is Maria's office, a cosy room housing her large iMac, green velvet desk chair, and multiple Moroccan rugs. The walls are brick, painted eggshell white. We have one large window in the reception and two in Maria's office with views out to the restaurants and shops below. The location is insane, one floor above Fortum and Mason in Piccadilly Circus. I truly believe that's why Maria chose it, seeing as I pick up her lunch from there every day. I usually walk to and from work as my flat is in Embankment, it only takes twenty minutes.

I wince as I pick up my phone seeing the message to Daniel has sent.

"Everything alright, ducky?"

Maria asks, approaching the desk to gently stroke my hair. She's got bouncy curls of grey, that used to be ginger when she was younger. After she hired me she joked that it was the deciding factor, and knowing her now I completely believe it. Her blue eyes are always encased with smoky eyeliner, making them pop underneath her massive tortoise shell glasses. Her eyesight is the one area of aging she has taken seriously, seeing as it's her livelihood. She only ever wears Stevie Knicks-esque shawls over black culotte trousers or maxi dresses, no matter the season, and smoky topaz rings on nearly every finger.

"Yes, all good, just a bit tired."

"You silly sausage. I told you to take a day off and adjust before you came back to the office!"

She did. Maria is actually a great boss, despite her eccentricities. The thought of being alone in my flat, during this season, with nothing but my thoughts of Daniel and Mum swirling round my head sounded much worse than an email-induced headache, so I told her I'd come back straight away.

"Well don't burn yourself out, ducky. If you want to work from home a couple days next week - do it!" She says, grabbing a blood orange San Pellegrino out the mini-fridge.

"Thanks!" I say, forcing a smile to try hide the panic until she's back in her office. As soon as she's floated out the room and shut the door, I glance back down at WhatsApp. TWO FUCKING BLUE TICKS?! How's that even possible?! It was only sent a minute ago. I hold my breath, seeing '*typing*' appear under his name. It could be blunt. Could be flirty. Maybe he'll say simply

"Thanks, best of luck with your career." Or maybe "I'm so glad you messaged, I didn't have your number and have been dying!" or maybe... wait... the '*typing*' has disappeared. And he's gone offline. Surely, surely he wouldn't just leave it on 'read'?

CHAPTER 16

I stab the Ikea meatball with the scratched silver fork, drenching it in creamy sauce. They used to be my all-time favourite, but now don't hold a candle to Mustafa's. Anya sits in front of me, a massive cactus between us - ready to join my little army at home. She's nearly finished her second plate of meatballs, I have no clue how she stays in such good shape. She's holding my phone flicking through it as she chews.

"Yeah, he's decent. Where are you meeting him?"

"I think a pub near London Bridge."

Anya glances up at me, her brow furrowed. "Are you sure that's a good idea?"

"He said he knows a nice place."

I shrug, popping the meatball in my mouth. After the WhatsApp humiliation of yesterday, I decided to actually meet up with one of the Tinder Nintendogs. I'd picked Matt, a 29-year-old banker. He had a cockapoo and a house in Barons Court. Wore nice shirts. Looked like the type to wash his hands, have a sizeable penis, change his sheets weekly - or at least have his cleaner do it. I needed to have sex with someone to try block the memory of the pool table from circulating my mind throughout the day.

Who knows, maybe Matt's the one? That would certainly wipe any lust for Daniel from my mind.

"Are you free tomorrow?" I ask, watching Anya swamp her last meatball in mashed potato before lifting it to her mouth, a blob falling onto her crisp white shirt. She's been in the office all day, and it's currently 6pm. The Ikea cafe is near empty, not surprising for a Friday night. Next to Anya sits a large wicker bag overflowing with bedsheets and towels. She'd changed her detergent last month and all her linens had "lost their fluff" she claimed, as she'd frantically stacked our shopping cart with pastel sheets.

"Shit." she mutters, trying to wipe off the brown blob. "Um, I'm actually not. Brian's booked an Airbnb in Cornwall."

I raise an eyebrow. "Is that the reason for those?" I say, looking at her freshly manicured nails.

"Stop. I don't wanna jinx it!"

"Fuck off! How could you not tell me that he's gonna propose?!"

"Because I don't want to jinx it!" she hisses at me, her blue eyes glittering with excitement.

"Well. All I'll say is an Airbnb in Cornwall sure sounds like it. You've been together four bloody years."

"Shhhh!" She blushes more, unable to stop her smile.

"He'd be crazy not to." I say, squeezing her hand. "You're golden."

I clutch my cactus to my chest as I emerge from London Bridge station, my belly in knots. It doesn't feel like the fluttery butterflies I got in Kenya, instead dark black beetles squirming and scratching at my stomach. London Bridge is a lot less festive than Piccadilly or Embankment, just a few Christmas lights dotted in random brasseries and shops as opposed to the massive twinkling canopies I'm used to walking under. I reach the pub, overflowing with men and women in business casual. I inhale deeply and enter, warmth billowing out the door as I fling it open. I start unwrapping my scarf, I'm wearing my black Doc Martens, a little black skirt that Maria had raised an eyebrow at when I delivered her chicken Caesar, a black polo neck and my favourite leopard fur coat. Anya got it for me three Christmases ago, after we'd watched *Last Christmas* at the cinema together and bawled our eyes out. It's now tradition to wear it every winter.

"Maddie!"

A deep, posh voices calls out to me. I spy him sat on a table by the window. As I expected, he looks clean, his dirty blonde hair perfectly coiffed, crisp white shirt probably straight off the shelves of TM Lewin. An expensive watch glimmers on his left wrist. He shoots up from his chair to pull mine out, which makes the beetles transform into moths.

"Thanks!" I say, sitting on the padded leather stool. I see his eyes quickly jump up from my legs and he smiles at me sheepishly.

"What can I get you?"

"Um. House red is great thanks!"

"House red it is!"

He says, making his way to the bar. I gaze out the window at the the familiar streets, The Shard dwarfing all the surrounding buildings. I've been to this pub before, quite a few times actually, just didn't remember it by name. Matt saunters back, a bottle of expensive looking red in his hand.

"What's this?" I enquire.

"House red, of course!" He winks. I hate to imagine how much it cost, especially in a pub this central. But it goes down smoothly as we do the usual rounds of a first date. Jobs. Pets. Flirty banter. We finish the bottle, and as soon as the last drop is poured he's on his feet to buy another.

"Just a glass, I don't need too much more!"

I protest as he saunters to the bar. My innards feel warm and fuzzy, like the wine has glossed me over with a layer of fleece. I run my hand through my hair, feeling my eyes well up. Not now. I open them wide trying to dry them out against the air. I look out the window and can't stop my eyes from focusing on the little strip of Guy's Hospital I can see. I used to come here after visiting her, drink a G&T before I went home. Sometimes three. It got to a point where I was on first name basis with one of the bartenders. Gary. I wonder if he's still here? I hope he isn't. I can imagine him smiling warmly, "Long time, eh! Guessing she's out of hospital?" The imaginary scenario makes my heart ache, and I polish off my remaining Pinot Noir to try numb it. Matt sets another bottle down in the middle of the table, and I look up at him shaking my head.

"I said just a glass!"

"Only the finest for m'lady!"

He says as he tops us up, some of the crimson liquid sloshing over the rim of my glass onto the sticky wooden table.

His hot tongue, flavoured with wine and tobacco exploring my mouth nearly does the trick to numb all the thoughts and memories accosting my brain. I'm leant on the cold wall outside the pub, and I pull him closer to me. One of his hands is round my waist, creeping down to my ass, the other lazily holding a cigarette. I caress his silky blonde locks, kissing him harder, urging the moths to take flight, evolve into butterflies. They stay sleeping, resting on the walls of my stomach.

"Shall we go back to yours?" I say breathlessly, coming up for air. He laughs, kissing my neck.

"The wife wouldn't like that, would she?"

I push him away, unsure if he's joking. "What?"

"What about yours?"

I laugh nervously "You're joking right?" He keeps kissing my neck, and a group of teenagers walk past us, wolf-whistling.

"About...what?" he says between kisses.

"Um...the wife?"

His lips haven't moved from my neck. "I said it on my profile, did you not read it?"

The moths transform to maggots, squirming and wriggling, chewing on my tummy walls.

"I thought it was a joke. Like sarcasm. Satire."

"No, babe!" he says, laughing as his hand massages my ass. I quickly push him away, disgusted I ever let him touch me.

"Prick!"

I start walking away. I can feel everyone's eyes on me outside the pub, some giggles, some whispers.

Matt calls out to me, "Come on! We had a good time! I spent fucking £160 on wine! Oi, you bitch!"

I quickly slam on my noise cancelling headphones, blocking out his words, tears welling up in my eyes making me see double. I fucking forgot my cactus, but I can't go back now. So I pick up the pace, trying to block out everything but Wham playing in my ears. I keep walking and walking until I reach the river and can't walk anymore. I sink down onto a bench, finally allowing the tears to fall. My body heaves up and down, the wine in my system not helping as the tears flood down my cheeks. I frantically open my phone to call Anya, but imagine her and Brian, snuggled by a fireplace in their Airbnb, or at a romantic dinner, or walking along the beach. I don't want to ruin her weekend. I'm sure he's proposing, and if he's doing it now the last thing they need is the blubbering maid of honour pestering them on the phone. My mind is blank of who else to call.

I don't really have any other friends, it's always been just Anya and me. I look at my recent calls and see Gia's name. I don't want to overstep, I don't know how close we actually are. I'm sure she has hundreds of friends, I'm probably just a good acquaintance to her. I look out to the Thames, lit orange by all the city lights. A party boat thumps past, full of people dancing and laughing. Fuck it. I press call, listen to it ring four times, and quickly cancel it. How embarrassing - I don't need to call Gia fucking Tucci sobbing after a bad date. I try distract myself by counting the red buses that zoom past over London Bridge, advertising perfumes and new blockbusters. I feel my phone vibrate in my hand and look down to see the caller. Gia. I gulp nervously and answer, clearing my throat trying to conceal my sobs.

"Hey slut!" she laughs into the phone.

"Hi. Hi!" I respond, my voice wobbly.

"What's wrong?"

"What? No, nothing! I was gonna make a pumpkin pie, and you're American-ish so called to ask for advice, but I've found a good YouTube video now so don't worry!"

I struggle, wincing every time I hear my voice crack. She must think I'm such a loser.

"Maddie. Be fucking for real. What's up?"

"Honestly nothing!"

"Don't piss me off. It's 11.30 your time. I know you're not baking a fucking pie! What's happened?"

I feel the words brimming in my chest, ready to overflow and escape my mouth. I exhale and let them.

"I don't know. I've just had a weird few days. I thought this guy really liked me, but then he ghosted me. So, then I just went on a date with this other guy to try get over it, and he picked a pub by London Bridge, which is by the hospital where–"

I let out a snotty blubber, unable to form words.

"Hey, it's ok. Just take a deep breath. I'm here."

I breathe in, following Gia's instructions.

"The pub was by the hospital where my Mum died. Last Christmas. And Anya's busy all weekend and I just feel so lonely and sad and... I didn't think it'd be this hard a year on."

Relief flows through my body, finally saying the words out loud. Gia's quiet for a moment, and I don't know what to say. "I'm sorry – you're probably busy with your life and I'm just a random girl you met on holiday-"

"No, hang on," she says, distracted. I sit, nervously biting my lip. Fucking idiot. She's probably blocking me.

"Get to Heathrow."

"What?"

"Get to Heathrow. I've booked you a flight to see me."

"What?!"

"If you're feeling sad, at least feel sad with me in Manhattan! You have your passport right, I remember you said you lost your license in Kenya…"

"What?! Yes – but I don't have my clothes, my toothbrush, my skincare…"

"Fuck it, we'll buy you stuff when you're here!"

"I can't affo–"

"Bitch, don't make me brag, but come on. I'm fucking rich! Please. Don't feel indebted – you're practically doing me a favour, I have no plans this weekend and would love the company."

"I find that hard to believe." I sniffle, looking up how long it'll take me to get to Heathrow, butterflies zapping around my stomach.

"None that I actually wanted to do."

I sent Gia my passport details, and she said her agent had connections that could help get my ESTA fast tracked. I honestly have no clue what anything meant, other than that I'm heading to New York. Either Gia may be one of the best people I've ever met, or she's made her fortune trafficking lonely women's organs. I can't help but laugh as I go through security, having nothing on me but my satchel containing my headphones, phone charger, book, lip gloss and a bottle of water. In my short skirt and leopard print with no luggage, I must look like an escort or a drug mule. I send a text to my neighbour, Agnes, a lovely 55-year-old divorcee asking her to feed Sprout while I'm away. I also grab Gia some English Breakfast Tea and a little Beefeater teddy bear from Duty Free, in some meek attempt at thanks for what she's done. As I'm queuing to board my 4am flight to JFK, my eyes widen re-reading the ticket. I should've got her the Harrod's teddy, she's booked me First Class!

First Class is even more insane than I ever imagined. Complimentary pyjamas, blankets, and toiletries are laid out neatly waiting for me on my seat. As I sit down, I look up to see the roof of the plane dotted with tiny LED lights making little constellations, taking me back to the night on Gia's balcony in Kenya. And the pool with Daniel. I swat the image from my mind and play with the seat controls next to me. To my shock the seat merges into a full sleeping position.

"Sorry Ma'am, your seat needs to stay upright till after take-off." An air hostess smiles down at me.

"Oh sorry, I was just testing it!" I giggle, fumbling with the remote to switch it back.

We take off, and as soon as the plane taxies a flight attendant trots around offering everyone a glass of champagne and caviar. I skip the caviar, not sure of how the unfamiliar taste will sit on a stomach full of red wine and anticipation, but happily accept the champagne. Before I take a sip, I gingerly make my way to the toilet, pyjamas and toiletries in hand. My eyes widen even more as the door opens, revealing an airplane bathroom double the size of any I've seen. I gently place my pyjamas next to the pristine sink and start investigating the contents of the complimentary wash bag. Toothbrush, toothpaste, face wash, exfoliator, moisturiser, eye mask. I stifle a squeal of delight. I scrub off my makeup but save brushing my teeth for after my champagne. I tear off my clothes, nearly toppling over trying to pull off my tights quickly, aware someone may be bursting for the toilet outside whilst I'm doing a whole bedtime routine. The pyjama's fleecy material sends shivers across my body, grateful for the cosy warmth after an early December evening sporting a mini skirt.

Even though sleep is all I want, especially in a seat probably comfier than my own bed, I couldn't say no to the free meal that probably cost a day's wage. I've never had plane food like this, caprese salad, spinach and ricotta ravioli, a warm crusty bread roll, and a whole cheese board! As I sip my champagne, scrolling through the infinite inflight entertainment, my heart skips a beat seeing Gia's face plastered on one of the '*New Releases*'. How has this become my life? I pass out as soon as I pick a movie, Monsters Inc, my champagne flute still half full.

CHAPTER 17

I stare out Gia's window, my eyes boggling at the view. The blue morning sky is shrouded by towering concrete skyscrapers. Gia's apartment has the quintessential New York view, the Empire State dwarfing all adjacent buildings, the deep burgundy lights of the New Yorker Hotel a stone's throw away, and the edge of Central Park just peeking through to the left. Gia's apartment is a swanky one bed on the 32nd floor. the colour palette is yellow and white, making the space feel even larger than it is. Her dining table is pushed against the floor to ceiling windows, housing four light wooden chairs.

"Your flight was actually perfect timing! You got 8 hours sleep and arrived early morning! It's almost like you teleported!" Gia says, setting down two cappuccinos in front of us, the creamy foam jiggling. Her kitchen is decked out with tons of fancy equipment, including a barista level coffee machine. I cup my hands around the ivory mug, letting the warmth seep into my palms. The bright blue sky is deceiving, it's 6 degrees centigrade.

"I've planned a two-day NYC bootcamp, I'm gonna try show you everything worth seeing and feed you everything worth eating in 48 hours."

"Oh my God ok – are we going to the Sugar Factory?" I jest playfully.

Gia retches into her coffee, her curls bouncing around her face. She's taken out her long braids, her natural silky ringlets reaching just above her shoulders.

"I wouldn't be caught dead at the Sugar Factory, thank you."

I take a large gulp of my coffee, nearly scalding my tongue on the rich, nutty liquid. It would've been worth it.

"I swear this coffee is ten times better than anything I've had in London. If acting doesn't work out, you'd make a great barista."

"With the scripts my agents been sending me, I'll consider." Gia laughs, flicking through a brown notebook, landing on a long list written in blue ink. Her handwriting is exactly what I'd expect, large and swirly. She runs her finger down the list, reading out the activities. I can't believed she planned all this for me.

We spend the morning getting the must-see tourist attractions out the way. Gia says they're a necessity, some things I might not love but would certainly regret if we skipped. We got city bikes to get around, riding to Radio City Music Hall, The MET (a compulsory yogurt was eaten on the steps to live out my Gossip Girl fantasy, which Gia found very entertaining), and walked the High Line. Gia's outfit makes me smile every time I look at her - the classic celebrity disguise. She wears low rise blue jeans, a cream long sleeved top, brown Afghan coat, a blue Yankees baseball cap and large tortoiseshell sunglasses. She's finished off her disguise with a black surgical mask on her chin, which she pulls up anytime someone stares for too long. She still looks radiant. I'm stuck wearing the only outfit I brought with me and can feel the cold breeze nipping incessantly at my legs. Part of me wishes I'd worn my airline pyjamas. After we left the High Line, we walked along Fifth Avenue admiring all the Christmas lights, which easily rival London's. Massive twinkling baubles, levitating glowing candy canes and rainbow LED lights bejewel the outsides of the shops, bars, and restaurants. I had to repeatedly duck inside shops to take advantage of their heating, my thin miniskirt defeated by the unrelenting cold.

Gia raises an eyebrow at me while I do tiny bounces up and down inside the Mulberry store, as two skinny sales associates watch disconcertedly.

"Are you seriously that cold?"

"Yes! I'm sorry! I dressed for a quick drink in the pub and then sex. Not New York Winter!"

Gia cocks her head, and then grabs my hand. I stop jumping and stare back at her.

"I'm sorry. I'm embarrassing you!" I panic, glancing over to the sales assistants who quickly avert their gaze. Gia grips my hand tighter, her cashmere glove a warm relief, and yanks me out the store. "I'm so sorry, I was being stupid! Bouncing is just the quickest way for my body to warm up, an–"

"Taxi!" She yells, hailing down one of the yellow cars zooming past.

"Where are we going?" I ask nervously.

She's probably sending me back to JFK. Gia flings open the door and we quickly huddle in, Gia smiling at me, her emerald eyes twinkling. She leans forward to the cab driver, a plump man in a large knitted sweater and black beanie.

"Macy's on 34th please!"

Gia waltzes me around Macy's, stopping at any hanging rail she notices my eyes lingering on.

"This is honestly insane, stop spending money on me!"

"No! Think of it like this - you're a beautiful Barbie, and I'm getting enjoyment from dressing you. You're nurturing my inner child." Gia giggles from behind a rack of faux fur.

After an hour of browsing Gia stops triumphantly outside the UGG section, much to my surprise.

"Aren't they a bit... Jersey Shore?"

"Don't speak that blasphemy in here!" she hisses, playfully hitting my shoulder. "There is no better shoe for New York Winter; ask the Olsen twins."

She buys us matching pairs of the classic brown mini ones with a platform sole. We both slip them on and retire our original shoes into the UGG bag, groaning in delight at their warmth.

We sail through endless racks and shelves of silks and satins, and I finally decide on a luxurious, cream, cashmere jumper. It just hangs off my right shoulder and has a little halter neck made of freshwater pearls. I haven't heard of the brand, so am hopeful it's on the cheaper end of Macy's stock. For bottoms I grab a pair of thick, tawny corduroys, ones I'm sure will block out the biting Winter wind. As we approach the counter, Gia quickly grabs a pair of green cashmere gloves from a nearby rack

"These are the same brand as mine - they're unreal!"

I throw the outfit on in the bathroom, feeling ready to brave the chilly outdoors with my designer armour. I reckon the whole ensemble probably cost a month's pay cheque, so I guess if times get tough I can always pawn it. My guilt about Gia's generosity towards me has subsided, after watching her impulse buy a Cartier panther ring that cost $38,000. She's waiting for me outside the toilet, and I strut out as if I'm Cindy Crawford.

"Oh my God. Show stopping. Legendary. You look gorgeous!" she squeals in excitement.

For lunch Gia insisted we have a Central Park picnic, especially now I'm decked out in warm attire. The picnic consists of two large slices of New York pizza - one margarita, one pepperoni, two slightly questionable street hot dogs and two different flavours of cheesecake from Juniors. I picked Raspberry, Gia went for Belgian

Chocolate. I insist on adding a bag of caramel nuts to the list, much to Gia's disappointment.

"You know they never taste as good as they smell…"

Gia sighs, as I pay the hefty $6.

"I'll be the judge of that." I laugh, as I thank the vendor taking the sticky paper bag from him, ever thankful for my new gloves. "How did you know to get green ones?" I ask, realising only now she'd actively chosen my favourite colour.

"I'm perceptive." She says, tapping her nose.

We sit perched on a large rock, our banquet splayed out in front of us like a dragon's bounty and eat and talk until the sun starts to sink below the trees, speckling the green grass with little puddles of gold. We pack up the rubbish, and walk through the leafy pavements past roaming labradors and bundled up children racing around on scooters.

"I know you said I'm crazy for buying you a ticket, but I think you're even crazier for coming." Gia says, gazing at me over the rims of her oversized glasses.

"Maybe." I say, chucking the rubbish into a nearby bin.

"Do you wanna talk about last night?"

"I don't know. Maybe." I say, suddenly feeling the cold again. I release a shiver, and Gia links my arm, stroking it affectionately.

"There was this guy I thought I liked. Probably still do–"

"I think that's the lesser evil. I mean about your mum?" Gia says, squeezing my arm. "Sorry, I'm not trying to pressure you. If you don't want to talk about it that's totally fine."

A tiny girl with blonde pigtails races past us on a dinky pink bike, her mother laughing as she runs after her, trying to keep up. I feel a sharp pang in my chest.

"It was just me and her for most of my life. We moved around for her job when I was little, she was a wig stylist for touring West End shows. We settled in Cornwall when I was 7. She wanted me to grow up near the sea. She loved swimming. She was always really healthy, I didn't eat Monster Munch until I left for uni–"

"Wait… Monster's Munch?"

I laugh. "Monster Munch! It's an English snack, it's kind of like puffy oniony things."

"Ahh. Ok. Delicious."

"They are! Mum always hated them. I think because she was really health conscious - she always ate well, exercised, barely drank. And then she got cancer. And they couldn't fix her."

"Fuck. I'm so sorry." Gia pulls me into a big hug. The tighter she cradles me the faster the salty liquid gushes from my eyes and drips to my lips. I bury my head in Gia's neck, embarrassed about any onlookers seeing me break apart. The scent of her Tom Ford and vanilla hair oil soothe me, and I feel the heaving of my chest slow. I pull away, quickly wiping my eyes.

"God, I'm really making a habit of public crying, aren't I?"

Gia rubs my back and laughs, her eyes glassy.

"At least you're not an ugly cryer. It's actually quite majestic. I may need you to do it again so I can study it for my next role!"

I swat her shoulder affectionately.

"Fuck off!"

We laugh more, nearing the edge of the park.

"What type of cancer was it?"

"Ha. It was rectal. And she never let anyone forget it. She'd always joke about how her bum was trying to murder her."

Gia smiles. "I would've loved to meet her. She sounds funny."

"She was. She would've liked you."

"What triggered you so badly last night?"

"The pub I met that guy in, I used to go there after I'd visit Mum. Sometimes before. The hospital was pretty much next door."

"Ah."

"I'd made a point to try avoid areas that would remind me of that time, but I think I was so desperate to forget about the guy, it didn't really cross my mind. I thought since it's been nearly a year I'd be fine."

"When did she die?"

"The anniversary's actually next week."

We've reached the edge of the park, the bustling traffic zooming in front of us. I feel more liquid trickle down my face and reach to wipe it away. I didn't even realise I was still crying. I look to Gia, who's face is wet with drops too, and then my head, my hands, everywhere. We both gasp in shock and look up at the grey clouds that have quickly taken over the sky, rain pelting down.

"Our UGGs!" Gia laughs, hand over her mouth. We race through the cold to the edge of the pavement, waving frantically at the first taxi we see. Luckily it's free, and comes to a halt next to us. We clamber in, laughing hysterically as Gia slams the door shut, a loud boom of thunder rippling through the city.

CHAPTER 18

I gingerly emerge from the bedroom to find Gia pouring the contents of a silver cocktail shaker into two tall martini glasses.

"I knew you'd pick that!" Gia grins, plopping an olive into each drink, some liquid splashing out the second glass. She pops another olive in her mouth and licks her fingers. I'm wearing another dress of Gia's, this time a deep purple halter neck that stops mid-thigh. I'm aware the purple probably clashes with the red of my hair but couldn't resist the shimmery fabric. It reminded me of when the lilac gossamer of a butterfly's wings just catches a ray of sunlight. I slicked my hair into a low bun to try smooth out the clash, the gel darkening my hair into a deep copper. Gia's wearing a white 70's style jumpsuit, with flared bottoms. It's a halter neck too, and there's a large gold ring sitting between her small perky breasts, revealing a risqué amount of cleavage. Her chestnut curls are falling around her face, framing it perfectly. She's matched it with large gold hoops, her new Cartier ring, and gold eyeshadow in the corners of her siren-esque eyes, their green glimmering in contrast.

"Somethings missing…" Gia says, looking me up and down, pressing a finger to her glossed lips.

"What?"

Gia retrieves a red Cartier box from the drawer in front of her and slides it across the marble kitchen counter.

"No. Stop. You're insane, I can't!"

"Just look!"

I sigh heavily and open the box. Inside the red velvet sits a delicate gold chain, adorned with teeny amethysts every few links. I feel my breath stuck in my throat.

"Gia, this must've cost a fortune! I seriously can't accept it. You've already gotten me so much!"

"Okkk, you don't have to keep it… just wear it tonight!"

Gia saunters around the island towards me, and gently lifts the chain from its burgundy box, the amethysts glimmering as they catch the light. I laugh awkwardly as Gia walks behind me and clasps it around my neck.

"Jesus. I'm in *Pretty Woman*."

Gia laughs. "Fuck you! I'm way hotter than Richard Gere!" She laughs, spinning me round to admire the necklace. "Perfect. Told you I knew you'd pick that dress."

I see her eyes momentarily gaze down from the necklace to my chest, but I don't blame her. The way they sit in this dress I was struggling not to stare at them in the mirror myself. We grab our drinks and sit on her long velvet canary sofa, which is adjacent to a marble fireplace with a large flatscreen perched on top. A wicker egg chair hangs from the ceiling next to me, and I swing it gently it with my hand as I marvel at the view. The skyscrapers twinkle, towering over the zooming red and yellow matchbox cars that drive through the city's grids. I take a sip of my martini, not telling Gia it's my first one. The iced vodka sends a shock through my body, and I struggle not to pull a face. Gia notices and giggles into her glass.

"Not a fan?"

I swallow the bitter liquid and pull a strained smile. "No, uh, it just caught me off guard. She's strong."

"Oh yeah. She's very strong. That's why she's the perfect pre-game drink."

"Please can you tell me where we're going."

Gia taps a duck egg blue nail to her chin playfully.

"You genuinely want to know? You don't want the surprise?"

"Not a fan of surprises. Would really like to know." I say, grimacing my way through another sip.

"Ok fine." Gia leans in close, as if she's telling me a big secret. "We're going to The Bureau!"

I can feel the mushroom risotto we grabbed for dinner sloshing around my gut, mixing with the strong martini and multiple glasses of wine I'd consumed over the last couple hours. I don't go clubbing much, but when I do one of the big memories of the night is standing in the queue freezing my nipples off for an hour. In the cab on the way to dinner I'd done a quick Google search. *"The Bureau - NYC's most exclusive nightclub"* read one of the article headlines. I'd braced myself for a good two hours in the Manhattan cold, but on arrival Gia had simply waltzed up to the bouncer, greeted him with a kiss on the cheek and beckoned me through the large wooden doors. Of course. I was with Gia Tucci. As if she'd wait outside for five minutes. We built up the courage to peel off our warm coats and leave them in cloakroom, luckily the alcohol in my system warming me from within. Gia took my hand and led me up the maroon stairs, my ankles teetering slightly in the sparkly silver heels she'd lent me - half a size too big.

The Bureau has rich mahogany walls, the panels of wood warmly lit by the red fabric lamps sat upon on the dotted circular tables framing the edges of the club. Some tables are enclosed in red velvet booths, others burgundy armchairs. In the middle of the room is an old-fashioned wooden stage, currently occupied by drinkers and dancers in glittery dresses and fancy shirts. The people seep from the stage onto the surrounding dance floor, as Peggy Gou thumps through the speakers. The stage is framed by glamorous red curtains and has little orange lights lining the edges in the shape of clams. Gia's warm hand still holds mine as we make our way through the dance floor, people parting like the Red Sea. We finally reach the bar and I lean my arms on the cool, silky, wood, a vast change from the sticky countertop of my local Wetherspoons. I look up to Gia, the dim red light somehow still making the green in her eyes pop.

"What are we drinking?"

Her eyes sparkle, and she waves over the bartender.

"Two Manhattans!"

CHAPTER 19

I run my hand along the rough red brick of The Bureau's walls in an attempt to ground myself. I'm stood in the smoking area, a Marlboro Vogue balanced between my fingers that I'm occasionally pretending to take long drags from. I'm hoping everyone is too enthralled in their own stories to notice. Currently we're all listening to one told by a man named Oscar. He's rattling on about his latest trip to Whole Foods, and how he truly believes alcoholic kombucha is taking over. Soon all the clubs will be serving it, he claims. It really is a story that could be told in two sentences, but Oscar has managed to weave it into a Spielberg movie. He's a funny looking man, with dark chestnut hair falling around his hollow cheeks, almost like a Tim Burton character. He wears a green velvet suit, an old school tattoo of the Virgin Mary just peeking out the top of his ivory silk shirt. I think Gia said he writes a daily column, which I guess is why he's so good at transforming mundane stories into epic tales. I try tune back into his monologue, watching his hands move enthusiastically helping explain each twist and turn, the cigarette he delicately holds flailing back and forth dusting ash onto his velvet. I blink, his hand starting to look fuzzy, morphing from one into two into one again. I grip the cold bricks harder, unsure why I believe this will help sober me up. I can feel Gia's eyes on me, I hope I'm not embarrassing her. I look to her apologetically, swaying a little as I do, but am relieved to be greeted by a subtle eye roll towards Oscar. I struggle to withhold a giggle, relieved she thinks he's a pretentious twat too. All the other nepo babies of New York have flocked around him, grasping onto every detail of the Whole Foods saga. Gia leans into me, her soft curls brushing my neck making a small shiver run down my spine.

"Water?" She whispers.

"Please!" I respond sheepishly, a little embarrassed she can tell I'm past my limit. She stubs out her cigarette on the bricks I've been secretly clutching, takes my hand and leads me back up the stairs where the music pulsates from.

Gia and I return to the dance floor, in my hand a pint of iced water, hers a vodka martini.

"I'm sorry. Do you think I'm really lame?" I say, taking a big glug of the water. I misjudge the distance from the glass to my mouth and feel some of the liquid trickle down my chin. Gia laughs and wipes it, her finger lingering a second too long. Maybe I imagined it.

"Not at all. I'm practically paid to go out and party to promote stuff, my tolerance isn't normal."

"Ok. Thanks. That's good." I say, wiping the last drops of water that made their way down to my chest away. Gia watches, her eyes glimmering as she takes a sip of her martini.

"Shall we dance?"

I don't know how long we've been dancing for, all I know is I don't want to stop. I haven't been clubbing in a long time, despite Anya's begging. Everything feels different tonight, the drinks taste sweeter, the smoke smells delicious, I can feel the music pounding through my body. Gia and I did take half a pill of ecstasy in the toilet an hour ago, so maybe it's that too. I'd sobered up, and proposed getting another drink from the bar when she suggested it. I didn't tell her, but I've never actually taken drugs before, unless you count the skanky weed my high school friend Dawn convinced me to smoke with her one day after school. The journey home had felt awful, like everything was moving in slow motion except for my anxious thoughts. I vowed never again, but something in me shifted tonight. I felt ready. I felt safe. Gia dances in front of me, the flashing lights illuminating every curve of her silhouette. She looks at me and giggles, cupping my face with her hands. They're so soft and warm, making me lean in, smushing my face into them more. This makes Gia giggle harder.

"Are you feeling it?"

My face is still smushed between her palms, and I'm the one relentlessly giggling now. "What does it look like?" I respond, unleashing a loud cackle.

Gia splutters with joy and pulls me into her for a hug. I feel a hand on my ass, and my heart thumps.

"Are you making a move on me?" I say shyly into Gia's hair. "What?" She responds, releasing me from her grip. I stand for a moment confused, no longer feeling Gia's body on mine but still the hand on my ass, now squeezing slightly. I whip around to see a tall man in a black suit, his shirt unbuttoned revealing thick chest hair stood behind me, grinning from ear to ear. Even though he's a lecherous pig, I can't deny that he's handsome. He runs the hand that was seconds ago touching my ass through his brown curls, clearly trying to show off his muscled physique.

"Can I buy you a drink?" His deep voice rumbles, his hand now returning to my body, this time snaking around my waist.

"No, thanks. I'm just here with my friend." I squirm, removing his hand and turning back to Gia. I feel his touch slither back around my torso, and he steps closer so our bodies are touching again. I'm sure I can feel him rubbing himself on my back and feel my skin crawl. The E made good touches feel great, but bad touches feel awful. Gia sees my face crinkle, and before I can turn around to tell him to back off again, she's pulled me away and positioned herself between us. Gia's gold stilettos make her just reach his height.

"What's your problem dude, she told you to fuck off, so kindly fuck off?" Gia says, smiling at him sweetly. He laughs, biting his lip and straightening his posture, an attempt to make himself taller than her.

"Chill out babe, don't be jealous, there's enough of me to go round."

Gia laughs through gritted teeth. "Ok, you got me. Have you ever heard of a tornado shot?"

"No, I haven't."

They're standing even closer now, her lips nearly touching his.

"Do you want one?"

"Sure."

Gia beckons to the shot girl parading around the club, and I dig my hands tighter into the ridges of my water glass. Is she really into this slimeball? I get flashbacks of being abandoned in the club by Dawn during freshers week so she could go home with some guy, dancing on my own waiting for her to come back. She never did. Gia grabs three shots off the tray, handing over $100 to the girl.

"Keep the change." She passes one to me, and one to the man.

"To new friends!" He says, raising his shot.

"Sure." Gia says, raising hers. We all throw our heads back and sink the cold vodka. Before I've even fully swallowed mine Gia's grabbed my water and thrown it in the slime ball's face. He looks hilarious, mouth open in shock, eyes blinking to get rid of the water, almost like a koi fish. I'm still processing the water being thrown before Gia's raises her hand and a large "SLAP" rings over the bass of the music. Slimeball holds his hand to his cheek, his eyes flickering between embarrassment, rage and shock, unsure of which they want to commit to.

"That's a tornado shot, baby." She says, as she grabs my hand and swiftly walks us towards the exit, one of the security quickly moving through the crowd in pursuit.

CHAPTER 20

We tumble out the yellow cab, collapsing with laughter crouching on the curb. I cling onto Gia's plush fur coat to help balance my teetering sparkly heels.

"His face!" Gia wheezes, wiping tears from her eyes. "His FUCKING FACE! I've never seen something so funny!"

I can feel a stitch forming under my left rib from the laughter but can't stop. I can't stop as Gia fumbles a blue nail to type in her apartment code, I can't stop in the lift - the deep inhales I take between laughs filling my lungs with the sweet smell of Gia's vanilla oil and musky perfume. I try to stop as I flop onto the canary couch, slowing my breaths to try relieve my stomach from the cramp, shutting my eyes and massaging my temples. I hear Gia kick off her heels and the tap start running, the splashing water echoing off her bronze sink. I feel like I'm falling backwards down a massive tube. Normally I hate this feeling and do everything in my power to sober myself up when I feel it wash over me - but tonight it feels electric. Everything I touch feels magnetic, the velvet sofa like a warm, purring, cat beneath me.

"Here", Gia says, handing me a thick blue glass of icy water from behind the sofa. The cold glass feels unbelievable, and I press it to my forehead feeling the cool particles transfer from the indigo cup to my flushed face, seeping into my pores and coursing through my body. I nearly chug the whole thing, obsessed with how my body is receiving every sensation.

"Is this really what Molly feels like?"

Gia sits next to me, tucking in her long caramel legs and resting her head just next to mine. I can feel her soft breath tickle my nose as she breaths in and out.

"Yes. But I'm lucky. My manager gets it for me, she doesn't want me bugging out on some laced pills ending up plastered on the pages of US Weekly."

I scoff, currently enthralled with the pattern of her carpet. "Yeah. This must be the stuff Pablo Escobar does."

Gia laughs, and I feel myself slightly lean in to the feel of her warm breath.

"I'm not sure Molly was his drug of choice."

Her breath tickles me more, and a roar of laughter spills out my belly. It manifests in a deep snort. Gia laughs, and I laugh more at her laughter, an elvish, high pitched giggle. We both collapse down onto the rug, my belly aching with every cackle. Each little fleece of the rug makes my back light on fire, as if they're caressing every follicle. We both catch our breath and lay on the floor panting.

"That might be one of my favourite sounds." Gia says breathlessly.

"What?"

I listen and realise it's raining again outside. How did I not notice? Now all I can hear are the little droplets pattering softly against her glass windows, like a tiny percussion band.

"Me too. I love the rain."

Gia laughs and rolls onto her belly, her head just above mine. We're in the same position as Spider-Man and Mary-Jane when they have their iconic kiss.

"Not the rain. I do love it. But, I was talking about your piglet laugh."

Again I feel her warm breath graze over my face, caressing every tiny hair. I can smell her cotton candy lip gloss. I feel like I have Spider-Man senses.

"I don't ever want to forget this night. I'm so sad The Bureau didn't allow photos, knowing my drunk brain I probably won't remember anything." I sigh, reaching up to play with one of Gia's curls hanging above me. "Thank you. For everything."

"I have an idea." Gia grins.

She gets up, her long body towering over me, holding out her hand. I grab it, feeling her warmth surge through my fingertips up my arm.

I'm sat on the sofa, chugging my second glass of water while Gia finishes setting up her camera, wobbling slightly as she twists it into the tripod. It's an old digital camera, Gia apparently stayed up all night on eBay to outbid the other competitors for it. She looks through the viewfinder, tilting it down.

"I mean, there is a professional photographer in the room so if you need help…" I taunt between gulps. Gia laughs.

"A little role reversal is always fun. You should be in front of it more often."

She says, holding my gaze. Our eye contact is broken by a bright flash released from the camera, and Gia rushes to plonk onto the sofa next to me. "It'll take 10 frames now, all 10 seconds apart. Ready?"

"Ready!"

For our first pose we fling our arms up, mouths open laughing.

FLASH

Gia throws her arm around me for the next one, hugging me tight.

FLASH

"Charlie's Angels!" Gia shrieks, and we quickly sit back-to-back holding finger guns.

FLASH

"Prom!" I squeal, Gia and I laughing as I sit with my back to her, as she holds her hands awkwardly around my waist like a 15-year-old couple at their first dance.

FLASH

"What else should we do?" I say, turning to face Gia, her hands still around my waist. She's looking down at me, her lips parted, green eyes twinkling. She really is so beautiful.

FLASH

The flash makes me jump, and I jolt forward knocking us both over, Gia under me. She giggles, her body moving under mine making my skin tingle.

"Are you ok?" She laughs, a curl falling between her eyes.

167

"I really am." I say, brushing it away, my finger tracing over her eyebrows.

FLASH

I feel the energy shift, like everything in the world has gone static except for us. I look down at her plump lips, and find myself lean forward, grazing them with my own, feeling her breath sharpen. We press into each other, our lips meeting properly, my tongue slipping out my mouth and into hers.

FLASH

She releases a small moan, and I push my body harder into hers, Gia's hands now exploring my waist, slowly moving lower. I'm now the one who moans, Gia gently biting my bottom lip as her hand travels down to my thigh, and then inside it, slowly travelling upwards.

FLASH

I run my hands through her curls, then down her neck, then to her breast. I feel her back arch beneath me, as I drag my lips from hers, kissing down her chin, tracing down the ridge of her neck with my lips.

FLASH

Gia gently moves her warm hands from my body and cups my face between her palms.

FLASH

"I think we should go to bed." Gia says breathlessly. I feel the butterflies take flight.

"Ok." I say nervously, leaning down to kiss her again. To my surprise, she ducks her face away and laughs.

"No! Not like that! I mean sleep."

I bite my lip, the butterflies sinking.

"Why? Do you... not like me?"

Gia strokes me cheek.

"You're gorgeous. But you're also my friend. And you're wasted. I don't want you to do something you'll regret tomorrow."

I swiftly sit up, the room spinning again, quickly placing a hand to my head.

"I'm not that wasted!" I protest, even though I can hear my words slur.

Gia laughs, and gently pushes me so I'm lying down on the sofa, eyes gazing up at her butterscotch ceiling lamps. Gia gets up, and I hear her tap sputter on again.

"If you really want to make a move on me, there's tomorrow. But my hunch is it's the Molly making you horny, not the company."

Gia laughs from the kitchen. I bite my lip, unsure of her statement. Suddenly a shock of cold lands on my forehead, and I look up to see Gia gently placing a wet dishcloth on my forehead. It feels like the cool fabric is melting through my skull, comforting the mini headache that has started to form. Gia walks round the sofa, and pulls a large cable knit blanket over me, tucking in the sides.

"Sleep, we'll talk in the morning." She says, squeezing my hand. Like it was a command, I feel my eyes close and fall into darkness.

I wake up on Gia's sofa, bright rays of morning light streaming through her windows, the cold compress still on my head, now warm. I reach up and peel it off, barely remembering how it got there. I guess I started the hangover prevention early? I sit up, much too fast, and feel the contents of my stomach gurgle. I quickly reach for the glass of water on the coffee table in front of me, chugging it down. A long arm gently sets a cappuccino down where the water glass was, and I look up to see Gia, fresh as a daisy. She's in a cream silk robe, her hair in a towel and little jelly eye masks under each eye.

"How're you feeling?"

"How do you look like that?" I exclaim, gratefully reaching for the coffee.

Gia laughs. "Like I said, I get a lot of practice."

I take a long sip of the warm liquid, swirling it round my mouth, feeling its heat seep into every tooth.

"I have something to ask you. You might think I'm crazy. You're totally allowed to say no." Gia says, as she picks up a brown cardboard box sat by her front door.

"Ok. I'm scared. Do you want a kidney?"

Gia laughs as she places the box on my lap, gesturing for me to open it. I drain the last sip of coffee from the mug and set it down on the table, raising an eyebrow at her suspiciously.

"What's this?"

"Open it!"

Gia smiles, sitting down next to me. I feebly finger the cardboard, prying it open. My mouth gapes, inside the box a new silver MacBook Air.

"Gia, I can't-"

"Just listen. Ok, first off, it's refurbished, and I can keep it once you've finished using it! I'm about to buy this house in Carmel, but would love a second opinion from someone who I know'll be honest-"

"So you bought me a refurbished Mac so you could... show me the listing?"

Gia laughs and clasps my hand.

"I was thinking, there's no better treatment for a hangover than the sea. What if you asked Maria if you could work remotely for a couple days and come with me to Carmel to see the house."

I gulp, the butterflies fluttering their wings. I know Maria will say yes, especially as she knows the anniversary is coming up. I rub my eyes, unsure if I'm awake or dreaming.

"How long for?"

"As long as you want! Flights on me! Pleaaase?" Gia pulls a puppy face, and I consider whilst chewing my lip.

"Ok. On one condition."

Gia squeals in excitement. "Anything."

"Food. Greasy food."

CHAPTER 21

The seats of the jet look like an episode of Hoarders, food wrappers and pizza boxes scattered everywhere. I'm splayed out on one of the cream leather chairs, wearing my comfy airline pyjamas and a pair of Gia's big sunglasses. I'm clutching a burrito, juice dripping down my fingers which I voraciously lick off. Gia laughs from the seat opposite me.

"I'm sorry." I say between mouthfuls. "I have to."

"No, it's great. Super elegant, perfectly fitting for a private jet!" She teases.

I sit up straighter, picking off a stray grain of rice from my top. "Ok. Sorry. You're right. I think I'm still a bit drunk."

Gia grabs a slice of pizza from the box on the table between us, the melted cheese hanging off it in little threads. She angles it to her mouth and takes a big bite, some of the cheesy cobwebs sticking to her chin.

"This is the best inflight meal I've ever had." she says, licking the strings from her lips.

"How long till we land?" I ask, through a mouthful of guacamole.

"4 hours." Gia replies, her mouth full too.

FLASH

Gia giggles, spinning the camera to show me the photo. I look a mess, mouth wrapped around the burrito, a glob of sauce on my upper lip.

"Fuck you!" I exclaim, quickly snatching the camera from her to delete the picture.

"Noooo, please don't delete it! It's a memory!"

"I'll consider." I grumble, flicking to the next photo as I dab a napkin over my lips. I nearly choke on my burrito, the memories of last night rushing back, staring at the photo before me. I'm straddling Gia, our lips pressed together, eyes closed. Gia raises her eyebrows.

"I wasn't sure if you remembered. I guess not." She shrugs, popping a French fry into her mouth.

"Oh my God. I totally blanked. We didn't…"

Gia spurts, covering her mouth to stop the fry flying across the plane.

"No! No. We kissed, and then I tucked you in and we went to bed. To sleep."

I massage my temples, a multitude of emotions swirling around my mind. Gia's laughter softens, and she reaches over to touch my knee.

"Don't stress. Molly is literally known as the love drug. You're not the first girlfriend I've had kiss me when she's drunk. And probably won't be the last."

"I can't believe how fucked up I got!" I exclaim, burying my head in my hands. Gia pries them apart, peeking through my fingers.

"It doesn't affect anything. This is just your hangxiety talking. We're golden!"

I laugh feebly.

"Was I at least good?"

Gia cackles, reaching for another slice of pizza.

"The best!"

CHAPTER 22

I wake to find Gia still fast asleep next to me and relax into a long stretch under the thick feather duvet. I look to my right and see the embers of the fire from last night glow a muted orange. We'd gotten into Monterey Airport at 7pm, refreshed from an afternoon of salty food and sleep. Gia had rented a white convertible Porsche for our trip, and it was waiting for us outside the airport for collection. We'd sped along the coastal roads, my hair flying in the wind as we drove. You could smell the sea in the breeze, and I relished every second it lapped at my face.

We didn't see much of Carmel as we ate dinner at the hotel, aptly named 'The Fireplace Lodge' as every room contained a little stone fireplace. I had salmon, Gia, sea bass, and we lounged in the room next to the roar of the fire watching old Friends re-runs until we fell asleep.

I quietly rise, trying not to wake Gia, creeping into the bathroom. I let the shower run till the water starts steaming, and plunge myself under it, the heat rushing through my body, warming my core. The complimentary soaps smell like lavender, and I scrub the purple gel all over, inhaling deeply. I run the last month of my life through my head like a movie, astounded at how much has changed. I try make sure Daniel stays in the deleted scenes, but can't stop my memories occasionally flicking back to the pool table.

I must've been in the shower longer than I'd realised, as when I finally emerge from the bathroom, lavender steam wafting after me, Gia's sat on the bed, a tray of room service breakfast beside her.

"I got food!" She says, through a mouthful of croissant.

I laugh, and plop myself down on the bed next to her. "I hardly feel like I have room for anything after yesterday!" I exclaim, though it doesn't stop me picking up a fork and shovelling in a mouthful of eggs.

We barely make a dent in breakfast, but once we can eat no more, we get dressed, my corduroys unsurprisingly snugger than when we'd bought them. Gia lends me a blue "NYU" sweatshirt of hers, its fleecy inside somehow still soft despite its age. Gia wears a long white skirt, a camel coloured jumper and a big brown puffer coat, her hair slicked back in a low bun. I let mine air dry, the salty sea air giving it a slight wave.

As I'm packing my satchel for the day, Gia tips out the mason jar from our breakfast tray, little sachets of brown and white sugar falling onto the bed. She makes her way over to the fireplace, and gingerly pushes some of the ashes into the jar before screwing on the lid. I raise an eyebrow at her, and she laughs awkwardly, dusting off her hands.

"It's weird. I use it for meditation." She giggles, nervously scuffing her UGGs against each other.

"That's the first questionable celebrity quirk you have, so I'll let you off. No Scientology though!" I tease back. Gia laughs, tucking the jar into her tote bag.

"Noted."

We head out to the car, the golden morning sun giving me my first real look at Carmel-by-the-Sea. I'm speechless. Carmel looks like a film set; part seaside town, part fairytale. All the buildings are small and cottage like, many painted different pastel colours, all with quirky, intricate windows. Some of the roofs are thatched, some are slate, many adorned with flowers, moss, and vines. All the shops are little boutique stores, no big chains. They all sport colourful hanging signs, some art galleries, some cafes, some clothing stores, all unique and enticing. We drive through the little streets, the blue expanse of the sea getting ever closer.

For a crisp, December Monday morning, the beach is near empty. A jogger runs along by the sea, a woman walks her two small dogs, and Gia and I stroll down to the water. We left our shoes in the car, and my feet sink deeper into the soft white sand with each step. We reach the waves, and stand in silence, both admiring the view. The sea is a glimmering turquoise, complimented by the lush, green, coastal scenery of the bay. It's dappled with patches of deep blue, where clumps of seaweed sway gently below the surface. Small, cold waves lap against our toes, as we look out to the horizon.

"I can see why you'd want to live here. It's magic." I say, drawing swirls in the wet sand with my big toe.

"I can't wait for you to see the house. Thank you for coming with me."

We both plonk down to the sand, and I squint looking up at the cloudless blue sky. Gia presses her sunglasses into my lap, and I smile at her in thanks.

"Is it similar to the beaches in Cornwall?"

"In some ways. I remember the beaches there being massive, but that may have been because I was so small."

Gia laughs, resting her chin on her knees. "I'm so over New York. It's so fast. I want to live somewhere where

I can grow my own vegetables, rescue some cats, swim in the sea."

"Don't. That literally sounds like a dream."

"You know you'd be welcome to visit any time. You've gotta see it in spring, all the cliffs become thick with wildflowers. Every colour you can think of." Gia says, tilting her gaze towards me, smiling softly.

She's not wearing any makeup, and the little freckles that dapple her nose are highlighted by the bright light. I clear my throat, looking out to the sea, each wave sparkling with the reflection of the beating sun. When the salty breeze stops, it's almost warm enough to take off my coat.

"Did you bring any water?" I ask, suddenly feeling flushed.

"In my bag." Gia says, her eyes set on a flock of seagulls flapping across the sky. You can just hear the gentle beating of their wings over the crashing waves. I root through her tote, my hands landing on the mason jar. I snicker and pull it out, inspecting it suspiciously. "Please explain how exactly ash helps with meditation."

Gia smiles sheepishly, gently taking the jar from me. "I might've lied."

I raise an eyebrow at her as I retrieve the water bottle from her bag, unscrewing the lid.

"I'm sorry if I overstepped, you're welcome to tell me to shut up at any point. I know you said this week was the anniversary, and that she loved the sea. I thought maybe if you wanted to do a tribute, you could sprinkle these in the ocean. I know they aren't hers, but I think she'd still feel you doing it. And you might feel her." Gia finishes, gently setting the jar in the sand between us. I feel my eyes go glassy, the waves of the sea blurring into a twinkling blue symphony of colours. I quickly rub my eyes on my sleeves, trying to dry them.

"Shit. I'm sorry, it was a bad idea." Gia scrambles to retrieve the jar, but I reach my hand out stopping her.

"It's beautiful. I'm just..." I try, my voice wobbling. I can feel my chest go tight, gripping the jar till my fingers go white.

"Do you want to do it now?" Gia asks, stroking my hand with her gentle fingers as we both hold the cool glass. I manage a nod. I think if I speak it'll come out as a wail.

"Do you want to do it alone?"

I stay silent, trying to calm my heaving chest, unable to make words. Gia slowly rises, and kisses the top of my head.

"If you need me just wave, I'll be right over there." She says, gesturing down the shoreline.

I wait till I can no longer hear her soft footsteps padding over the sand, and bury my head in my knees, letting the sobs course through my body, taking me over. I sob until it feels like I don't have any more tears left, peeling my eyes back to the waves. I roll up my trousers till they're just above my knees, and wobble to my feet, left hand still clutching the mason jar. I step into the sea, feeling numb from the cold despite it pricking up all the hairs on my body as I wade deeper, a small sprig of seaweed tickling my calf. And then I think.

I think back to the pancakes she'd make us every Friday, on the old frying pan that they'd always stick to but she didn't have the heart to replace.

I think back to the sound of her laugh, the way she'd squeal with joy as we ran into the sea, no matter the time of year.

I think of every time I was sick, how she'd press her lips gently to my forehead to see if I had a temperature.

I remember and think and remember and think, as I slowly tip the jar into the wind, watching each speckle of ash as it takes flight for second, before gently dancing down to the blue ocean below.

CHAPTER 23

I sit on the wooden stool, mouth agape as I stare at my phone.

"I can untag you, if you want." Gia says, as she squeezes edamame beans out their green shell with her teeth.

Gia had left me alone by the shore till I waved her over, after about an hour of memories and tears and love relentlessly poured out of me. It had just hit 1pm, and I was ravenous. I felt like I'd completed a marathon; sweaty, hungry, tired and fulfilled. Gia drove us to her favourite sushi spot and had just posted a story of me as I flicked through the menu. That was only seven minutes ago, and I've gained 3,000 followers.

"Or just turn your notifications off!" Gia suggests, in between sips of her miso soup. I put my phone on airplane mode and set it aside, my heart pounding slightly.

"I think I forgot how famous you are." I say, as I drench a California roll in soy sauce.

"I think I do too, when I'm with you."

I laugh awkwardly, my sushi roll nearly crumbling with the amount of soy dripping off it.

"That's a compliment!" Gia adds quickly, watching me struggle with my chopsticks. I've never quite got the hang of them despite years of practice. She masterfully grabs a piece of salmon nigiri, delicately dips it in the soy and holds it out to me. I smile sheepishly, embarrassed she clocked.

"Hurry, it's gonna fall!" she laughs, and I quickly lean in and eat it from her chopsticks, giggling. Gia smiles and pours us more sake, I can already feel the first tiny glass we had. That doesn't stop me raising it to my lips, savouring the warmth whilst admiring the view. We're sat at a table by the window, which is accented with little rainbow stained glass dragonflies. You can see the sea down the road to the left, and directly opposite are more colourful artisan stores. My eyes are set on a little cheese shop I've already made Gia promise we'll go browse after, the windows full of wax wheels, all different hues of reds and yellows and oranges.

"Aw, Daniel thinks you're cute."

I nearly splutter out my sake.

"What?" I manage between coughs, my eyes watering as the alcohol singes my windpipe. Gia pushes a glass of water towards me, not looking up from her phone.

"He responded to my story."

"I didn't know he had Instagram?"

"He's very aloof. Weird username, elephantsandcoffee94."

"What did he say?" I ask, trying to mask the desperation in my voice.

"He said: Cute." she shrugs, swimming a pink piece of sashimi round her little bowl of soy and lifting it to her mouth.

"That's it? Like, it's cute that we're together, or that I'm cute?" I probe frantically. Gia's eyes slowly lift from her phone, an eyebrow raised.

"I'm not sure... do you want me to ask him?"

I quickly compose myself, taking another long sip of sake. "Oh, what? No!" I laugh, maybe too hard. "That's sweet." I say, gritting my teeth as I plunge another roll into my sauce. I can feel Gia's eyes studying me, and quickly gaze around the restaurant looking for different direction to steer the conversation. My eyes land on a pinboard, plastered with photos of the elderly Japanese chef behind the sushi bar, posing with tons of A List celebrities. "You didn't tell me this was such a hotspot." I say, gesturing to the board. Gia turns, a smile spreading across her face. Relief washes over me. Distraction successful.

"Look at the third row down, left side." She says shyly.

I squint, and next to a photo of Arnold Schwarzenegger is one of a young, teenage Gia, her curls dyed blonde.

"Oh my God! You look so different! And your photo is in between Arnold Schwarzenegger and Anna Paquin!"

Gia laughs, her cheeks slightly red.

"That was after my first ever role, I was 19. I'd just finished shooting in LA and my mom brought me down here as a celebration. I fell in love with it instantly. No one knew who I was, we came here to eat, and my Mom wouldn't stop bragging, showing them pictures of me on set. We didn't know how my career would turn out. The waiter laughed and insisted on taking a picture and adding me to the wall."

She takes a sip of her sake, still staring at photo. "Sometimes I wonder if they didn't stick it up, maybe none of this would've ever happened."

I roll my eyes. "That's a very cute story. But you are extremely beautiful and immensely talented. This would've happened whether you were on that board of not. It wasn't luck, it was fate."

"Maybe like it was fate meeting you. I haven't had a friend like you in a long time." Gia smiles softly, offering me another sushi roll with her chopsticks.

As promised, once we finished our lunch, we headed straight for the cheese shop. We spent about thirty minutes tasting each cheese, learning where they came from and what wine to pair them with. We decided on a creamy Brie and popped into the little wine shop next door to buy one bottle of Champagne and one California Sauvignon Blanc, as recommended by the sales assistant. We strolled down the street, popping into art galleries, clothes shops and jewellery stores. I insisted on buying Gia some little green sea glass earrings, a feeble attempt at thanks for all she's done. She put them on excitedly as we left the shop, as if they were worth $30,000 as opposed to the $30 I paid. The light made the deep green glass glimmer, matching her eyes almost perfectly.

Our last stop was down a winding cobbled path, past chicken coops and colourful beehives. The bakery looked like a witches grotto, and we had to duck our heads as we entered through the small wooden door. The warm scent of freshly baked bread engulfed us, and despite how much sushi we'd eaten I found my mouth watering. Stacked behind the counter were baguettes, loaves of brown, white, seeded, and little colourful pastries adorned with seasonal winter berries. Gia grabbed us some homemade crackers, a crispy baguette and two berry tarts. As we made our way back up the path to the main road, fighting the urge to tear off a chunk of the warm baguette, Gia looked at me excitedly.

"I think we're ready!"

The roads shrink smaller as they wind further along the cliff top. I look down to the beaches below, the blue sea crashing into the rocks, spluttering apart into white foam. As we drive on the sea slowly calms, the cliffs and jagged rocks transitioning back to sandy beach. Gia brings the car to a stop, pointing at numerous grey rocks scattered along the shore.

"Seals!" she exclaims, beaming.

I squint in disbelief and watch one of the rocks blubber its way slowly into the water, its fat rippling just like the little waves of the beach as it shuffles along.

"Oh my God!" I say, clutching my hand to my mouth, removing Gia's sunglasses to get a better view. I giggle in disbelief, snapping as many photos as I can for Anya.

We watch the seals in silence for a moment, and I almost feel like I'm on safari again.

"Ready?" Gia asks, and I nod.

As the Porsche purrs to life, numerous little grey heads lazily look towards us as we drive on down the road.

Gia slows as we approach a black iron gate, green tendrils of ivy wrapping round every rung. She leans out the car to key in the entry code, her jumper riding up revealing her toned, caramel torso. I quickly avert my eyes, feeling my cheeks flush, the memory of me straddling her flashing across my mind. The gate buzzes open, and as the car crunches down the gravel driveway, lush green grass either side, my eyes widen taking in the little mansion before us.

The house is built on the edge of a small cliff, about 30 feet above the white beach below. The grounds are made of lush, green grass, scattered with Monterey Cypress trees and rose bushes, all trimmed back for the winter. The house is two stories, built of aged beige stone, and a mossy brown terracotta roof. The windows are mammoth, framed with deep brown oak and all dappled with colourful panels of stained glass. A large wisteria vine climbs around the oak front door, creeping its way up to the roof and across the sides of the house. I feel myself let out a little gasp, as Gia brings the car to a halt.

"I'd want a little chicken coop there, so I can have fresh eggs in the morning," she says, pointing to foliage on our right, "and round the back of the house the little vegetable garden, so I can eat more seasonally. Come on!" She's already out the Porsche unpacking our food. In a daze I exit the car, tripping a little as I step out unable to take my eyes off the view.

"Wait till you see it from the back!" Gia says, as she passes me the brown paper bag containing our baked goods, striding ahead whilst fishing the keys out of her tote.

"Is the realtor gonna meet us here?" I ask, as Gia pushes the silver keys into the lock and it gently clicks open.

"I think so!" she says, distracted, as she holds open the door for me.

I walk inside and gasp again. The bottom floor is open plan, and the entire back of the house is made of glass, the vast expanse of the coastal scenery sprawling before us like a painting. The floorboards are a warm, light oak, and the walls cream. There's a flight of wooden stairs leading up to the second floor on my left, the banister made from panels of blue and green speckled hand-blown glass. In front of us is the little kitchen, which houses an old-fashioned brown fridge, a gas stove and pale wooden countertops surrounding a small wooden island. A retro bamboo room divider shrouds the kitchen from the living room and dining area, which takes up the right side of the room. A large stone fireplace sits on the right wall, surrounded by comfy, pale blue sofas and a large turquoise armchair. The floor is dotted with sea grass carpets and a large cream sherpa rug by the fireplace. The dining table sits to our right, a circular oak piece painted distressed white, wicker chairs surrounding it. I walk across the room, mouth agape, peering out the sliding glass door to the stone patio outside, housing a swimming pool, hot tub, barbecue and seating area. I notice some small stone steps leading off the edge of the cliff and turn to Gia.

"Where do those go?"

"Down to the beach!" she says excitedly, familiarly retrieving a box of matches from the kitchen drawer and making her way to the fireplace.

"Are we allowed to light it?" I ask, gingerly sitting on the sofa, sinking into its soft cushions. Gia smirks sheepishly as she strikes the long match, an orange flame bursting to life. She slips it in between the logs, and we watch as the baby flames slowly lick at the wood, painting their edges with black soot as it starts to crackle and grow. She turns to face me, clasping her hands.

"Again, I'm sorry. I wasn't completely honest with you. I may have in fact already bought it." She winces, plonking down onto the sofa next to me.

"What?"

"I know! I'm sorry! I just thought you'd love it, and love being by the sea, and when you said the stuff about the anniversary. I thought you could use a break. A real break."

I open and shut my mouth, unsure of what to say.

"You're the first person I've brought here." Gia says, picking at her nails. "I'm scared to tell my New York friends. I think they're gonna be mad at me for leaving. But I've wanted to share it with someone so badly, it all seemed like perfect timing. Are you mad?"

I flick the tassels of the blue pillow, playing with a stray thread.

"I'm the furthest thing from mad. Definitely shocked. But not mad."

Gia looks up at me and smiles.

"Your friends are your friends for a reason. They'll be sad you're further away, but they know you. This place is just so... you. It's exactly where I'd imagine you to live. Don't feel guilty for doing what's best for you."

Gia quickly rubs her glassy eyes, rising to her feet.

"Wine?"

We decide to bake the Brie, as the chilly December evening sets in and sit bundled up in blankets on Gia's patio, drinking and eating our purchases from earlier. I tear off another chunk of baguette, the crumbs dusted all over the swirly blue glass table and dunk it into the soft Brie. I pop it in my mouth looking up to the sky, small slithers of clouds slowly forming over the hazy evening blue.

"We might have to open another bottle," Gia says, pouring the last of the wine into my glass instead of hers. I roll my eyes, tipping half of my glass into her own, and she smiles.

"Thanks. Do you want me to grab us anything else?"

"Could you actually get my phone, I think it's in my satchel?"

"Sure!" She says, elegantly slipping off the thick blanket from her shoulders as she rises, draping it over the back of her chair.

I raise the glass to my lips and swirl the last bit of wine around, the fruity notes making my tongue sing. Daniel replied to Gia's story. Of me. It could've just been friendly; he could reply to all her stories for all I know. Or it could've meant something, I could mean something to him. I press my palm against my forehead trying to distract myself, think about anything else. I focus on the sound of the crashing waves below, the birds singing, the tapping of my nails on the table. I look back up to the clouds, now a hue of purple leaking into them. The start of the sunset. I hear the pop of the champagne behind me, and before I know it Gia's topping up my glass. She wraps herself back in the Aztec blanket and slides my phone across the table, fumbling with her own trying to connect it to the outdoor speaker.

I touch the screen to check the time, and nearly fall off my chair. On my screen, sits a large message from Daniel. My eyes go fuzzy, unable to make out the words.

"I, um, need the loo." I say, bolting to my feet.

"Ok." Gia says absent minded, still struggling with the bluetooth.

I stumble inside, nearly tripping up on the blanket over my shoulders. I peel it off, tossing it on the sofa as I make my way to the bathroom. I lock the door and plonk myself down on the toilet seat, taking a deep breath. It was a big paragraph. I brace myself, unlocking my phone and opening WhatsApp. My stomach drops, and I feel my wine rise.

All that sits in my chat with Daniel, is my old message. And an automated message from his end:

"This message was deleted."

I feel like screaming. I swipe down, checking if the preview is still in my notification centre. It's gone. I sink my head in my hands, overwhelmed with frustration and confusion. I should've read the preview, why didn't I read the fucking preview? I tuck my phone in my pocket, lean over the sink and splash water on my face. No. He doesn't get to have this control over me. I can't let him ruin my night. I won't.

I leave my phone in the kitchen, grab my blanket from the sofa and join Gia back outside. She's taking long elegant drags from a cigarette, looking out to the sea. She's clearly managed to get the speaker working, as Buena Vista Social Club softly plays. I take a hefty swig of my champagne, and gingerly take a cigarette out the pack. Gia smirks and raises an eyebrow at me.

"I know you don't smoke," she says, eyes twinkling.

"I do tonight." I say, fumbling getting the lighter to strike. Gia laughs and shrugs, taking it from me. She holds it by my face, shielding it from the wind with her other hand, her cigarette balanced between her lips. I lean in close, lighting mine, and take a large drag. I actually inhale, feeling the smoke scrape against my lungs like little sharp fingernails, and release a loud splutter. Gia laughs more.

"Maybe I don't, actually." I cough, stubbing it out in the ashtray.

CHAPTER 24

I clumsily make my way down the stone steps, clinging to the frayed rope handrail next to me. I'm barefoot, and can feel the little grains of sand that dust the steps, and the soft pine needles fallen from the canopies above. As my right hand clings to the rope, my left grips the bottle of champagne, the condensation on its cool glass exterior making it slowly slip through my fingers. I quickly push it up with my knee, losing my balance slightly and clutching Gia's shoulder ahead to steady myself, both of us giggling as I teeter. Once I've found my footing I muster the courage to look up as we descend, marvelling at the view. We'd polished off our bounty of food, and heated by the alcohol and full stomachs decided to swim in the sea. We're currently climbing down the steps at the bottom of Gia's garden, leading to the secluded beach below. Now halfway down, I'm able to see what lies along the cliff top past the tall trees concealing Gia's grounds. Peppered along the cliff other luxurious abodes sit, all with their own small set of steps leading down to the cove. Gia confidently jumps down the last couple stairs, the glass flutes in her hand clinking together. She holds out her free hand, which I gratefully take to steady myself down the last step. The waves gently crash on the shore, dappled with deep pink as the sun slips below the horizon. Gia leads me to the edge of the sea, and we sit down in the sand pouring a glass of champagne each. The fizzy bubbles dance around my mouth as I watch the sky, pastel clouds concealing the indigo night that's creeping in.

"I think I've seen more sunsets in the last month than I have my whole life." I say, taking another sip.

"Another reason why I can't wait to live here. I think Californian sunsets are the closest to Kenyan ones I've seen."

I set my flute on the sand, digging a little hole to steady it and lie on my back. All I can hear are the waves, and all I can see is the sky. I lift my finger, tracing over the dips and curves of the clouds, admiring how all the colours blend into each other. I wish I had my camera. I hear a scream and jolt up to see Gia running into the water, her clothes left strewn on the sand next to me.

"Is it cold?" I yell.

"Fucking freezing!" Gia shrieks. "You have to come in – it was your idea!"

She's right, it was. I reluctantly rise, and start peeling off my layers, the sea breeze biting at my bare skin.

"I really don't want to – it feels really cold!" I call out, nibbling my lip.

"I'll warm you up!" Gia yells playfully.

I feel a spark shoot through me, blurry memories of our kiss burning in my brain. I'm brought back to reality as Gia splashes a wave of water towards me, only a couple drops making it far enough to hit my body. Those few drops are enough to send a shiver down my spine and I quickly brush them off to try warm up. No backing down now. I quickly tear off my bra and underwear and race into the sea, the cold shock coursing through my veins, making my skin prickle. I reach Gia, and stand with my arms crossed, waves lapping around my waist.

"Ok. We did it. Shall we go in?" I beg, teeth chattering.

"Not until we've dunked. Full experience."

I shake my head pleadingly, looking up to the glowing warmth of the house.

"Think of it like we're baptising my new home. A new chapter."

"Ok fine, just quickly!" I say, starting my mini bounces.

"3, 2, 1!" Gia shrieks, as we both plunge under the surface. I feel the icy water caress every inch of my body, the cold making my heart beat faster. I lay still for a moment, letting the waves gently toss me back and forth, like I'm a piece of seaweed, at one with the motion. I let the ocean rock me, as if I'm held in her arms once more. Maybe I am, maybe she felt me earlier. I feel a tear leak out my eye, merging with the salty water surrounding me. Suddenly I'm scooped from my cocoon, back into the cool breeze panting. Gia looks down at me, her brow knitted in worry as she holds me.

"Maddie?!"

"What?" I splutter.

"Sorry! I was worried! You were down there for ages!"

"This keeps happening to me!" I feebly cry, tilting my head up to the sky in defeat. The pastel clouds have dissipated, replaced by the deep indigo sky peppered with stars, a bright full moon making the waves sparkle. I look up at Gia, who I realise is still holding me. Her brown hair is wet and slicked down her back, little droplets of water hanging on her eyelashes. The faint moonlight paints her face, she looks like she's glowing. I feel the warmth of her torso on mine, and look down to

201

see our bare bodies touching, I'm sure I can feel her heart pound. Maybe it's mine? As if I'm no longer in control, I find my hand creeping up her back, my face leaning towards her, ready to –

A large wave crashes over us, toppling us over into the sea. We crawl to the shore on our hands and knees, spluttering laughs as the waves continue to attack us from behind. Once we've reached the edge, we lie on our backs, shivering looking up at the stars.

We climb up the steps double the pace we descended, our clothes clinging to our damp salty bodies. We finally reach the top, and I rush to the sliding door, the fireplace just behind it beckoning.

"Stop!" Gia yells, halting me in my tracks, my hand gripping the door.

"I don't want sand in the house, let's quickly use the outdoor shower!"

"Ok!" I shiver, padding across the patio to where she's standing. She sets the champagne on the grass, and fiddles with a tap on the side of the wall. I didn't notice it earlier, but amongst the flowerbeds lining the house is a little bronze shower head, and a stone basin concealed in the rose bushes. I reach down, helping myself to a large swig of champagne to try warm up from within.

"This reminds me of how we met." I say, wiping my mouth on the back of my hand.

Gia turns to face me as water spurts out the shower, cocking her head. "Full circle." She says smiling, taking the bottle from me to have a sip. Gia undresses and jumps under the cascading water. I stand fully clothed, shivering as I take another swig of champagne, waiting my turn.

"Just come in with me, you're freezing!" Gia calls, as she tilts her head under the shower, the little speckles of sand gently releasing from her hair and running down her back. I feel those pesky butterflies take flight, but don't protest. I peel off my clothes, now practically fused to my damp body and gingerly step in. The rush of warmth makes me lightheaded, and I groan with pleasure as I let it rush over me. I open my eyes to see Gia, delicately rinsing each arm under the water. I can see why drunk me kissed her. Her eyelashes dark and long, her full lips slightly parted, the way the water rushes down her collar bone, to her perky breasts, to her toned abs. She stops rinsing, noticing my eyes on her chest and smirks down at me.

"Here," she says, pressing a pale bar of soap in my palm. She starts to retract her hand, but I feel my fingers grip it, pulling her body closer to mine, the butterflies flapping frantically. I gaze up to her green eyes, and then down to her lips, tilting my head back, inviting her.

"What are you doing?" she laughs. I keep hold of her gaze, intertwining my fingers with hers. Gia's laugh fades as I pull her closer. "Maddie, are you sure you want to do this?" she breathes, the sound of the shower roaring above us.

"I think I do. I think I might've for a while." I say shyly. Gia's lips part in a smile. And she cups my chin between her fingers.

"Me too." she sighs, before her lips come crashing into mine. Electricity rushes through my body, our hands both hungrily feeling each other. Every sense feels heightened, as her palms travel down my neck, to my waist to my ass. She pushes me against the cold stone of the house, running her tongue around my mouth as her right hand strokes down my belly, stopping just by my waist, teasing little circles.

"You're sure you want this?" She asks breathlessly into my mouth.

"Uh huh", I moan, her teasing driving me crazy.

"Say it," she says, kissing my neck. I tilt my head back in pleasure, a deep moan escaping me as my back arches, pushing my body further into hers.

"I want it." I gasp, as her fingers slip between my legs gently moving back and forth. I moan louder, and she speeds up, plunging her fingers deep inside me. I feel my body succumb to hers, unsure of where she ends and I begin. I feel the release crash through me, making my body shake as the water cascades over us. Gia holds me, as I lean into the wall barely mustering the strength to stay standing.

CHAPTER 25

The next few days are spent working, cooking, walking on the beach, swimming in the sea, and having sex. Possibly the best sex I've ever had?

After the shower three nights ago, we'd gone up to the bedroom and drifted off. Gia had offered me the spare room, which I firmly declined. We spent the rest of the night wrapped together, tasting and touching every inch of each other's bodies.

Today is our last day at the house, Gia's driving us to San Francisco this afternoon, where we'll spend the night before I fly back to London tomorrow. Gia is up in Monterey today, doing some promo for the Aquarium and their seal rehabilitation. Free of charge. She really is a rare one. I'm just wrapping up the day's work for Maria, sat at the dining table downstairs, fire roaring behind me. We'd gone into Carmel town to get me some more clothes, and I'm now wearing new comfy cream joggers and a baggy navy polo jumper. I've been racking my brain today for something nice to do for Gia before we leave, and have settled on cooking spaghetti meatballs, just like the ones Mustafa had taught us to make. It's gone awfully, and I wince as I look over to the kitchen. My clumpy attempts at pasta lay splayed on the counter, like thick beige worms, and my oddly shaped meatballs sit next to them. I ping off my final email and shut my laptop, rolling up my sleeves ready to try salvage lunch. I heat up some oil in a pan, and as I try to gently add the meatballs they fall apart, little edges crumbling right off. I sigh in despair, mashing them together. I guess it'll be bolognaise.

The sauce is nearly done, and I throw in my misshapen spaghetti into a pot of boiling water, nervously glancing at the time. She'll be home any minute. I always felt a little nervous around Gia, but ever since we've been... intimate, the nerves are different. I find myself worrying about what I look like, what I sound like, what I feel like. I nervously stir my sauce which bubbles in the pan, at least it smells good.

My timer goes off, and I struggle to lift the heavy pot containing my pasta worms, carrying it over to the sink to drain. As I do so, the door flings open making me jump, the pot jerking out my grip, scattering my spaghetti down the sink. I shriek as some of the boiling water splashes onto my hand, and Gia drops her bag to the floor rushing over.

"What the fuck happened?" she says, quickly turning on the cold tap and shoving my hand under it. I gesture to the spaghetti below, sadly splayed across the sink.

"I wanted to cook us lunch."

"There's spaghetti in the cupboard!"

"I wanted it to be special. Like Mustafa made…"

Gia laughs and kisses my forehead "That's sweet." She kisses my cheek, and then my neck. "Is there anything I can do, to help take your mind off the pain?" She says into my ear, gently stroking my hand that's sat under the cold tap.

"Um, maybe?" I say awkwardly. We usually do this in the evening, after a couple glasses of wine.

"Does it help if I touch you here?" She says, her hand winding under my jumper round my waist, gently grazing her lips on my neck from behind.

"What time did we need to leave again?" I ask, feeling a little lightheaded.

"A couple of hours." Gia responds, as her hands play with my waistband, flicking at my button.

"Should we pack?" I gasp, as her other hand joins it and undoes my trousers in one effortless motion, slinking them down, hand creeping between my legs.

"Do you want to pack?" Gia purrs, her hand now creeping up my back, stroking my hair, as her other hand delicately strokes the cotton of my underwear.

"I don't think so." I manage, and Gia kisses my neck harder. I feel my nerves dissipate and succumb to the pleasure, my knuckles white as I grip the counter, feeling Gia's body pressed firmly against mine. Her breathing is heavy, as her hand slowly slips beneath my underwear, finally touching me. Just as a loud moan escapes me, Gia's ringtone floods the kitchen making us both jump.

"Great timing," she mutters, recoiling her hand from my hair to retrieve it from her pocket. I compose myself and go to move, but Gia doesn't budge her stance, her other hand still between my legs.

"Hey!" she says into the phone, her fingers sliding lower between my legs, delicately teasing circles around my centre. I gasp and try wriggle away from her touch. I can feel her stifle a giggle from behind me.

"9 should be fine yeah, do you want us to bring anything?"

My face heats, and a stifle another moan as she finally grazes my core, lighting every inch of my body on fire.

"Shhh", she whispers into my ear, holding the phone away as she touches me more, kissing my neck. I can barely keep my mouth shut, her hips firmly planted into my back as she enters me, making my legs feel like jelly.

"Great, see you later!"

She hangs up, setting her phone down next to the sink. I release the loud gasp I've been holding in, and to my disappointment she slowly removes her fingers, swivelling me around to face her. I can feel my face beaded with sweat, and she looks at me hungrily as she cups my chin between her fingers.

"We gotta leave at 5."

"Mmmhmm," I nod, dazed.

"I just hope it's enough time." she says, stroking my neck.

"For what?" I ask, although I think I already know.

We pull over the hills of San Francisco at 7pm, greeted by a sea of twinkling orange lights. We have the roof up as it was a long drive, and I can't help but imagine what it would be like to drive around with the roof down in summer, fully immersed in the sounds and smells of the city of love. I'll have to come back. We were surprisingly quiet for most of the drive, but I suppose we're past the point of awkwardness together.

We slow at a red light, and I look over to Gia's face, painted deep crimson from the light.

"Are you excited for later?" I ask, fiddling with the straw from my drive-through Coke. She snorts.

"Yes and no. I'm excited for the project as a whole, but the cast mingling not so much. I'd much rather be just us by the sea. I find Tyler pretty nauseating."

"Which one's Tyler?"

"You'll know when you see him. He's better known for his singing."

I raise an eyebrow at her, sucking the last bits of watered down cola from my cup. Her face turns from red to green and we zoom on. Gia's in San Francisco tonight for the cast party for a new film she's in, although she's been very secretive about the whole thing. Or maybe she just doesn't like talking about it. All I know is we have to be there for 9pm, dressed smart. I feel a lump of anxiety clog my throat, struggling to swallow my sugary drink.

The December breeze bites my bare shoulders, and my teeth chatter against the cool crystal champagne glass as I press it to my lips. I left my coat in the pile of furs, leathers and wools by the front door, and would've had to speak to even more people on my route to retrieve it. I've borrowed a dress of Gia's, a white sequin number more fit for summer in the Hamptons than winter in San Francisco. We're staying at Brielle's, which houses a box of emergency Gia things for occasions such as tonight. Unfortunately, no Brielle, as she's gone back to see family in Houston for the holidays. I peer behind me into the glass house, my eyes immediately landing on Gia, laughing vibrantly in the middle of a group. Everyone was talking about the project, the industry, their successes... I needed a minute.

I turn away from the house, built into one of San Francisco's many hills and look back to the view. All the city lights move and twinkle beneath me, sprawling all the way out to the bay, dark and blue highlighted with silver moonlight. I inhale deeply, readying myself to head back in, before coughing on a pungent waft of smoke.

"Sorry, I can move."

I hadn't even noticed the man leaning over the balcony railing a couple feet from me. From what I can make out in the dark, he's tall, has a bleach blonde buzz cut, and is wearing a dark velour suit with no shirt underneath, a plethora of black tattoos inked over his chest. He balances a joint between his fingers and looks at me for a beat before offering it. "Unless you wanna join?"

"Oh, no I'll stick to this thanks!" I say, holding up my champagne.

"Classy girl." He retorts, taking another drag but not moving away. A few cars on the street honk. People inside laugh.

"Are you... in the movie?" I ask, trying to break the silence.

He laughs. "Yeah. I'm also a producer."

"Oh, amazing! I'm uh, friends with Gia. She's really excited."

"I should've known you were one of Gia's."

"Why's that?" I shift awkwardly on my stilettos.

"Her friends are always smoke shows." He says, blowing out a puff as he turns to smile at me. Now I'm looking directly at his face, I'm sure I've seen it before.

"You're a singer, right?" I ask nervously.

"Correct. I'm in Wings of Paragon. But trying my hand at something different."

"Well, I look forward to seeing the finished product." I say, spying Gia waving to me from inside. "I'll see you in there, I think Gia wants me." I say, going to move past him.

"You in town for long, classy?"

Maybe it's the champagne, or his fame, but I feel my heart flutter a little.

"One night only," I say, looking back at him as I press my hand to the sliding door.

"Guess I'll have to make an impression then."

"I guess so," I say, turning quickly before he can see me blush as I walk inside.

Gia catches me as I enter the warm, orange room, my ears accosted by the music and conversation. Her hair is slicked back into a bun, makeup natural and dewy as usual, with her signature gold glitter highlighting the inner corners of her eyes. She's wearing a cropped black jacket and matching skirt, opaque tights, and black pointed kitten heels. I nearly forgot how good she looked. Gia wraps her arm around my waist and leans into my ear.

"I missed you," she says, hushed.

"Me too, but you were busy!" I say, tilting away from her slightly, aware of how many people can see us.

"I know, I'm sorry it's so boring for you. We just gotta take a couple more photos and then a few of us are thinking about ditching for tacos."

"Tacos?" I say, pressing my finger to my lips.

"Uh huh. So, drink the *Cristal* dry, snoop around the house, and I'll grab you when it's time to go. Or you can stay with me and chat to people. Whatever you want." She says, stroking my back gently. I catch a man's eyes linger on us, noticing Gia's caress and I quickly slide out of it, feeling my cheeks flush. Gia follows my gaze and looks from the man to me, her eyes darkening slightly.

"I think I need the bathroom," I say, quickly slipping away from her and down the hallway.

I've had one and a half more glasses of *Cristal*, less than I'd usually drink but didn't want to risk making a fool of myself in front of Gia's industry people. I've mainly been looking at all the paintings around the house, and my phone. I feel somewhat invisible amongst this crowd, and they're pretty much treating me like a ghost among mortals in turn. I drain my champagne flute, looking up at the modern splatters of paint on canvas before me, not quite sure I get it. I'm in the hallway, next to the pile of coats, feeling a little like a discarded accessory myself. I crack my neck and run my fingers through my hair, just as a pair of familiar arms wind their way around my waist. I smile and turn to face Gia, who's beaming behind me.

"You hungry?"

"Yes!" I giggle, as she pushes me against the wall, her lips crashing into mine. She tastes like a mix of cigarettes, champagne, and cherry lip gloss. I kiss her back, pulling on her jacket, feeling her chest on mine. Footsteps echo down the hallway, and I quickly push her away.

"We are allowed to kiss here. Hollywood's well versed in don't ask don't tell." Gia teases as I fix my hair.

"I know. Sorry. I'm weird in professional environments."

"Uber's here!" someone yells from the living room, and more footsteps approach.

Gia grabs our coats from the pile, and we head out the door towards the waiting Tesla.

"Shotgun!" a guy in a tux yells as he jostles past us, the blonde man from the balcony in hot pursuit. Gia rolls her eyes.

"Tyler and Max - they're like blood brothers, even though they only met two weeks ago at the table read."

"Tyler's the singer you mentioned, Wings of Paragon, right?"

Gia raises an eyebrow at me as Max clambers in the front, Tyler accepting defeat sliding into the back.

"You a fan?"

"Oh, no, I actually met him earlier... he seemed fine."

Gia laughs. "I'll check back in with you at the end of the night on that one."

"Is it just us four?"

"Oh no, a few others are coming, just different taxis." Gia says, gesturing to another Tesla that's pulling into the drive. We reach ours and Gia opens the door for me. I clamber in, catching my heel on the edge of the car nearly falling onto Tyler's lap.

"Careful, classy!" he says, blue eyes flickering as he scootches over. The drive only takes ten minutes, and luckily I'm the one squished in the middle - preventing Gia from having to interact much with Tyler, and Tyler from seeing Gia's eyes roll back into her skull every time he speaks.

Somehow in the mayhem of seating fourteen people, Gia and I have ended up opposite each other in the middle of the table. To my right is Tyler, and my left a young female producer with a hawk like face, who's only acknowledged me when she asked me to "Pass the wine, doll." Gia is shoulder to shoulder with one of the writers, who happens to be an old university acquaintance, so they've been excitedly trading old memories and news of other classmates since we sat down. Next to Tyler is his "blood brother" Max, so my main company for the night has been this meal. I'm on my first margarita and have already ordered my second plate of tacos, hoping the night will draw to a close soon. Part of me wishes I'd stayed home and ordered Postmates, letting Gia brave this alone. I suck any remaining sauce from my fingers and look round for the waiter with my next plate of social armour. Gia made a comment about bringing Mandy to one of these a couple years ago, who sat moody and bored on her phone for the whole night, so I've tried to refrain from using mine. The restaurant is dimly lit by multicoloured candlesticks wedged into empty tequila bottles, colourful wax dripping down their sides and onto the tables. Live music belts from a Latin band in the corner, and some people are getting up to dance, which makes it particularly difficult to keep an eye out for the waiters. I see one approach our table, clad in black, steaming dish in hand.

"Jumbo Shrimp Taco?"

"Yep!" I respond instantly, raising my hand to make sure he sees me. Even though I've already stuffed down a whole plate of their tacos, my mouth doesn't stop watering when another's placed in front of me. They're about double the size of normal tacos, absolutely slathered in sauce, chargrilled prawns, guacamole, spicy salsa, vegetables... need I go on? I twist my hair out the way and take my first bite, sauce dripping down my hands. I quickly glance up, relieved to find Gia and her crowd engrossed in a conversation about the social pressure of being a trust fund kid before licking the tendrils of dark juice from my forearms.

"You don't fuck about with tacos, do you classy?" Tyler laughs next to me, catching me mid-lick. I feel my cheeks go hot and reach for a napkin to dab the rest.

"Not so classy anymore, huh?" I laugh nervously.

"No, it's chill. I'm usually the same when I'm not wearing velvet," he says, giving me a wink before taking a sip of his margarita.

"You're not classy?"

"Sure. I mean I can't resist licking things, but that as well."

I laugh into my margarita glass, looking up at him. "This is probably the best taco I've ever had, it's not my fault they're making me feral!"

"Naaah, for real? I'll have to take you to Alejandro's in LA sometime, they're unmatched."

"Is that so?"

"It is, m'lady." he responds in an English accent, and I giggle as I take another bite.

"Needs some work, hope you're not playing a Brit in this film." I tease, and he roars with laughter.

"Hey Gia, I like Maddie!" Tyler half yells at her across the table.

"Thanks, me too!" Gia yells jokingly back. It's good to see the margaritas have made her more agreeable to him, defrosting her icy glare from the cab. I turn to look at him and find his eyes fixed on me.

"You've got a little…" Tyler leans over and licks the corner of my lip, making me stifle a shriek.

"What the fuck?" I squeal, shocked.

"You had some sauce! I'd hate to see it go to waste!"

"You're gross." Gia says, rolling her eyes. I wipe my mouth with my hand and laugh, unsure what to do.

"Gia, as her friend, may I have your blessing to ask her on a date?" Tyler asks, looking from me to her. It's almost like you can see the ice refreeze in her gaze.

"She's a grown woman, dude, ask her yourself."

"Maddie, can I offer you a great date full of good company, and even better tacos than this?" Tyler says, taking my hand.

"I'd love to, but I'm leaving tomorrow." I giggle nervously. He is *really* cute.

"When I'm next in London. Or we could always bounce early tonight, I can think of a couple fun things we could do." He says, leaning closer, placing his hand on my thigh. I see Gia's eyes flutter down, and she swallows sharply.

"I'm gonna go to the little girls room," she says shortly, rising from her seat and stalking off.

CHAPTER 26

The heat from the mint tea seeps through Brielle's thin mugs to my palms, and I struggle not to drop them as I push open the bedroom door with my hip.

"Careful, it's hot!"

I say as I set them both down on the bedside table. Gia doesn't look up from her phone, lying cocooned in the poofy yellow blanket pulled up to her chin. She's barely spoken to me since we got home, I'm hoping she's just tired.

"So... tonight was fun?"

"Uh huh." She doesn't look at me and keeps scrolling. Weird.

"Did you have fun?"

"Uh huh."

"Cool." I say shortly, lifting the blanket to get into bed.

"There's another bedroom down the hall." She looks up at me coldly. "If you want."

"Why would I want?" I say, reaching for her knee. She recoils, and I feel my heart sink. "Can you tell me what's happened? I thought we had a good night?"

"You certainly did."

"That's bullshit. You were happy chatting and laughing with everyone all night - your people need I remind you, not mine?"

"And while I was having to talk with my people, who are people I have to ensure like me so they keep hiring me, I had to watch you and Tyler eyefuck each other the entire evening."

"Oh my God, we were not!"

She turns off her phone and looks at me, her eyes glassy. "Be so for real with me Maddie."

I sigh. "Maybe we flirted a little..."

"A little?!"

"Ok we flirted! So what?"

"How would you feel if I flirted with someone in front of you?"

I shrug. I honestly don't know. I don't know what any of this is. Gia squeezes her eyes shut and blocks them with her fists. "God, I'm so stupid." I go to stroke her arm, but she bats me away. "I'm so tired of being an experiment. A phase. And I can tell that's probably all I'll ever be to you."

"I never said that!"

"You don't have to! All I could think about tonight was you. Were you having a good time? Were you

223

thinking about me? What I wanted to do to you when we got home. And the whole time I was looking at you, you were looking at him."

A lump's formed in my throat the size of a golf ball, and I feel like a caught fish on a boardwalk, flapping about the planks struggling for air.

"Gia, I really like you. I do. I'm sorry, you know this is all so new and... overwhelming for me."

She takes a deep breath and clasps my hand. "I know. I know it is. And I'm sorry. I'm not trying to pressure you. It took me years to come to terms with who I am. But I can't be someone's experiment again. My heart can't take it." I gulp, lost for words. Despite the sounds of the city, the silence in the bedroom is deafening. Gia rubs her eyes and sits up. "I think I should sleep in the guest room tonight, and you should think about what you want. If it's me, that's great. If it isn't, then tell me. So I don't fall any harder."

I scan her face, those deep green eyes, full lips, little freckles. I want her. I think? I close my eyes and lean in but feel her pull back. She cups my face, slowly stroking my cheek.

"I'm serious Maddie. Have. A. Think. Take the time you need. Then tell me what you want." She leans over, planting a soft kiss on my forehead, before getting out of bed and padding towards the door, reaching for the coral mug.

"Night. Thanks for the tea."

The door shuts. And then I'm alone.

CHAPTER 27

I swear, one day these last ten steps will be the death of me. I haul my suitcase, heavy with my new wardrobe up the wooden stairs. In return, it bangs into my ankle with each step. That'll bruise. As I reach my door, I sink to the floor catching my breath. A crumpled piece of paper falls out my pocket, I don't need to look at it to know what it is. I didn't see Gia this morning. When I woke there was a bag of pastries and a lukewarm coffee next to my bed, but no Gia. Under the bag of croissants and pain au chocolates, was a little note.

"Take the time you need. Have a Merry Christmas. Hopefully speak in the new year. Safe flight, Gia xo"

I don't know why I bothered keeping it, it's hardly a love letter. But for some reason I found myself clutching onto it for most of the flight, terrified of losing it through security or dropping it during customs. I scoop it up and take a deep breath. The main thing keeping me moving is the warm bath that awaits. Even in the stairwell, the London December breeze is freezing me through to my bones. I push the key into the lock, my fingers near numb, and burst through the door. Sprout comes racing over, and I scoop him up burying my face in his warm, soft fur. He smells like a fresh Spring meadow.

Our cuddle is interrupted by my stomach releasing a large growl, so I pop Sprout down and plod over to the fridge. I'm so tired the bright light inside it makes me squint, and although Anya's kept Sprout alive she hasn't left any surprises for me this time. I grab an old yogurt that looks edible enough and sink down into the sofa, too tired to think about Gia but too enamoured by her to not. Who knows what any of it was. A phase? A distraction? Love...

I'm snapped out of self-pity when I notice the large bouquet of half dead flowers on the coffee table in front of me and smile. The white roses are now mostly crispy and brown, petals that gave up scattered across the oak. Anya's never been great at keeping plants alive, I'm still in awe of how she's managed Sprout.

Once I've finished shovelling the sour yogurt into my mouth, I yank off clothes and enter the bathroom, lazily turning on the hot tap. Steam slowly fills the room, dappling all the white tiles with specks of condensation. I shut my eyes, pressing my head to the cool ceramic listening to the tap run, letting it drown out the frantic thoughts scurrying round my mind.

I race through Covent Garden, different variations of the same Christmas songs belting out of every shop and restaurant I pass. It seems spending Christmas Day at home with family is a thing of the past, as Central London is swamped with tourists and locals alike, friends meeting for lunch, families out seeing the lights, everyone laughing and drinking and rosy-cheeked. I pick up the pace and my boots clack on the icy cobbles, careful not to disturb the perfectly prepared chicken nestled inside the largest Tupperware I could find last minute on Amazon. I'm dressed for a smart Christmas Day celebration with Anya and her now fiancé Brian at his Notting Hill townhouse. I, however, find myself being a glorified food delivery woman for my eccentric boss. I could have said no, Maria absolutely didn't force me into this. But I felt bad. It's her first Christmas totally alone, as her daughter decided to stay in Australia last minute as her grandkids came down with the flu. One of Maria's eccentricities is a phobia of raw meat, meaning she never normally prepares her own roast chicken on the 25th. I couldn't bare the idea of her home alone picking at a nut roast, so volunteered my culinary prowess to deliver her an oven ready chicken, prepared with love on my way to Brian's. I'd assumed at the time I'd be the only one travelling on Christmas Day, how wrong I was.

I reach Maria's by 1.20, an hour behind schedule and throw myself at her big blue door. She has a gorgeous old apartment on Dean Street, I've only been inside once but it's like stepping into one of her coffee table books. High ceilings, deep blue furniture, Moroccan rugs, candles and plants everywhere.

"It's – me – and – chicken!" I pant into the buzzer, and the door flies open. Again, old London flat, no lift.

Maria greets me at the door arms flung wide, bringing me and the chicken into a bony hug.

"Come in darling, come in!" she says, her emerald kimono rippling after her as she walks through to the kitchen. The floors are tiled green and white, and she managed to get permission to install a large skylight, with spirals of wrought iron swirling between the glass panes.

"She's all ready to go, stuffed, basted and greased!"

"You're a star! What would I do without you?" she says, gingerly putting on her oven gloves before opening the lid of the Tupperware.

"The bottom can go in the oven, so you don't have to transfer it."

"Smart ducky you are!" she says, inspecting the seasoned bird. I actually enjoyed doing it, using the recipe me and Mum made every year.

"You know you're still welcome to spend it with me and–"

"Nonsense! Work life balance darling, besides, I'm 67 and have never spent a Christmas alone! I'm rather excited. Sherry for your troubles?"

"I really mustn't, I'm already late."

"Alright sweetie. I'll see you out."

As she ushers me to the door, she grabs a white folder off the marble kitchen counter with her cobalt nails.

"I thought I ought to give you this. How would you fancy working over New Year? Little trip, all expenses paid?"

I clasp the white folder, taken aback.

"Me? Another shoot alone?"

"Yes, you got on quite well with the Kenya project. I'm getting tired of all the travelling, and my daughter might try make it to London for New Year now."

My heart glows, this is basically a promotion. Or could at least lead to one.

"I'll look over the project and make sure I feel confident with it, but I'd love to!"

"Fabulous ducky! I'll see you next week. Merry Christmas!"

She plants a kiss on my cheek and shuts the door, and it's all I can do to not shriek with joy. As I race down the steps I flick through the file, excited to see where I'm off to. And my heart stops. I grip the banister to steady myself, little black specks clouding my vision. Watamu. Kenya. A hotel named Utulivu. A Kimani Hotel.

"What?! Do you think he knows?"

I shrug, letting out a large puff of air. I sink further into the armchair and undo the top button of my skirt. I feel like I'm made up of 30% Christmas lunch, 30% wine and 40% anxiety. Anya tucks her legs under the thick knitted blanket on the sofa and holds her glass towards Brian for a top-up. He's been patiently watching the TV Christmas specials at low volume while Anya and I chat.

"I feel like he must? Or maybe he doesn't? Either way, he obviously gave Maria a glowing report of last time." I say, draining my glass. Brian rises to fill it without question, and I smile at him in thanks.

"Do you think he might've... requested you?"

My heart pounds at the thought. "I did wonder. But why?"

"Maybe he feels bad about everything?"

"Surely a WhatsApp is cheaper than a whole new shoot." I drum my finger against the crystal glass, eyes flicking to the TV. "Besides, he's old news anyway. I'd rather not waste my breath."

Anya nudges Brian under the blanket with her foot and raises and eyebrow at me. "Old news, huh. We thought there might be someone new on the scene!"

I roll my eyes at them and look to the TV.

"Let me guess, a proper New York Wallstreet guy? Or a struggling Brooklyn artist? Or could it be a blonde, chiselled Californian surfer dude–"

"Anya, stop! There's no one else." I try stifle my guilt with a large gulp of wine, but nearly choke on it instead. I barely know what's going on with my feelings for Gia, let alone how to vocalise them to Anya. The Eastenders theme blares from the TV and I can feel my chest heave and suddenly need to be away, alone. "Sorry, I just need some air for a second."

"Alone?" Anya asks. I smile and nod, and excuse myself into the garden.

I sink down on the cool slate patio, pressing my palms into the stone trying to calm my racing pulse. For London, Brian's Notting Hill townhouse is a mansion, two floors, three bedrooms and a garden. I feel spoiled, all the sunsets and oceans and views I've taken in over the last month make Brian's meagre holly bushes look almost an eyesore. I can hear laughter and music coming from all the other semi-detached houses on the street and try focus on all the sounds instead of the beating of my pulse rattling in my ears. It's funny, Gia is the one person I know who would make me feel better now. And yet she's one of the causes of my nerves. And Daniel. The pressure of a solo project, a real solo project. And Mum. I'd done a good job of blocking her out all day, trying not to think of the ghosts of Christmas pasts, the meal prep, the table setting, the cracker pulling. Eastenders was a big one for us though. It was stupid really, we never watched a single episode aside from the yearly Christmas special. We'd make up our own backstories and names for all the characters. It was special. It was ours. But this is Brian and Anya's Christmas, their first Christmas engaged. I don't want to impose more than I already am. If Gia and I were talking we could FaceTime now until the episode's over, or I know she'd at least know what to say to get me through it. But we're not. We've hardly spoken since I got back. I told her I'd reach out after New Years when I'd had time to fully think. She said she understood and wished me a Merry Christmas.

I hear a tap on the glass doors behind me, and Anya does a crying face from inside, gesturing to a cheese board now in the centre of the dining table.

"Come help me or I'll eat it all myself!" she whines, muffled by the glass. I smile and stand up, dusting off my skirt.

CHAPTER 28

I slather a thick layer of sun cream on my face, making sure to rub in every last white splodge. I learnt my lesson well last time. I'm in the same Nairobi hotel as before, its scent now familiar, almost comforting. Looking back, I can't believe how nervous I was, in this exact room not two months ago. I seemed so much younger somehow. I'm wearing my same denim shorts, white vest and white linen shirt on top. No chance of a farmer's tan here. One thing I did on the eight-hour plane ride instead of sink back Sauvignon Blanc was master the French braid, and am proud of the two twin plaits that glide down my back.

I leave for the coast tomorrow, so have one full day in Nairobi, which I don't intend on wasting. I'd gone out for a morning coffee at the cafe under the hotel called Java House, and sat on their patio soaking up the sun with my book and an iced latte. It almost felt like a holiday. Kenya is great as I don't tend to think about Mum, no old haunts to remind me of her. It does however reek of Gia and Daniel, two souls who I'm trying to block from my thoughts entirely, at least for today.

Today, I basically am on holiday. My intercom rings and I scramble over my splayed suitcase to answer it.

"Good day Ms. Wilson, your shuttle is here."

"Thank you!"

I scurry towards the door, rifling through my bag to make sure I haven't forgotten anything. If I'm treating today as a holiday, I thought I may as well do some touristy things, and when I'd googled fun things to do in Nairobi, Daphne Sheldrick's Elephant Orphanage had been number one. I grab my blue baseball cap off the floor, slide my keycard into my satchel and am out the door.

Being in the top touristy thing to do in Nairobi, the orphanage is packed. It doesn't stop the wonder of the experience though, being so close to all the little baby elephants. I can't help but think of the teeny one Daniel and I found, and hope she made it. General Admission gets you entry to view the meet and greet show, where the handlers bring out baby elephants of all shapes and sizes, all with tragic backstories but hopeful futures. Being a solo traveller, I managed to jostle my way to the front of the crowd, securing a spot right by the wooden rails, able to reach out and stroke one of their dusty backs. It was a little overwhelming, the sea of people, but knowing that each person's admission goes to keeping the elephants alive made it worthwhile. I was sandwiched between one large, sunburnt American man in khakis, and one large, sunburnt English man in khakis, both with loud families on their other sides. By the time the last elephant scurried off after its handler, tail wagging between its little legs, I was parched and tired, having fought for my spot in the front. Finally my sides ease as the people disperse and head for the gift shop, and I make my way to one of the benches in the shade ready to glug down the contents of my water bottle. It's 28 degrees today, but after standing in direct sun for half an hour it feels about 35. Fuck it, I'm here alone. I lift off my cap and douse my forehead in the last of my water, the instant relief making the hairs on the back of my neck stand up. I should head back to my shuttle soon, the numbers of revellers dwindling. I look out to the pen, housing two muddy waterholes that the elephants played in, and bare abandoned branches that have been stripped of their leaves by the older calves. To the right of the pen is bush, and to the left what must have been Daphne's house, the founder of the orphanage. It's made of grey stone, and has a large wooden balcony on the second floor with a couple figures, who had enjoyed the show with refreshments. Must be the VIP experience, I think as I jealousy squint at the tray of biscuits and juice on the table. I rise and make my way towards the exit, lingering by a table of green and beige fleeces, all embroidered with two little elephants on the right breast. Despite the heat, the fleece feels amazingly soft.

"How much are these?" I ask, biting my lip. Technically could be a Christmas present.

"8,000 shillings ma'am." The handler dressed in green behind the table responds. Pretty pricey, but I guess it's for charity?

"It does get chilly up at the coast, at least in the evenings." A deep voice purrs from behind me. A voice I definitely recognise. I whip round, half in disbelief, half in fright. There he is, stood right behind me, same silver chain and flowy linen shirt.

"I thought it was you but wasn't sure, had to come down and double check before I waved like an idiot."

I can barely make words. "You were at the show?"

"On the balcony. I should really ask for a refund, I was extremely distracted from the elephants by a small redhead holding a wrestling match against two stocky men."

My mouth opens and shuts, and I feel sweat bead on my nose.

"Then again I've seen it enough for a lifetime."

"How come you're not in the Mara. Or the coast?" is all I can muster.

"I was in the Mara, yesterday. Came down today, coast tomorrow."

"I'll take this one, thank you." I say, turning back to the handler. He smiles and bags up the green fleece.

"I knew you'd go for the green." Daniel smiles, his eyes twinkling. As if there was no history between us.

"How perceptive you are." I say, giving the handler the money in exchange for the fleece and turning to leave. "I've gotta get my shuttle, I guess I'll see you in Watamu." I say flatly, eager to end whatever this interaction is. To my dismay, he walks after me.

"Ok, Maddie, wait. Let me drop you back at your hotel, or arrange you a new shuttle. I think there's something you'd like to see."

Despite my better judgment, I stop.

Even though it's been under two months, she's nearly double her original size. I can feel my vision go glassy as her trunk clumsily sniffs around my linen as she playfully nudges me with her head.

"She remembers your scent, see." Daniel says from outside the pen, watching us.

"I can't believe how big she's gotten!" I kneel down in the hay so she's taller than me and stroke her ears as she flaps them back and forth.

"Kijani. That's her name now."

"Hi Kijani!" She bumps into me again, nearly toppling me over. I push myself back up and look into her deep brown eyes. She's alive. She's here. She's big! A handler enters the hut, milk bottle the size of a toddler in hand. Like she can sense it, Kijani bolts from my side to his, trunk vigorously wrestling for the bottle.

"We had no problem getting her to eat, which is good," the handler says smiling.

"I can tell!"

"I'm glad you got to see her," the handler smiles. "It's getting near nap time, but please feel free to come again." he says, struggling to keep a firm grip on the bottle as her trunk wraps around it vigorously.

"I can't thank you enough." I say, stroking her fuzzy grey head one last time, trying to memorise each bump and hair. We thank the handlers and head across the red dust paths to the car park.

"You really seem to have the whole of Nairobi under your thumb."

Daniel laughs sheepishly. "I work closely with the Sheldrick Foundation because of Tukio. And donate some of our revenue. In turn I get access to the balcony and to see them in their pens."

I nod, and we continue in silence till we reach my shuttle.

"Thank you. You could've just ignored me. Or let me leave earlier. It meant a lot to me to see her."

"I would never have done that."

I struggle to hold in a scoff as he slides open the van door for me, he clearly had no issue doing it the last time he watched me drive away.

"I'll see you in Watamu." I'm unsure of what else to say.

He nods and goes to close the car door.

"Have you got dinner plans tonight?"

I suck in a breath. "None as of yet."

"There's a great Japanese, Furusato. Meet there at 8?"

"Um – I –"

He slams the door shut with a smile, leaving me no time to object.

CHAPTER 29

I could've easily not come. No one forced me, all it would've taken was a text. But I can't stifle that little ember that lit when I saw him, whether it be rage or lust. I dab fresh powder on my cheeks, concealing the nervous flush of pink. Soft Japanese folk music plays over the restaurant speakers, calming me somewhat. I've been here for twenty minutes, he's obviously running late. Typical. I lift up my breasts so they sit perfectly in my skin tight black maxi dress, luckily not out of place in the fancy restaurant. My hair is down but wavy from my previous braids, and for once I feel gorgeous. Really, truly, gorgeous. I take one last look in the bathroom mirror, and head back to my table, bracing myself to see Daniel sat there.

But when I return it's empty aside from the jug of tap water and bottle of sake I ordered. I sit back down and pour myself a top up of both, peering around the restaurant. I can't help but think of the dinky little one Gia and I went to in Carmel. Furusato is much larger, with high wooden ceilings, glowing yellow lanterns suspended from it. I'm in a little nook by one of the open windows, with full view of the entrance and the large four-man sushi bar to my left. I wonder if Gia's been here. She probably has. I check the time on my phone. 8.30. I take a big gulp of sake and go to scroll Instagram to look busy. But my phone is on 20%, I can't afford to waste the battery. So, I sit and wait. And wait. At 8.45 when the sake's enveloped me in a warm haze and my stomach has started growling I text him.

"Where are you?"

At 9.10, my phone pings.

"Swamped with a work thing. Can't make it. Order whatever you want and expense it to me."

I nearly laugh out loud, my vision practically turning red. He was the one with something to make up to me! And he stood me up? Not that this was a date… I can feel my blood boil with humiliation and anger. If this wasn't the opportunity for my first solo project I'd quit on the spot. But I know Maria either wouldn't let me or wouldn't forgive me if I did.

I order the sushi platter to share for four people, which arrives on a giant wooden boat. The waiter looks at me skeptically, and I make sure to finish it all out of spite. At him and at Daniel. I then order the chocolate lava cake and a double of their top shelf Japanese whisky and roll back into my hotel bed full and drunk.

The flight to the coast took less than an hour, and thankfully was on a much larger plane than the ones that fly to the Mara. Though a little bumpy, I savoured every second of it knowing I wasn't in Daniel's presence. The drive from Watamu Airport took forty minutes, again precious, solitary time. I spent most of it gawking out the window at the stark differences of the coast to Nairobi. Palm trees scattered everywhere, rickshaws zooming around with vibrant hand painted murals on their sides.

The shuttle slows as we pull into large white gates, and my stomach seizes up. After driving up a bumpy sand road the hotel comes into view, and I look out to where I'll be staying for the next week, and where I'll be seeing in the New Year. The van door swings open, and the driver smiles and nods at me as he goes to fetch my suitcase. I didn't have the time or the funds to upgrade the purple monstrosity, and wince as he lugs it towards me. I smile and press 100 shillings into his palm and walk through the large white archway to reception. Inside is a wooden desk, housing a neat tray of pamphlets about the coast and activities, a marbled jug of iced water with floating lemon wedges and sprigs of mint, and a ginormous sculpture of a sword fish mounted on the wall above that almost gives me a fright. The floor is the same smooth limestone as most of the buildings in the Mara, and I'm grateful for how it softens the sound of my clunky suitcase rolling over it. The receptionist smiles as I approach.

"Ms. Wilson?"

"How did you know?"

"Mr. Kimani said to look out for a purple suitcase!" she laughs nervously. I grimace a smile.

"I'm Rita, if you need anything please feel free to ask."

"Thank you. Is Da– Mr. Kimani around?"

"Uh, yes ma'am. I think he arrived a couple hours ago. Would you like me to pho–"

"Oh no it's fine!" I feel my stomach sink. I was hoping I'd beat his arrival and have a few hours without the constant need to look over my shoulder and find him skulking in a corner.

"Great. Here is your room key, 108, I'll have a concierge accompany you there now with your baggage. Your room is down that pathway on the left," she says, pointing out the reception archway to a small path over lush grass. "Just up these stairs here," she gestures to six stone steps on my right "is the common area, the bar, and beyond that is the restaurant. But you can order restaurant food to anywhere you are seated if you just flag one of the staff members over."

"Amazing, thanks so much."

Despite my foul mood, I can't help but marvel at the route to my room. We walk along a winding path of white stones, surrounded by lush green grass, tropical bushes and frangipani trees. Each room is a little hut, with its own outdoor patio with a view out to the sea to my right. It looks like how I'd always imagined Hawaii would be. The concierge swipes my room card before handing it to me, and a strong wave of AC hits me as I enter. The floors are the familiar yellow limestone, with a woven sea grass rug on top. The mahogany four poster bed is draped in a decadent mosquito net, all tied up neatly at its corners. Each side has a bedside table, again reminiscent of the Mara with a vase of fresh frangipani, hand blown water glasses and a large beeswax candle. In front of the bed is a dresser with a TV mounted above it, and a full-length mirror by the door leading to what I assume is the bathroom. I stifle a smile as I walk to the bed and spy an intricate towel sculpture elephant seated in the middle. I'm sure it was a coincidence, but I stroke its little head all the same. The concierge awkwardly clears his throat by the door, and I turn embarrassed, having completely forgotten he was there.

"Sorry, thank you so much."

He smiles, placing my keycard on the dresser and shuts the door behind him as he leaves. I exhale and flop onto the bed, careful not to squash my towel companion.

I can feel my hair dampen with sweat as I lounge by the pool, a little droplet tickling the back of my neck as it glides down. I don't technically start work until tomorrow, so intend to treat today as another holiday. Alone, solo, holiday. I know better than to try tan, so am lying on one of the blue sun loungers that shroud the turquoise circular swimming pool. I prop myself up on one arm, and thankfully the screeching twins that were diving and splashing relentlessly since I arrived are being bundled up in Disney towels by their parents and led away. As I sit up and stretch my achey bones, excited to finally swim, I see Rita making her way towards me. She waves, and I suck in a breath, unsure of what she wants. I quickly adjust my olive bikini, far from work appropriate.

"Ms. Wilson! I was just on my way to your room."

"Oh?" I bite my lip, not sure what to respond.

"Mr. Kimani has requested dinner with you, is 7.30 good?"

My stomach churns. So much for my day of solitude. But he's technically the client, so I can't refuse.

"That's fine with me. Shall I meet him at the restaurant?"

Rita smiles warmly, almost like she senses my apprehension. "I believe so. Sorry to bother, please enjoy your swim!" she says, turning to leave.

"Thank you!" If only there were some rocks I could put in my pockets. I'm tempted to stand him up, leave him there waiting like he left me. I walk to the water's edge and slowly lower myself in, the cool a welcome relief from the red hot rage I can feel simmering in my belly.

I gingerly wait by the stone arch in the white wall separating the bar area from the restaurant. Wanting to make the most of my alone time, I didn't bother going back to the room and changing, so I'm wearing a white beach tunic over my olive bikini and my Birkenstocks. My hair is up in a messy bun, wilder than usual from the chlorine and humidity. He doesn't deserve anything more, not after the humiliation of the other night. I glance up at the TV, mounted next to the wooden bar. 7.35.

Typical. I plonk down on one of the oak bar stools and order a glass of red. If he's going to be God knows how late again, I'm at least waiting with a drink. The bartender gently sets the glass in front of me, and I raise it to my lips for a hefty swig.

"Do you always need a drink to be in my company?"

I roll my eyes before swivelling around to face him.

"Just wasn't sure how late you'd be." I bite back. Daniel chuckles, which infuriates me more.

"Come, let's eat." he says, holding out a hand. I ignore it, reaching down to grab my satchel. As I lift it, my SPF50 clatters onto the floor. Daniel kneels down to fetch it, handing it to me, his eyes flicking up and down my attire.

"Day by the pool?"

"I was hot." I shrug, grabbing it from him and walking towards the restaurant.

"Not there, follow me," he says, gesturing to the large outdoor balcony on stilts 10 feet above the beach below. He grabs my wine and leads the way, and we walk across the patio in silence, the wooden planks under our feet creaking softly. The balcony houses multiple tables and sofas, about half inhabited by other guests. We keep walking until we reach the very end of the balcony, where a small section juts out shielded by a wicker gazebo roof. Little wind chimes of sea glass hang from it, slowly tinkling in the breeze. Under it is a table for two, with a crisp ivory tablecloth, three of the signature beeswax candles, a brown folder and a vase of frangipani.

"Hope you're not planning on proposing." I say icily, ignoring the chair he's pulled out for me and sitting in the other. He chuckles again. Prick.

"Not tonight."

If I didn't hate him so much, I'd feel violently underdressed. As he slides my wine across to me, I spy a waiter approaching with two steaming bowls.

"No chance to look at the menu I guess."

He smiles, filling my water glass before his from a glass jug, similar to the one on the front desk.

"I remembered how much you liked Mustafa's food. This is one of his recipes."

The waiter gently sets down the dishes and my heart sinks. Spaghetti and meatballs. I feel a pang in my chest as I'm transported back to being with Gia.

"Unless you were just being polite?"

Daniel raises an eyebrow, my emotions clearly painted across my face. I quickly shake them off, pronging a meatball.

"No, it looks great."

I pop it in my mouth and try muster up memories of Ikea and Anya to replace their association with Gia. Neither of us talk, maybe out of stubbornness, so instead I look out to the view. It's low tide, making the white sandy beach below double its size. The deep blue waves gently crash in the distance, as the last sliver of orange sun dips below the horizon.

"I'm sorry about the other night."

My gaze whips back to him.

"It's fine." I say icily.

"It's not. I handled it badly, and I'm sorry. I hope you ordered half the menu to spite me."

I smirk as I take a sip of my wine. "And some top shelf whisky."

"Wouldn't have expected anything less," he says, flicking through the folder. "I'm sure Maria has briefed you on the basics, but we're aiming for a twin site for the coast and the Mara, hopefully making the hotels more integrated and getting clients to try both."

I nod, twirling a string of spaghetti around my fork.

"I made this folder with the plans for each day and what I think would work well. Tomorrow there's a snorkelling excursion in the afternoon, and I thought you could utilise the morning to get photos of the rooms."

"Sounds good." I'm still twirling the spaghetti, unable to raise it to my lips, my mind stuck in Carmel.

"Then the day after is our pre–New Year's barbecue; food, drinking, dancing. You know the drill. For the Thursday I thought you could do the rest of the hotel and the surrounding area, potentially going into Watamu town and get some shots of things to do there. And the Friday is the New Year's party, which is always our busiest. And then Saturday is home."

"Amazing. Thanks for making me the folder, very professional." I jest. He raises an eyebrow and sips his water.

"Well, I anticipated you could use some assistance in that department."

I feel my cheeks heat. "What does that mean?"

He laughs, rubbing his hand on his neck. "Come on Maddie, you know."

"Enlighten me."

He laughs.

"Ok. Well. Showing up on your first day in those tiny shorts and a see-through top."

"That was my travel outfit." I scoff, "It's not like I could've worn business casual in 30 degree heat being tossed round the back of a van."

Daniel smirks, his eyes flicking down me. "So tonight, is this your travel outfit? And travel glass of wine?"

I cross my arms, attempting to conceal any part of my bikini which may show through my tunic. "I assumed work started tomorrow. Anyway, it's rich for you to talk about professionalism."

He leans back in his chair, surprised. "And what does that mean?"

"It means would you call it professional to drunkenly kiss and touch your employee? Or is that just what you do with everyone?"

His eyes darken, and he leans forward.

"I'm sorry. It was a bad joke. I do think you're professional."

I can feel my blood simmering in my veins. "You're just saying that now because you've realised how hypocritical it was."

"That night... it was a mistake. I'm sorry."

My heart pummels down my chest. A mistake. A drunken mistake. That's all I ever was to him. "I just... I don't understand this."

"What?"

"All of it. Why would you request me again?"

Daniel straightens, confused. "Request you?"

"For this job. Instead of Maria."

His brow furrows. "I didn't?"

"Yes, you did?"

"I don't know what you're on about," he leans forward, his gaze softening. "I had a follow-up call with Maria, and mentioned I'd be interested in doing a new site for the coast. She pitched you coming alone and doing it, to help you learn the ropes more with a client you've already worked with. I assumed you knew?"

My stomach now joins my heart in the deep pit below.

"She didn't tell me." I say feebly. The little orange solar powered lights all flicker on, the evening sky darkening. "Thanks, for dinner. The plan sounds great. I think I'm going to go to bed." I say, slipping the folder into my satchel and rising slowly. I'm worried if I move too fast I may faint.

"At least stay for dessert?"

"Goodnight, Daniel."

CHAPTER 30

The boat bobs up and down against the waves, and I shield my camera from the bright sun, flicking through the photos. It's the first time I've done underwater shots, and I think I'm in love. I'd had to hurriedly watch a few YouTube tutorials this morning on how to work the new camera, but they turned out professional. I snort at the word. And quickly swallow the embarrassment that follows. He didn't request me. I shove the thought aside, focussing on the neon pink parrotfish I got a closeup of. It was almost like she was modelling, constantly zipping past me as I swam, begging to be photographed. I hear his deep laugh rumble off the boats roof, followed by high pitched cackles. I grind my teeth, thankfully the boat's on the way back. To my dismay, Daniel joined the snorkelling excursion with two young Italian sisters both stick thin and bronzed, and their Adonis-bodied brother. They were the children of one of the hoteliers down the beach and seemed to know Daniel well. I flick to the next photo of one of the girls, lounging on the roof of the boat, laughing at someone off camera, her hair whipping in caramel swirls behind her. I suppose they do look good in the photos. Another laugh roars from above, and I relax into the corner of the boat, grateful to be away from them all. It's a relief to not have the fake smile plastered across my face, making my cheeks ache. I tuck my camera back in my bag and lean my shoulders on the wooden edge of the boat, watching the palm trees and houses that line the beach slowly pass. The boat isn't the fastest, an old wooden fishing boat refurbished and painted a deep blue. The bottom has a strip of glass down the middle, catching glimpses of the reef below as we travel. There is a ladder at the back leading up to the wooden roof, where Daniel & Co are lying in the sun and having a beer. I wasn't invited, but I guess I didn't ask.

The boat finally stops, and I clamber off it quickly wading through the water trying to put a good distance between me, Daniel and the Italians.

"Maddie, can you send me any good ones?" Lucia, the one who did the majority of the posing whether I asked her to or not yells after me.

"Of course, lovely meeting you all!" I wave back from ahead, not changing my pace. I can feel the sun beating down on me and am grateful I chose to wear my tunic on top of my professionally chosen one piece, providing me some form of protection. Shower. Room service. Nap. A clump of seaweed gets tangled around my ankle, the sensation making me hold in a shriek, and I slow to trying to kick it off. As I do, I hear a loud splashing through the water behind me, and I whip around to see Daniel effortlessly jogging through the waves towards me. Great. I turn away and keep walking but hear the waves quickly get louder.

"Maddie, wait a sec!"

So I do. He catches up to my side, reaching out offering to carry my large bag which I've had hauled up by my chest to avoid the lapping waves around my knees.

"I'm good, thank you." I say, forcing a smile and gripping my satchel tighter, almost like armour to my chest.

"Alright." He says, and we walk on. He's wearing deep blue swimming trunks and is carrying his soggy linen shirt under his arm, a beer in hand. I try not to notice how the sun makes his skin shine, his muscles rippling as we walk.

"Are you happy with the shots?"

"Yeah, very. They came out really nice, and it worked well having some... models?"

Daniel laughs. "They've been on my case about a boat day for ages, so I thought two birds one stone."

I nod and smile, unsure what to say. The awkwardness hangs like the sticky humidity in the air.

"Look, about last night–"

"Honestly, it's fine."

"It's not, I was rude. And I'm sorry you didn't know the full situation with Maria. It wasn't about the discount, I liked your work last time. I was happy to agree as I *really* liked your work."

Thankfully we've reached the shore, as my legs feel like jelly, my mouth sandpaper dry. "Discount?"

"Shit... I assumed you'd have talked it through with Maria by now..."

"She's been busy." I say through gritted teeth. "I'll send you some previews tonight, I'm going to go have a shower." I quickly say, forcing a smile hopping up the wooden steps to the hotel as fast as I can. I feel him grip my hand and turn to yank it away. His dark eyes are soft, almost pleading. "What have I done to make you hate me this much?"

I roll my eyes, pulling my hand away. "I don't hate you."

"Dislike me."

"Is that really a question?"

He just stands looking down at me, as the soft ocean breeze whips a little strand of hair in between my eyes. He raises his hand as if to brush it away, before clearing his throat and running it through his curls instead.

"We can agree that we don't like each other, but we have to get on. At least till Saturday. So, let's be civil, make this a project to be proud of, and then we never have to see each other again."

I bite my tongue to try distract from the pain in my chest.

"Sounds like a plan." I smile sweetly before turning away, heading back to my room.

I stuff the last handful of room service French fries into my mouth as I finish up my draft for Maria to look over. I turn up the music in my headphones, trying to drown out Daniel's words. Agree to not like each other. I knew I didn't like him, but him outright saying he doesn't like me? I don't know why it hurts so much. I shouldn't be letting it. A deep crack of thunder rumbles outside, and I look through the mesh of my mosquito net to the window, its panes spattered with rain. I've never seen a tropical storm, the palm trees swaying to and fro, the swimming pools rippling with raindrops, the deep rich smell of the earth and salt and sea. I peel my eyes from the window and hit send, but the email bounces back. Shit. My Wi-Fi has one bar, I'm guessing made worse from the storm. Rita had mentioned sometimes it dips in the rooms, but the reception always has it. I sigh and fold my laptop, carefully slipping through the soft mosquito net. I stuff it in my bag, pulling my new green fleece over my head, preparing for the trip to the main area. It's just gone 1am, so I'm sure it'll be desolate. I slip on my trainers and burst out the door, running quickly across the stone path, raindrops hitting my face. At least my hair was already wet from my shower.

I pant to a halt as I enter reception, the graveyard shift receptionist who I haven't seen smiling at me.

"Wi-Fi?" They ask.

"Yes! Is it still good here?"

They nod.

"Amazing, thank you!"

I plop down on the little sofa near the reception, hidden from the main area by the small wall next to the steps leading up to the bar. My email sends, and I'm met with an incoming FaceTime from Maria within seconds.

"Hi ducky!" She's in her office, sipping what I assume is peppermint tea from an extravagantly large mug.

"Hiya!"

"They look wonderful!" she says, scrolling through them, "Just wanted to call and say well done! Is it all going to plan?"

"Thank you! Um, yes, for the most part..." I say, nibbling my lip. "I actually wanted to ask... Daniel said he didn't request me for this?"

Maria sets her mug down and laughs, cupping her cheeks in her hands.

"Oh God, did he now? I suppose the cat's out of the bag, eh?"

I laugh nervously. "So, what exactly happened?"

"Well darling, we had a little follow up chat and he said how happy he was with the Mara work, and how he quite fancied doing the same for his beach hotel. And I'd been thinking how I'm getting older, and travelling is such a faff, how lovely it was to be able to send you out occasionally if I don't feel up to it! So, I thought, since you two have a rapport and you could use a bit more experience before I send you off on other projects it worked perfectly!"

"Right. Why didn't you tell me?"

"I thought it might hurt your confidence, ducky! I thought if you went in, all guns blazing, you'd feel more at ease!"

"Ok, well, thank you for the opportunity. It's very sweet!"

"Darling, it's just as much for me as it is for you!" she laughs, taking another sip of her tea.

"And he mentioned it's discounted?"

"Yes, I thought it'd be a bit unfair for me to charge full price when I'm not there by choice this time!"

"That makes sense." I sigh, playing with the leaves of a monstera plant next to me.

"Anyway, by the looks of things you're getting along swimmingly – pardon the pun! I won't keep you any longer, say hi to darling Daniel for me," she says, blowing kisses at the camera making all the bangles on her arm jangle.

"Speak soon!" I blow a kiss back, and then she's gone. I sigh, taking off my headphones and putting my laptop in my bag. I hear laughter rippling through the foyer from the bar, at least they're still open. I quietly pad my way up the stone steps to order a mint tea, influenced by Maria's steaming mug, and freeze. Daniel and Lucia are alone at the bar, her hand stroking his thigh as they laugh and talk. I knew there was something between them. He laughs and leans in, and I turn quickly on my heels. That's the last thing I need to see tonight, to rub salt in the wound of being a discount charity case of a photographer. I forget the tea, grab my bag, and run back to my room under the dark clouds of the storm.

CHAPTER 31

I can smell the soft smoke wafting into my room from the barbecue, and hear the gentle thump of music as I get ready. I twirl my hair up into a claw clip and smooth out my blue linen dress. It's a halter neck, so covers up my cleavage and flows down to just above my knee. One might deem it *professional*. It's just gone five, and the barbecue is in full swing.

Even the reception is heaving, as I squeeze through clutching my camera at my side. I make my way up the stairs, passing a young couple enthralled with each other on one of the sofas and loiter by the bar. The number of people is intimidating, and I nervously turn on my camera. Although it's my armour, making it obvious I'm here for work, it also draws more attention to me than I'd like. Three tipsy blonde girls clad in bikini tops and teeny denim shorts wave at me from the bar!

"Oooh, get one of us!"

"Uh, sure." I say, flicking on my camera and fumbling to quickly put the lens cap in my bag. This definitely won't be one for the website, I think as one of the girls cups her friend's breasts. They coo at me in thanks and I quickly walk away before anyone else asks for a portrait.

I step onto the wooden balcony, a gentle breeze whipping at my face and exhale in relief. I set my camera on one of few empty the coffee tables, feeling around my bag for my lens cap. Shit. I imagine Daniel walking in, seeing me crawling around the bar floor in between people's legs hunting for a lost piece of equipment. I wince, panic setting in, squinting through the doorway trying to see if I can spy it on the floor. I suck in a breath, heading back inside as a hand softly touches my shoulder.

"Can you take one of me?" a posh English accent asks.

"Sorry, not right now." I say, not bothering to look at who's speaking.

"Even for a trade?" the voice continues. I turn, to see a tall, tanned blonde man, balancing my lens cap between his thumb and forefinger.

"Oh my God, you're a lifesaver! Thank you!" Relief washes over me as I slip it back onto my camera. "I'll happily take one of you now."

"Don't worry, I haven't had nearly enough of these to curse anyone's camera with my face." he says, gesturing to a beer in his hand. The statement is laughable, he could play Prince Charming in a live action Shrek.

"If you say so."

266

"I would however, love it if you drank one of these with me? Strictly because my friend has abandoned me for a girl he's just met and I feel like a bit of a plonker standing on my own." He gestures to the couple I walked past on the stairs, who now look like they're having a battle with each other's tongues.

"I would love to, but I'm on the clock." I say, gesturing to my camera.

"Damn. Well maybe when you're off it."

We smile awkwardly at each other, and out the corner of my eye I catch Daniel by the bar, Lucia at his side. I know it's wrong, but I jump at the opportunity to make him jealous. Or maybe just piss him off. I lean in to the unnamed man, so our faces are inches apart.

"Make that a promise." I flirt, stroking the bottom of his waist as I walk away. I can feel Daniel's eyes fixed on me, even as I'm outside making my way towards the barbecue.

Down on the white sand, the beach by the hotel has been peppered with little bowls of multicoloured sea glass, all holding little flickering tea lights. Two chefs man a large barbecue grill, flipping burger patties, sausages, ribs and vegetables. White pouffes scatter the sand, half of which are occupied by guests munching on their bounties of food. A large bonfire has been erected, its dancing orange flames flickering against the blue of the sea. Music tinkles from the outdoor bar on the balcony above, and a man spins his girlfriend around in time to the music in the queue for food.

I mooch around for a few hours, snapping photos of the food, the bonfire, the guests, all whilst avoiding Daniel as much as possible. Even though I'm making the conscious effort to ignore him, I can feel his gaze locked on me whenever we cross paths, like a lion who wants to get rid of a pesky bird that won't stop flapping around his ears. As the sun starts to sink down on the horizon, slowly turning the sky a deep orange, I feel my stomach start to rumble. Happy with what I took, I sling my camera over my shoulder, making my way down to the beach to see if there's any food left. Approaching the grill, I can see there's a mound of vegetables but no meat. I let out a disgruntled sigh, and stack my plate high with courgettes, peppers and mushrooms. I should've taken a break earlier. All the seats are now occupied, everyone wanting to watch the sunset from the beach. As the sun dims, the light and shadows from the bonfire prance around on the sand, the little tea lights flickering, their orange flames contrasting with the deep blues and greens of the sea glass. The palm trees sway slightly, as an evening breeze sets in, the warm scent of salt and seaweed caressing my face. I walk down to the cluster of poofs nearest the sea, and sit down a few feet away from them. Even though my meal is only vegetables it tastes amazing, but I may need to grab a burger later from room service before bed. I bite into one of the peppers, savouring the smoky chargrilled tase as I watch the waves slowly creep up the sand towards me.

"Can't have you getting that lovely dress all sandy, can we?" that same posh voice from earlier says from behind me. I turn, and see he's holding a pouffe under each arm.

"Where'd you get those?" I smile, rising to my feet. I had been looking forward to decompressing alone while I eat, but I suppose if anyone's going to join me, he's the best option. He sets down the pouffes, dusting them off before sitting on one.

"I know it's probably frowned upon, but I was using one for my feet. When I saw you sit on the floor guilt set in."

"Oh, so you're just doing this for your conscience?"

"Oh absolutely, it's completely self-serving."

I laugh as I sit down, the cushion certainly much comfier than the sand.

"I'm Hugh."

"Maddie."

"Lovely name, Maddie. And dress." he says, grinning as he runs his fingers through his hair.

"Thank you." I say, covering my mouth as I wolf down the remains of my vegetables. "This is incredible," I say gesturing to the set up, "I can't imagine how they'll top it for actual New Years."

Hugh laughs, leaning back, his hands behind his head, his Ralph Lauren shirt clinging to his biceps. "I know, but they always do."

"So, you're a regular?"

"Yeah, around New Years at least. It's like a tradition to come here for most of us."

"Oh, so you live here?"

"My family have a ranch out near Kitengela, goes back a few generations."

"I'm guessing if it's tradition, you won't be here alone?"

"No, I'm not."

I nod, looking out to the sea. "Then how come you're sat with me instead of your friends?"

"Well Maddie, my friends aren't nearly as good looking as you," he says with a laugh, nodding his head toward a tribe of other Polo clad men.

"I suppose that makes sense," I say, setting my plate down in the sand. He leans a little closer to me as I do.

"Tell me, why is someone so gorgeous behind the camera, surely you'd make a better living in front of it?"

I scoff, "God, what an awful line."

"Are my moves not impressing you?" he bellows, laughing.

"Haven't seen any moves as of yet," I tease. He rises to go, gently slapping my knee.

"Right, come on?"

"What?"

He holds his hand out to me, and I gingerly take it, heaving myself off the pouffe unsure of what we're doing.

"We're going to go and take your last snaps, get you off the clock, and then you're finally going to join me for that drink you owe me."

I raise an eyebrow, but suddenly feel that familiar glare lock on me from the balcony above.

"Ok, deal." I say, not letting go of Hugh's hand, hoping Daniel's watching, not quite sure what I'm trying

271

to achieve, or at least not willing to let myself acknowledge it.

The stars dust the night sky, as though the deep indigo has been splattered with a white paintbrush. It's nowhere close to the ones in the Mara, but it's incomparable to any I see in London. I peel my eyes from the sky, the small action making me dizzy and topple sideways. I land on something warm, and feel a hand gently stroke my hair.

"Oh, it's you!" I giggle, looking up to see Hugh, the edges of his blond hair blurring in my vision.

"Let's get you up! Can't enjoy your wine if you're sideways, can you?" he says, sitting me back upright. I feel my stomach churn as he does, and blink heavily to try rid myself of the feeling.

"All better!" he says, passing me my large glass of red. Its sides are sticky from the amount that's spilled, little grains of sand sticking to the edges. We're sat around the bonfire, who's flames have slowly simmered down to glowing embers. How late is it? I reach into my pocket for my phone to check, but it's not there. I quickly scan around looking for it, my eyes skipping from each one of Hugh's friends who I'm now sitting with. They're all men, aside from a small huddle of girls in the middle who look about 19, laughing and flirting with them.

"Have you seen my phone?" I slur to Hugh, who I now feel stroking my back as he talks to his friend on his left.

"In my pocket babe, you kept dropping it, remember?" he responds, not looking away from his friend. I rub my head, I don't. How much have I had to drink? I suddenly realise just how drunk I am and have to dig both hands into the sand to stop myself from toppling over back onto his lap. I feel my glass fall against my dress, the red seeping into the fabric wetting my leg.

"Oh no, you dropped it!" Hugh says, stroking my leg as he reaches for the half full bottle next to him. "Here, have this!" He says, lifting the bottle to my lips and pouring. I instinctively drink it, but he doesn't stop pouring and I feel wine escape my mouth and trickle down my lips and chin. I splutter away, unable to drink anymore and a couple of his friends laugh.

"Not a big drinker, are you?" Hugh says, wiping my lips with his thumb.

"I can– I jusst… only ate vegetables today…"

"She's probably had two bottles, Hugh!" One of his mates says across the fire, taking a swig of his beer. His face is so blurry I couldn't tell you what colour his hair is. I feel everything spin and tingle, and my stomach twist on the amount of red wine it just ingested at once.

"I think I…" I trail off, feeling the sick rise in my throat. I fumble to stand up, tripping away from the group through the darkness towards the stilts of the hotel balcony. I heave, painting the sand with splatters of deep crimson. I wipe my mouth, hobbling back to bonfire, embarrassed and tired.

"Can I have my phone? I think I need bed." I can feel myself swaying and slurring as I speak, it looks like there's three Hughs sat below me rather than one. Not sure which Hugh is real, I go to poke one and my finger prods air. This makes me stumble forward, leaning on his shoulders to balance myself. He stands up, taking my hands.

"Ok, time for bed."

"Phone?" I hold my hand out, but he laughs.

"A gentleman wouldn't let a lady walk back to her room alone after dark, especially when she's had a little too much to drink!" he says, slipping one hand around my waist and setting his bottle of beer in the sand.

"Goodnight lads, see you later. Or in the morning!" I think I see him wink at his friends but can't be sure.

Hugh leads me up the stairs to the hotel, gently tugging on my arm as I cling to the banister, scared I'll fall.

We walk along the path through the foliage, past the other hotel rooms. All the lights are off, so I'm guessing it must be late into the night. Hugh steers me from his hand around my waist, which caresses up and down my back. I don't know why his hand on my skin is making me so queasy.

"Honessstly, my room isss really clossse. You go back to your friendss!" I say, gesturing to my room in the distance, the porch light still on.

"Nonsense, we're nearly there. Let me at least tuck you in," he purrs into my ear, making the skin on the back of my neck prickle. I lose my footing, and stumble off the path, clutching onto a palm tree to balance myself.

"Why am I thisss drunk?" I mutter, still gripping onto the tree, feeling all my blood rushing to my head. Hugh saunters up behind me, turning me around to face him.

"God, you're so beautiful," he says, raising my chin with his fingers. Suddenly he crashes his mouth into mine, pinning me between him and the tree trunk. I try

275

turn my face to escape his kiss, but he grips the back of my head, keeping me in place. I try push him off with my hands, but he towers over me, my feeble attempts to push him off idle. He runs his other hand over my chest, squeezing firmly. All my sensations feel heightened, his touch making my skin crawl. His hand slides from my chest lower, lower, towards my legs.

"Please, stop." I try to say, my words swallowed whole by his kisses. I do the only thing I can think of, and bite down. He lets out a scream, pulling away.

"What the fuck, Maddie?"

I can feel tears welling up in my eyes. "I just want to go to bed."

He lets go of his grip on my hair, his hand sliding down to stroke my cheek. "Don't be silly, you've been flirting with me all night. You want this."

I try worm out from between him and the tree, but he has me firmly pinned with his body weight.

"I wonder if you'll scream when I make you come?" he chuckles, his hand slipping from my cheek to my thigh, and then moving up my dress.

"Get off me." I say, louder, hoping someone will hear it.

"Shhh. You do love the chase don't you!" I can feel him grow against my leg, and he moves his hand from between my legs to his belt, slowly undoing it. I writhe against the tree, trying to wriggle free to no avail. I squint my eyes shut, no clue what to do. Suddenly there's a loud thud, and his weight flies off me. I open my eyes to see Daniel stood over Hugh, who's nose has just started dripping blood to the grass below.

"What the fuck, bro?!" Hugh bellows, his eyes wide with shock.

"Get up," Daniel grumbles at Hugh, offering him a hand.

I look down at my dress, covered in red wine and a few specks of vomit and feel my cheeks heat with embarrassment. I probably did give Hugh all the signals, I know I was flirting with him all night. Daniel's probably friends with him for all I know. I suddenly feel dizzy, and sink to the grass. Hugh takes Daniel's hand and heaves to his feet, dabbing his nose on his sleeve. Somehow Daniel makes Hugh look small, towering over him. Hugh lunges at him, punching him across the jaw. Daniel reels back a step, raising a hand to his bleeding lip. A small laugh escapes him as a bead of blood trickles down his chin from his busted lower lip.

"You thought that was a good idea, did you?" he asks Hugh, who's nursing his nose glaring at him. Daniel looks at me, disgust flaring across his face as his eyes flick up and down my body.

"Did you want this?" he asks, his voice gruff. I stay silent, unable to make words or hold his gaze, his chiselled jaw feathering. "Maddie. Did. You. Want. This?" he says slower, not looking away.

"I don't... I don't think so." I gulp, unable to look back at him.

"Right." He says, suddenly swinging back and clocking Hugh again under the chin. He staggers back, falling onto the grass whimpering.

"Stop, man! I'm sorry ok!" he squeals, as Daniel looms over him. He raises his right boot, stepping on Hughs wrist. He squeals more, snot, tears and blood dripping over his face.

"You're going to leave tonight." Daniel says, crouching down, squeezing Hugh's cheeks together as he talks, digging his boot in more. "You're banned from this hotel, and most likely will be from the rest of Watamu."

"But I didn't–" Hugh tries to protest, but Daniel's boot presses further, turning his wrist white.

"And you won't touch another intoxicated woman again, or believe me, I will hear about it. And so will your family."

He lets go of his face, little pink fingerprints left on his cheeks from his firm grip. Daniel rises and releases his wrist, Hugh slowly crawling away from him. "I'll have a concierge come and get your bags, and a taxi arranged for the airport." He says, brushing off the sleeves of his shirt. Hugh scampers off, not saying a word. Daniel turns to me, and my eyes find the floor, too embarrassed to look at him. I feel faint, everything fuzzy. I see his boots walk closer to me, and he kneels down on the grass before me.

"Are you ok?"

"I'm fine, sorry, I was just going to bed…" I say, trying my best to cover my slurs. I glance up at him, surprised to find his eyes soft, brows knitted together in worry.

"Let's get you to bed then," he says, gently taking my forearms and hoisting me up. I feel myself wobble, my knees feeling like jelly.

"Can you walk?" he asks, and I look down to see they're shaking.

"I don't know," I say, gripping his bicep to steady myself as I take a step, feeling my ankle buckle. I drop to the floor, overcome with dizziness, unable to feel my fingertips, digging them into the dirt. My eyes grow tired, and then his large arms gently scoop me up, and I succumb to the darkness.

CHAPTER 32

My eyelids feel heavy as I peel them open, as if they'd been weighted down in my sleep. My mouth feels like sandpaper, parched for water, and I roll onto my stomach to reach my nightstand. The motion ignites a pang of nausea, and I clutch my hand over my mouth. I peel away the layers of mosquito net to reach my water glass, my eyes landing on the bedside table. A circular pedestal, little shards of sea glass mosaicking the top. This isn't my nightstand. I shoot up, eyes scanning around this room that isn't mine. It's mammoth, with huge gaping windows out onto the beach. The walls and floors are made of the familiar beige sandstone, a plush orange and white rug under the mahogany four poster bed. The sheets are crisp and white, despite the pillow having a few black smears thanks to my mascara. At the bottom of the bed is a tan leather sofa, facing a white wooden chest of drawers with a TV on top. Either side of the chest of drawers are two large white doors, with marbled blue and white door handles. I look back to the dresser, and next to the TV is a large plant on one side, and a framed photo of Daniel and a woman. Daniel. I clutch my knees to my chest, visions and memories of last night washing over me. And my last conscious moment, where

Daniel scooped me up in his arms. I smell the sheets, and sure enough they're coated in his signature sandalwood. So, this is his room. I gulp. My eyes suddenly land on my stained dress, neatly folded on the sofa. I glance down my body and find myself in a baggy T shirt about five sizes too large, and my pants. Does that mean… he dressed me? I feel my cheeks flush at the thought. Thank God I wasn't wearing a thong yesterday. I clamber out of bed, and gingerly attempt to open the door on the right of the dresser. It opens to reveal a bathroom, and I race towards the tap. I'm about to stick my head under it and drink, and then suddenly realise I don't know if the water is drinkable. I sigh and look in the large mirror. My hair looks wild, and my mascara's collected along my waterline like mini panda eyes. I gaze longingly at the bathtub, which is tucked into a nook with a large window out to the sea, one that's currently open letting in a delicious crisp breeze. It's a battle to not strip off and get in, but I should probably head back to my room. Why am I here?

I pad over the smooth floor towards the sofas. The other door by the TV led me down a small flight of stairs, into a living area. Large windows are set into the limestone, overlooking a small strip of beach and the lush greenery of the hotel rooms. It's set slightly higher up and further along, letting you see all the way to the rest of the public beach and hotel. There is a little desk pushed under one window, housing a laptop and stacks of papers. In the middle are two cream sofas, with a large mosaic coffee table between them. Daniel sits on one of them, his back to me. I can see a steaming espresso set on the coffee table. I notice the other sofa has a duvet and pillow made up on it. God, did he sleep there? Unsure what to do, I pull down the T Shirt as much as possible and clear my throat.

"Um, morning."

He whips around, shutting his book. "You're up!"

"I'm up," I say, scuffing my feet awkwardly. A memory of them buckling under me last night plays in my head and I feel my face flush.

"Look, I'm really sorry about–"

"Nothing to apologise for," he says as he rises. "Coffee?"

"I should probably get back; I need to take some more photos of the pool today."

He pops a coffee pod into the machine, and it whirs to life, a rich nutty scent wafting towards me as it spurts out dark coffee into a little cup.

"Milk?" he asks, turning off the machine just as the cup fills.

"Like that's fine. I'd actually love some water, if possible," I say, gingerly sitting on the edge of the sofa. He nods, and fills up a pint glass from a jug in the fridge. I play with my nails, avoiding eye contact as he sets them on the table before me.

"Thanks," I say, shakily reaching for the water and chugging some down. I can feel his eyes locked on me once again as he sits down, his tall form taking up much of the sofa.

"Are you ok?" he asks. I feel my stomach churn, embarrassment flooding me.

"Yeah, I just drunk too much. I'm sorry, I'm so em–"

"You didn't."

"Didn't drink too much?" I gesture at my face and laugh awkwardly. He doesn't avert from my gaze or offer a smile. I sit down.

"No. You didn't drink too much." He leans forward, gently placing his hand on my knee, and I feel my heart thump in my chest. "I'm sorry, I feel responsible."

"Why? It's my fault I didn't get to the food in time. I just should've eaten more before–"

"That wouldn't have helped. That man, his friends. I've been aware of their type for years. Kenya Cowboys. Young white Kenyans with acres of land and generational wealth who feel entitled to everything, and everyone. I've heard rumours about them... spiking women at parties."

I feel my heart hammer in my chest and have to lean back to stop feeling faint. Daniel's warm hand gently squeezes my knee.

"I'm sorry I didn't spot you sooner. I can get a doctor in to check you over, or you can fly home. Whatever you need. I'm just so sorry."

I squeeze my eyes shut, placing my hand on my heart to try slow it down. "Do you know what with?"

"From what I've heard ecstasy, and obviously a lot of alcohol. How do you feel now?"

"Like shit."

"That would be a given. Do you still feel, under the influence? Intoxicated?"

"No," I say, my heart finally slowing. At least it was hopefully the one drug I've taken before. I look up to Daniel, and really look at him for the first time in a while. His dark eyes are soft, so vulnerable. My eyes flick down to his soft lips, the bottom one now overpowered by a large slit.

"Oh my God, your lip!" I say, leaning forward, gently stroking it.

"It's the least of my worries," he says, and I'm sure I feel him lean into my touch. I quickly retract my hand, glancing out the window towards the scattered hotel rooms. I can just make out the palm tree where it must've happened, where he must've seen it from.

"Hugh and his friends have been escorted off the premises and banned," he says, softly removing his hand from my knee. "But I completely understand if you want to go home."

I gaze out to the sea, the waves crashing under the soft morning light. I don't feel ready.

"I don't want him to be the reason I leave. That's giving him the power," I breath out heavily, and Daniel rises, smiling softly.

"Take the day off and think it over. It's fresh. I'll give you some space and send the doctor to have a look."

"You... don't have to go. I'm the one imposing, this is your room," I say, standing to leave, tugging down the shirt as I do. Daniel's eyes follow my hands and then he quickly glances away, out one of the windows.

"Don't be silly. You're safe here. And welcome," he says, nodding at me as he walks out the door.

The doctor arrived just after lunch, which Daniel had sent up to his room for me along with some of my clothes. More specifically, three different lunches with a note saying, *"I didn't know what you'd want so thought I'd send some options."* The doctor said I was fine, and that I just needed to stay hydrated and get lots of rest. I couldn't resist the bath with the view of the sea, so ran it until the bathroom mirror was steamed up and dunked myself in, my achy body feeling like it was re-entering the womb. I FaceTimed Anya from the tub but decided not to tell her. I know it would just worry her, and she'd convince me to come home. I won't give Hugh that control, won't let him be the reason I lose out on this opportunity.

I lounge in the bath for well over an hour, watching the waves roll in and the palm trees sway. I think back to last night again, but this time to Daniel. How enraged he was, how protective of me he sounded, how his arms felt wrapping me up like a little caterpillar sheltered in a cocoon. Once my skin is nearly as pink as a boiled lobster, I clamber out and wrap myself in a towel, melting into its softness. I wipe some of the steam off the mirror, and gaze at myself. My wet hair gently curls in waves down my back, and my eyes look rejuvenated without the clumps of black mascara clinging to my lower lashes.

I slip into my green tube top and long white linen skirt, slide into my Birkenstocks, and head out the room towards the main area. My brain scrambles as I walk through the foliage, the sweet smell of the frangipani wafting around me. I was sure he hated me. Despised me. Maybe he still does, but I saw something, I'm sure. In his eyes this morning, in his body last night. I track down Rita at the main desk, racking my brain for some way to thank him.

"I was just wondering, would it be possible to organise a sort of, picnic dinner?" I ask nervously, fiddling with one of the snorkelling flyers. Rita raises an eyebrow but smiles softly to herself.

"Uh, yes, I think so. Do you know what food you'd like?"

"Whatever is easiest! Or whatever Mr. Kimani's favourite is?"

"Ok," she says, writing something on a sticky note.

"Would it be possible to have it on the beach? Not the public one, the little one by his room?"

"I'm sure that can be arranged. How's 6.30, just before sunset?"

"Perfect! And could you let him know, just in case I don't see him?"

Again, another eyebrow raises at this, and I bite my lip embarrassed. She smiles and nods, and I hastily make my way back to my room.

CHAPTER 33

I light the final candle, just as the flame licks its way up the last bit of wood towards my fingertips. I quickly blow out the match, just as I can feel its heat lapping at my nails. I set the last tea light down and look proudly at my setup. The staff found a beautiful yellow, pink and white patchwork blanket which I've set up at the top of the beach, just under Daniel's room. I dotted a few tea lights around the edges and had a hunt in the little library near reception for any books I thought he might like. I'm sure he's probably read them all, but on the off chance thought it was a nice gesture. There's a couple cans of beer and a bottle of champagne cooling, which I made sure to pay for on the spot. Gifting him alcohol from his own inventory felt wrong. The chefs rustled up a mouth-watering pizza, which sits still steaming in its cardboard box. I can just make out his silhouette walking towards me across the beach and give my set up one last look over. I'm still wearing my outfit from earlier, but for some reason made time to put on some mascara and lip gloss before I got to work. Maybe I do know the reason, but certainly won't be acknowledging it anytime soon.

"What's all this?" he yells, about fifteen feet away. I laugh awkwardly, shielding my eyes from the sun. He's wearing one of his classic linen shirts, billowing around his muscular form in the gentle breeze.

"A thank you!" I say, gesturing to the set up as he approaches. "You're always working, and I thought maybe it would be nice to have some me time. And I did want to say thank you, for how you handled everything. And I'm sorry about our weird... history." I wince. He now stands before me, his eyes flicking between me and the picnic.

"You're silly. I don't need thanks for the bare minimum. Besides, I thought you wouldn't want to drink today?" he says, looking at the champagne nestled in the ice bucket.

"Well, I don't. And it isn't for me. This is all for you."

"So, you've ambushed me with a picnic and are going to make me sit and eat it alone?" he laughs, rubbing the back of his neck.

"Yes. No? You have books! I thought you'd enjoy the peace for once!"

He smiles and crouches down, flicking open the pizza box and whistling. " You seriously expect me to finish this alone?" His eyes twinkle as they look up at me, and I feel those old butterflies take flight.

"I mean, if you actively want company, I could stay."

"I wouldn't contest," he says, sitting down and stretching his long legs out on the blanket.

"You certainly sound thrilled by the concept," I tease, sitting on the other side. He tears off a slice and takes a bite, laughing as he chews.

"This really is quite ridiculous, Maddie. A grand gesture of thanks for me being a decent human being."

"You didn't have to let me stay in your room. Or send me three lunches. I'd say that's a little above decent."

He shakes his head, still looking out to the waves. "It isn't. I could never forgive myself if I caused you hurt." He says, before quickly clearing his throat. I cock my head, suddenly feeling all my past anger at him flicker through me once more.

"Well, that's not quite true, Daniel."

He peels his eyes from the sea to meet mine. "How so?"

I take a deep breath, ready to take the plunge. Lay my cards on the table.

"You have hurt me, before. What happened in Tukio, the pool table and then... you didn't even say goodbye.

You ignored my text; you've made demeaning comments. I'm over it now… I think, I think there's someone else I like. But I did like you. And that did all hurt."

His face darkens, and he reaches for a beer, cracking it open as the silence consumes us. He takes a large swig, looking out to the sea as he runs a hand through his curls.

"I know. I handled everything so poorly. If I could undo my actions, change them, I would."

I feel my stomach drop, completely put off the slice of pizza I'd just picked up.

"I just don't understand why you kissed me, why you… if you didn't want to."

He laughs.

"Believe me, I wanted to. Want to."

I cock my head, surprised. He takes another sip, shaking his head.

"I've wanted to ever since I first laid eyes on you in the Mara. But I knew it could never–" he trails off, tapping his beer with his fingertips. "That night in Tukio, I'd had a bad day, and a few drinks, and my willpower crumbled. I'd been thinking about you all evening, and then you walked in, as if I'd manifested it. I should've been stronger."

"Why?" My heart's pounding, the butterflies in my tummy frantically flapping around.

He shakes his head. "I didn't say goodbye as I couldn't stand the thought of watching you drive away. And that was cowardly, and I'm sorry. I ignored your text as I knew if we started talking, I wouldn't want to stop," he sighs, taking a swig of his beer.

"I thought you hated me." I manage, a million thoughts whirring round my mind. Daniel laughs, leaning in closer.

"I think you're extremely special. And if things were different..." He takes another sip of his beer.

"What things? Why were you so adamant it wouldn't work?"

He shrugs and rubs his eyebrows. "Distance. Work. Life. It's complicated..."

I can't help lean into him, and can almost feel the warmth vibrating from his body, smell his woody cologne. The sunset's just starting, and his eyes are warm pools of caramel in the golden light. His short curls glisten, and his chiselled jaw feathers as he looks at me. I reach out, and gently stroke over the cut on his lip. The cut he got for me.

"I don't think those are good enough reasons to give up on someone. I wish you would've just told me."

He holds my gaze, eyes frantically scanning my face.

"Fuck it!" he says, chucking his beer onto the sand and leaning into me, pressing his lips into mine. He kisses me hungrily, and I feel a small moan escape me. He pulls back and cups my chin, looking into my eyes.

"Sorry. I forgot about last night for a moment, is this ok?" he asks, his eyes searching my face. I run my hand through his soft hair, his touch setting my body on fire.

"Yes." I breathe, crashing my lips back to his. He kneels towering over me as he leans down to kiss me, and I find my hands running across his torso, feeling every dip of his muscled abs. Without breaking his lips from mine he skids the pizza box across the mat, gently pushing me down onto it. He grabs one of my hands and holds it above my head as he keeps kissing, sliding his tongue across mine. The other hand caresses my cheek, and slowly slides down to my neck. He holds it there softly as we kiss more, pulling away to look at my face.

"I've wanted you for so long." He says, his hand softly caressing my neck and then moving lower, to my breasts, and I release a little whimper as he gently squeezes one.

"Me too." I breath, my back arching with yearning for him. He leans towards me and runs his lips across my neck, as his hand gently pulls down my top exposing my breasts. The cool sea breeze makes my nipples prick, as well as the feeling of his lips travelling down my collarbone slowly to my left nipple. I moan loudly as he tongue flicks it back and forth. His other hand slides under my skirt travelling up my thigh, and I can feel myself throbbing for his touch. His hand slips between my legs and he moans finding the wetness that awaits him. His fingers tease around me, almost like he's purposely refraining from touching the spot that aches for him, and it drives me crazy.

"Please!" I beg, unable to stand it any longer. He chuckles as he kisses his way up back to my neck, his fingers slowly grazing my centre. I arch my back as a shiver rushes over my body, but as quickly as he touched me his hands are gone. I can't help but whimper.

"Please touch me again." I beg, barely able to muster the words.

"Like this?" He says, grazing my core again and I gasp. "Or like this?" He purrs, as he slowly pushes his fingers inside me. I moan loudly, unable to keep quiet at the sensation. He kisses me again, stifling my moaning as his fingers caress me. I feel my body shake and dig my free hand into his back, my whole being feeling like it's coursing with electricity. I feel a wave of pleasure crash through me and cry out, his hands holding me steady as my body writhes and shakes. He slips his fingers out of me and runs them across my lips, gently parting them and running them over my tongue.

"I thought I should make up for not letting you finish by the pool table." He smirks, removing his fingers and kissing my forehead gently. I feel like I could melt.

"Do you want company tonight?" I croak, glancing up to his room.

"Sure," he says, brushing a strand of hair off my face.

Despite how badly I want him, Daniel doesn't do anything but kiss me the whole night. We head up and watch Superbad in his bed, wrapped in each other's limbs. I love feeling his large body heave with laughter, such a rare sound to hear him make. I attempt to kiss his neck, run my hand over his pyjama bottoms, but each time he gently moves it back to his stomach. "For the sake of professionalism!" he joked after my second attempt, which had grated me. I still fell asleep tucked in his arms, occasionally wondering if I should pinch myself to see if it was all a dream.

CHAPTER 34

I cling to the side of the rickshaw as we're tossed back and forth over the potholed roads, unsure if Daniel's gripping my leg because he wants to touch me or if he's worried about me flying out the vehicle. He's hunched next to me, his height proving difficult for the dinky car. We'd parted ways this morning for work, I'd edited all the pictures I'd done so far and presented them to him in the afternoon. He seemed happy and suggested going into Watamu to show me some traditional Kenyan food. I'd agreed - thinking we'd be driving to the restaurant by car. I'm wearing a little beige dress that's not well equipped for a rickshaw ride, the airy material flapping about wildly making it even shorter, a couple minutes in I had to weigh it down with my satchel to avoid flashing my panties to everyone. The vehicle hums to a slow, and Daniel pays the driver before clambering out. I scoot out the same side as him and look around. We're in the middle of what would be the equivalent to a British high street, shacks and shops displaying a range of items from clothes to bags to leathers lining the street. We stand in front of a white brick house, with large blue letters painting on the side reading *Restaurant & Bar*.

Daniel takes my hand, and we step inside, greeting the host. He leads us up to the roof, which is set up with multiple plastic tables and chairs, and a couple stray cats mooching around. It's a stark contrast from the luxury of the hotel. Daniel grabs the laminated menus from the host which have certainly seen better days and passes me one as we sit down.

"This isn't what I expected!" I say, unsure of what most of the foods are on the menu.

"Why's that?"

"All your properties are so luxurious. You're obviously raking it in!" I say, glancing at a broken plastic chair to my left, now home to a sleepy cat. He laughs, playfully flicking at my hand.

"True. But my grandmother used to love bringing me here. And the food is unmatched. There are some places that are perfect as they are, and don't need to pretend to be anything they're not. This is good food accessible for everyone. I like to come when I can."

He really could be an arrogant ass, with his inherited wealth and good looks. But I truly don't think he is.

I leave the ordering to Daniel as he's a regular, and we lean back and sip our Tusker beers whilst looking onto the street below. We spy a larger American lady who's been staying at the hotel waddling down the street with an abundance of shopping bags, clearly unable to say no to each vendor who targets her. It pretty much seems to be every single one, and it takes her over twenty minutes to walk out of sight. We quietly cackle at her as the steaming plates of food are set before us, the smell making my mouth water. Beans, spinach, samosas, stews. It's like a holiday feast. I wolf down my first plate, occasionally peeking up to find Daniel smiling at me. I'm glad I wore a flowy dress as can feel my stomach bulge, but can't seem to stop eating. Once I've polished off the last samosa I lean back fulfilled, resting my chin on my palm.

"That was unreal."

"As good as Mustafa's?" Daniel asks, sipping his beer.

"Is it bad if maybe... better?"

Daniel smiles into his beer and shakes his head.

"Not at all. It's his father's."

My jaw drops. "Really? He must be old?"

"He is, but he loves it. Mustafa used to work here and applied for a job at Utulivu, once I tasted his food, I made him head chef for Tukio."

I smile, looking around the roof imagining a young Mustafa waiting tables and feeding the cats leftovers.

"That makes it even more special. Thanks for bringing me here, it's nice to see the real Watamu." I say, gazing over my shoulder to the vendors below, the children running down the street playing with a ball, the colourful kikoy fabrics hanging off racks. "Are you excited for tomorrow?" I ask, my food digesting enough to finally have a sip of beer.

"Yes and no. It's great fun, but also greatly stressful. Most people I know, as they come for the party every year, so I guess that takes some of the pressure off. I'm glad you'll be around though."

I don't need a mirror to tell that my cheeks have gone rosy pink. "Well, technically I'll be working."

"Well, maybe if you ask your boss nicely, he'll let you finish early." His eyes flicker mischievously.

"I suppose I'll have to give Maria a call then, make sure I keep professional." I tease. Daniel breaths out a laugh as he finishes his beer.

"I had something else in mind, but we can discuss the logistics later." I can feel my body heat, yearning for his touch again.

"Sounds like a plan."

Daniel leans back, gesturing to the waiter for the bill. "I realised I never asked, did you get the flowers?"

"The flowers?" I ask, confused.

"About a month ago. I sent them as a thank you... and weak attempt at an apology."

"White roses?" My heart flutters. Surely not?

"Those are the ones."

"I assumed they were from Anya! I didn't even look for a card." A smile creeps across my face, he really was thinking of me.

"Well maybe for the best, if you'd seen who they were from they probably would've ended up in the bin," he chuckles. "Do you and Anya woo each other with floral arrangements often?"

I laugh. "No, we just hadn't seen much of each other because of life, so I assumed. Thank you."

He shakes his head.

"I ordered them drunk and felt like a fool the next day. I'm almost glad I was saved the humiliation. That's tough about Anya, life tends to do that with people you care about. You must be excited to see Gia again, you two really hit it off!"

I feel my stomach drop. "What do you mean?"

"You two not been chatting? She's coming tomorrow?"

I feel sick, regretting eating so much feeling the food curdle in my stomach. "Uh, no, not so much recently."

Daniels looks at me sympathetically, almost making me feel guilty not telling him the truth.

"She goes through busy patches, but always makes an effort once they're done. She comes here every New Year, like I said, it's a tradition for a lot of people."

I run my hand through my hair, no clue what to do or how to react.

"I, um, do you know what time she's arriving?"

"Not sure, maybe late afternoon. Drop her a text, honestly, sometimes I have to quadruple text her to get a response," he says nonchalantly as he fishes through his wallet for some shillings.

"Yeah. Maybe I should."

Despite feeling Daniel's warm body lying beside me, all my yearnings for him have dissipated with the news of Gia, instead replaced by a sinking pool of anxiety in my gut. I glance at the clock on Daniel's bedside, 2am. I haven't been able to shut my eyes, let alone sleep. I stare at Gia's WhatsApp icon, transported back to everything we shared. I thought I'd have more time to figure this out, and that's without even adding Daniel to the equation. I've composed about twelve different messages, each one feeling worse than the last. I now have: 'Hey, heard you're coming to Utulivu tomorrow. Crazily enough I'm here for work! Will be nice to see you, I've been missing you.' Not too blasé, not too formal. My eyes have started to ache from staring at my phone for so long. I hold my breath and press send.

When I wake Daniel's gone, his side of the bed made. I roll over finding a cold cup of coffee and a note, reading: 'Lots of setup to do, stay as long as you want! See you at the dinner x'

I glug down the chilled latte, how late did I sleep in? My eyes flick to the clock, 1.20pm. I'm too anxious to check my phone, so instead peel myself from bed, getting dressed to head back to my room. There's a large dinner at 7 tonight followed by drinks and dancing, and then fireworks at midnight. It'll be fine. Just take photos, while Daniel and Gia are in the same place. And don't know about each other. And I don't know which one I want. My stomach gurgles, maybe coffee on an empty stomach was a bad idea.

CHAPTER 35

I smooth out my emerald satin slip dress in the mirror, it reminds me of the one I borrowed from Gia all those nights ago in the Mara. I'm wearing gold pointy heels, matched with all the gold jewellery I own, little hoops in my ears and two chains on my neck. I swept my hair up into a half updo, pulling a few strands out to frame my face. I took a page out of Gia's book and went for a dewy makeup look, highlighting the inner corners of my eyes with gold. I look radiant, which is a far cry from how my insides feel.

I'd gotten back to my room at 2 and ordered room service, anticipating having a few drinks on New Year's Eve would be inevitable. It had been a mission enough to actually eat the burger and fries, the nausea building up in my stomach imagining all the different scenarios that could play out tonight. I glance at the clock, 6.45. I should get going.

I hobble down the path, my heels scuffing occasionally on the ground. All the hotel rooms sound bright and merry, playing music and getting ready for the night ahead. I can just see the reception, already flooded with people pouring out from the bar. I wonder if she's one of them. She didn't respond to my text, which may have been the reason for my lack of appetite. I take a deep breath, clutching my satchel to my side, my knuckles going white. As I get closer I hear karaoke booming out from the arches, a woman belting out *'Head Over Heels'* by *Tears For Fears*. I gingerly enter reception, slipping in through the crowd. Do I look for Daniel? Gia? Start taking photos alone? Have a drink to calm my nerves? The lines have become so blurred between what is and isn't work I walk slowly up the steps, no clue what to do. And that's when I see her.

"Something happens and I'm head over heels, don't take my heart don't break my heart don't throw it away!"

She's not the best singer but has something deep and rich to her voice that makes me turn my head to watch. And of course. Of course, it's her. Gia's stood by the bar, martini in hand, microphone in the other. She's wearing a cropped black sparkly blazer, showing off her slender arms and gorgeous body. She has matching trousers, her black kitten heels, and a sparkly necklace, no doubt worth a fortune draped round her neck travelling down to her low-cut top. Her curls bounce around her face, and she sets her martini on the bar to tousle a hand through them. I'm frozen, unable to move or think of what to do, so I stand like an idiot and stare.

"*La, la, la, la, la.*"

The song's coming to an end, and she picks back up her drink, swaying her hand over her head along with the crowd, trickles of martini sloshing over the rim of the glass and running down her arm. She catches eyes with me, and nearly stops singing in shock. I wince, awkwardly waving. Cover blown, I edge my way into the crowd as she sings the last line. Her gaggle of friends pounce on her, but she says something to them and they leave her. Leave her alone, as she walks up to me.

Gia dusts her cigarette into an ashtray as a man squeezes past me, jostling my back making my water spill over the edge of my glass onto the floor. No matter how badly I want a drink, I'm going to wait at least till dinner.

"Yeah, Daniel told me when I arrived. I was wondering when you'd show up." She says, blowing out smoke.

"I mean... I told you too." I say, biting my lip nervously. She smiles.

"Really?"

"Yeah... I texted you."

"Oh! I'm sorry, I didn't let you know as I thought you wouldn't message me till the New Year. I'm having a little detox, from technology. Which unfortunately includes my phone."

I feel the tension in my belly loosen a bit. She didn't see the text. She didn't ignore me.

"Like cold turkey?"

"Yep."

"How come?"

Gia cracks her neck, taking another long drag. "There's just been a few articles, drama basically around that film. The one you came to the party for."

"Oh, like what?" I ask. Now I'm looking at her closer, she looks more tired than usual, that golden light she exudes not glimmering as strong.

"I don't even wanna get into it. Not tonight. Tonight I wanna have fun! And hang out with you!" she says, reaching for my hand across the table. Her fingers graze mine, I feel my heart jitter at her touch, but she quickly removes them, smiling awkwardly at me. "I'm sorry how we parted, I was probably harsh. You were my friend first, and I hope you remain my friend despite everything."

I find my fingers creeping towards her hand, stroking it gently. I'd forgotten how soft they were, how beautiful she is, how at ease I feel around her. "No, I'm sorry too. I shouldn't have entertained Tyler, I think I was just bored, which shouldn't be an excuse. I loved our time together and having you as a friend. Let's just have fun tonight."

Her eyes flick from my face down my dress, then back up. I'm sure they linger on my lips for a second and feel my butterflies flutter.

"Absolute deal. You look really pretty, by the way."

I can't help but blush. "Thank you, so do you, but you always do."

We hold each other's gaze, fingers still touching. Suddenly a little bell rings, and everyone rises to migrate to the balcony. Gia lets go of my hand, the air feeling cold in comparison to her touch.

The balcony's had all the tables pushed together to make a long one nearly the length of the whole patio. It's been draped in a crisp yellow tablecloth and adorned with colourful floral arrangements and candles. It's breathtaking. Guests are peering around the table, looking for their little name cards. The setup seats 100 guests or so, so it takes a few minutes of shuffling for everyone to get seated.

"Looks like this is us." Gia says, nodding to chairs in the middle of the table. I'm sat opposite Gia, and next to Daniel. My stomach does a somersault, I think it might be time for a drink. As we sit, Gia's little group flock to our right, and I smile to see Brielle and Cassie, who each envelop me in a warm hug and a squeal of excitement.

"No Mandy?" I say, raising and eyebrow at Gia who bites an olive from her martini. I can't help watching as a little juice drips down her lip, remembering where they've been. Her eyes twinkle noticing my gaze, and I quickly clear my throat.

"No, sadly for you not. She's latched onto some rich Russian and is spending New Years with him."

"Shame." I say, unfolding my napkin and placing it on my lap. Gia wiggles her eyebrows at me and laughs.

"I'll bet."

A warm hand touches my shoulder, giving me a fright. I turn to see Daniel, looking like the next James Bond in a perfectly tailored black suit, the front three buttons of his crisp white shirt unbuttoned, his chain just poking out.

"Thought it was only right to sit you two together," he says, pulling out his chair and sitting next to me.

"You spoil us." I say, quickly pouring myself a glass of white from the carafe on the table trying to steady my shaky hand. I'm put off red for life.

Before the starter I walked around the table, snapping as many pictures as I could. As terrified as I am about Daniel and Gia being left alone to talk to one another, I have a job to do. As the courses came out I went into the kitchen to get photos of the food in good light, and then shots of them on the table and being enjoyed. We're now at dessert and my second glass of merlot, and I've never felt so exhausted. Each time I'd return to the table I'd hold my breath, expecting to see Daniel and Gia exchanging stories of me, mouths agape. Luckily no such thing has happened, and I can now sit and relax at the table until the end of dinner. And by relax, I mean monitor the conversation intensely. I take a bite of my lava cake, swimming it in the molten ice cream on my plate. Brielle, Gia and Daniel are all discussing the differences between New York and California, and how excited they are for Gia, who catches my eye and nods at me in thanks. I raise my eyebrows as if to say *I told you so*, and she laughs as she licks the last bit of chocolate sauce off her spoon. I feel something creep up my leg, and glance down to see Daniel's hand rubbing my thigh. I quickly look up, scared Gia will see. Luckily it's concealed by the tablecloth. I sneak a glance at Daniel who's seemingly engrossed in the conversation, despite his hand inching further and further up my leg. I try ignore it, taking a large sip of my water that feels like lead sinking down my throat. I look up and catch eyes with Gia, who's still licking her spoon clean. Daniels grip tightens, now having reached just below my panties. I quickly stand, my chair scraping against the floorboards.

"Sorry, need the loo." I say, scurrying off. I race inside and bolt the lock, resting my head against the door. I try ignore the feeling between my legs, not knowing if it was Daniel's touch or Gia's gaze that triggered it. I go to the sink and let the cold tap cascade down my wrists, trying to cool the fiery blood coursing through my body. A gentle knock taps on the door.

"Just a minute!" I say, rubbing the cold water into my veins.

"It's me!" Daniel says quietly. I feel my pulse race as I unlock the door and peek through.

"Yes?"

313

"Can I come in?"

"Why?"

"Because you looked like a deer in headlights. I just wanted to check if you're ok," he says. I open the door more, letting him in before drying my hands on one of the soft mini towels rolled up on a tray like little buns.

"I'm fine. Just tired, a lot of people." I say, exhaling again. He enters, locking the door again behind him.

"Yep. I know that one."

"Please, you know nearly everyone at that table." I scoff, leaning against the sink. He walks closer, his hands in his pockets. God, he looks incredible tonight.

"I know them, but I don't really know them. I'm glad you're here."

"Well, you don't really know me."

He reaches out, playing with one of my loose strands of hair. "Not yet. But I'd like to."

He leans in, his lips touching mine. I give in to my body, kissing him back, letting my arousal takeover. His hands run down my body, grabbing my ass and squeezing. I break away from him, cupping his cheek in my hand.

"Don't ruin my makeup!" I say, laughing breathlessly. I stifle a squeal as his grip tightens, hoisting me up so I'm sat on the sink, my dress riding up my thighs.

"Course not, I'm saving that for later." He purrs, before his lips meet mine again. I can feel his length harden through his trousers, rubbing against me driving me insane. Suddenly there's a soft knock on the door, and I'm half snapped back to my senses.

"Uh... hello?" I say, trying not to gasp as Daniel rubs against me harder, making me ache for his touch more.

"It's me, you've just been gone a while, wanted to check if you're ok!" Gia says through the door. I practically jump off the sink, landing awkwardly on my heels as I pull down my dress.

"Just coming!" I yell out to Gia. I turn to Daniel, who's smirking behind me, and push him against the wall. "I'm gonna go, you stay in here, and wait for a minute before you leave!" I hiss at him.

"Yes ma'am." He whispers back, as I quickly readjust my hair in the mirror. I open the door and shut it behind me, Gia stood outside.

"Sorry, I just was aware you'd been gone for a while, and was hoping you didn't feel awkward because of..."

"Oh, no, not at all! I just needed a wee and got caught up scrolling on my phone!" I blurt, praying my lipgloss is intact.

"Ok. That's good. I might actually go too then!" She says, reaching for the door.

"Uh, no! Don't!" I say, intercepting her hand.

"Why?" She laughs.

"Because... I'll be lonely if you do!"

"Oh yeah?" She looks down at me, the corners of her mouth tilting up.

"Yeah." I say, pulling her round the other side of the wall hoping Daniel uses this moment to escape. Her body presses against mine, and I look up at her. She looks at me for a moment, before leaning in. I'm taken aback for a second, nearly pulling away, but the more she kisses me the more I remember my feelings for her. She quickly pulls away.

"Sorry. I shouldn't have done that. You're still thinking," she says, wiping her lips with her little finger.

"It's fine. I wasn't lying earlier when I said I missed you."

I peak round the corner of the wall to see Daniel sauntering back to his seat and exhale a sigh of relief. I turn back to Gia. "Look, I'm nearly finished for the night. Let's get a drink" I say, guiding us towards the bar.

CHAPTER 36

It's 11.30 and the bar is heaving. People shout their order across to their friends queuing for a drink, whilst dancing in the middle of the room. Hordes of other people have arrived from Watamu town and neighbouring hotels, the ceiling fans gently spin, doing nothing to cool the heat from everyone's bodies. I finished up shooting by 10 and have allowed myself a couple drinks and many dances as reward. I'm now plonked on one of the sofas, nursing a glass of water looking at the crowd. There's something so fun about people-watching, especially when everyone's having too much fun to notice you staring. I can just make out Gia, Brielle and Cassie by the bar, the multicoloured flashing lights catching her curls as they strobe. I'd danced with them for most of the night but wanting to pace myself decided to sit down for a few minutes, relishing being at the coast with views of the sea. As I take another sip of my water, a long arm holding a little drink comes into view.

"Want company?" Daniel asks, as I take the small glass. I remember it instantly, the lime wedge, pooled golden honey at the bottom and little pestle.

"A dawa!" I say, excitedly setting my water on the floor as he sits next to me, stretching out his long legs. He's taken off his suit jacket now and rolled up the sleeves of his crisp shirt.

"I thought it would be sacrilegious for you to be in Kenya again and not have one," he says, grinding up the lime wedge and the honey, the particles swirling round his drink. I do the same and lift it to my lips, savouring the taste.

"I don't know which I prefer. Utulivu or Tukio."

"Who says you have to have a favourite?"

"Very true." I say, leaning back into the sofa gazing out at the sea.

"Maybe we'll have to get you back to the Mara soon, to experience it as a guest."

"I'd like that." I take another small sip of my drink, admiring the bright moon.

"Tired?"

"A little."

"Ok mopey, it's New Year's Eve. Once the fireworks are done you can go to bed. But for now," he says downing his drink and rising, grabbing one my hands and pulling me to my feet, "You're gonna dance and have fun. Send off the year right."

"You sure I'm the one you wanna dance with?" I gesture to the loud group of scantily clad Italians twirling in the middle of the room.

"The only one," he says, leading me into the pool of people. We dance and dance, and it takes all my willpower not to reach out and touch him in front of everyone. I can tell he's feeling the same, his eyes hungrily flicking down my body as I move.

"It's taking everything I've got right now not to rip that dress off you right here, Wilson," he says, his eyes flashing as if imaging doing it. I giggle, almost wanting him to. But my eyes catch Gia in the distance, and my laughter quickly stops.

"Can we please keep this private, until we know what we're doing" I yell, as he spins me round to ABBA. Once my twirl is finished I land on his chest, his lips just above my head.

"Whatever you want," he squeezes my hand gently. Fuck it, I really want to kiss him. The flashing lights flicking from blue to pink outline each beautiful contour of his face, like he's a Roman statue. I lean closer, but out the corner of my eye see those familiar curls race through the crowd towards the balcony. Gia looks distressed, rubbing the back of her hand against her eyes and my heart pangs.

"I'll be right back." I say to Daniel, squeezing his hand before slipping my way between the dancing bodies to the balcony.

Gia is sat halfway down the steps to the beach, running her hand through her hair, nursing a half-drunk pink daiquiri. I brush some of the sand off the step and sit down quietly next to her.

"Hey."

"Uh, hey." She says, sniffling and quickly dabbing under her eyes.

"Now I'm the one checking on you." I smile, and she forces one in return.

"No need, just came to look at the sea."

"Uh huh." I say, clearly not believing her. We sit in silence, the crashing waves before us nearly overpowering the thumping bass from the party. "How's Carmel?"

"Amazing." She says, a genuine smile twitching at her lips.

"I told you they'd be happy for you."

"I know. You're right. You're always right," she says softly. I gently reach out, squeezing her knee.

"So, tell me what's up. Then I can be right in telling you what to do. You... you helped me so much with Mum. Let me somehow repay you." I say softly. She looks at me, her green eyes glassy and puts her hand on mine, squeezing it back.

"It's honestly silly."

"Not to me. If it's upsetting you, it's upsetting me. I know we're in this weird place, but I still care about you. A lot."

"Alright." Gia takes a deep breath and a glug of her daiquiri. "Well firstly, there's us. I've missed you, and it's been tough having this space. But I won't touch anymore on that as don't want to make you feel shitty, as I know you're going through it too. Secondly, you know I like to keep my private life... private. The industry is weird, and I feel like I'm constantly treading on eggshells with connections, my reputation, all of it. For this new project, I'm playing a lesbian activist from the 90's, and since news of the plot and cast has been released there's been some... backlash," she winces.

"How so?"

"People are saying that I shouldn't be playing this role as I'm taking away opportunities from people in the LGBT community."

"That's ridiculous!" I let out a loud laugh, but Gia turns to me sombrely.

"Yep. But they don't know. They don't know that I'm a part of it, as I wanted to keep a barrier between my work and my personal life. But I guess with this type of job you can't."

"You shouldn't be forced out, but fuck 'em! Who cares what they think. I say you come out the closet holding two middle fingers up! All your friends and family know, so why not everyone else?"

She laughs, twisting one of her curls round her fingers.

"It's just not that simple. Like I said, the industry is weird. America is too. Some places are going backwards, and even though coming out would mean I'd be appropriate for this role, it may cut me off from others. And also fuck 'em! I came out nearly a decade ago to everyone who mattered to me, I don't see why I have to go through it again to the whole world." She takes another sip of her drink, fiddling with the cocktail stirrer.

"I think whatever you do, it'll all be fine. If you don't want to tell the world then don't. But don't not tell the world because you'd worried about acceptance or cutting off other opportunities. The only people and jobs who

323

would cut you off for who you love aren't ones you should want anyway. You're the bravest, strongest person I know. Don't give these shitty, small-minded people the strength to bring you down."

She sighs, looking up to the night sky trying to dry her eyes.

"Yep. You're always right,"

"Although I'm hardly one to talk, as clearly I have no clue what's going on with my sexuality or who I am. Or the backbone to figure it out."

Gia laughs, a single tear painted silver from the moonlight trickling down her cheek. I lean in, gently brushing it away. She looks down, her eyes meeting mine, and I feel electricity run through me. I lean in more, letting her familiar scent envelop me as my lips graze hers. She's still for a moment, but I don't pull away. She slowly kisses me back, running her hand across my cheek to my hair. I know it might not be right, especially now Daniel and I... but I can't deny that there's something between us. Something so strong, so warm, so safe.

"Ok, everyone out for the fireworks now!" The DJ says through the speakers, a cheer rippling through the dance floor. I pull away from Gia, just as the horde of people start pouring out, heading down to the beach to watch. We rise, and I brush the sand from my bum as Gia takes my hand.

"You wanna go watch?" She asks.

People start jostling past us down the steps.

"I actually might stay up here, but you go!"

"Are you sure?" she raises an eyebrow at me.

"Completely. I think I need to be alone."

"Ok. Thank you. For finding me," she says, squeezing my hand before letting it go, joining the crowd walking down the stairs. I find my way back up to the balcony, and walk along it to the very edge, just by the start of the sea. I lean over the rails in the dimly lit corner, looking out to the mass of people below. A loud bang erupts in the sky, and I raise my gaze to see red and green sparkles burst and glimmer against the night. The crowd cheers, illuminated with colourful light from each firework. I can make out couples, holding each other swaying softly with the display. Groups of friends laughing and cheering, clinking their drinks in celebration. Families, hoisting their children into their arms or onto their shoulders for a better view. For some reason, looking out to all these people, all these stories, all these tangible, glowing lives is even more interesting than the fireworks above. I can spy Gia, Cassie, Brielle and the others beaming up at the sky, their faces painted orange then pink then red from the bursts of colour above. I swallow, averting my eyes and looking back to the sky. BANG! A mammoth firework comes next, one of the ones who's prongs fizz out in a million sparkles, like a meteor shower scattered in the sky. The reflection of the fireworks ripples on the waves, making the display look twice as large. Just at the edge of the beach is Daniel, stood talking with his Italian friends. I wonder if he's wondering where I am, if he wanted to kiss me on the countdown. BANG! Pink and white fill the sky and I smile. She loved the pink ones. I squeeze my eyes shut, sending out waves of love as the pink sparkles slowly flutter towards the sea fizzling out. I know she'd be proud. And helpful. I have no clue what to do about Daniel, Gia, my feelings. I wish I could tell her, hear her laugh burst through my flat, tell me what to do. As the sparkles erupt and fall, I imagine each one to be a memory of her, the sea, the span of my life. No matter where I am, she'll always be there, dusted across my moments in memories. I promise myself this, as I gaze up.

CHAPTER 37

"Mount Kilimanjaro!" Cassie bellows, nearly toppling over with conviction.

"Correct!" I say, flipping the card around to show everyone. Gia groans in defeat.

"Another point for moi!" Cassie sings, gleefully rolling the dice. I drain the last of my cocktail, my eyes growing sleepy. I glance to the clock above the bar, 2am; I'm exhausted. We're among the last people standing of the night, and Brielle suggested a board game to round the evening off. That was at 1am, and everyone's still going strong.

"Ok, my turn to read! You fuckers better be ready!" Brielle says, dramatically picking a card.

"I may have to love you and leave you." I say, cracking my neck.

"Noooo!" the girls echo, and we all laugh.

"I don't want to, but I'm so knackered. And need to be somewhat fresh for tomorrow."

Cassie reaches out, squeezing my knee.

"It was so so nice seeing you again, please keep in touch!"

"I will!" I say slowly rising, my back aching from sitting on the floor.

"Do you want me to walk you to your room?" Gia asks. After my second cocktail at around 1.30 I'd told the group about Hugh, and she's hardly let me out her sight since.

"I'm fine, but thank you." I say, squeezing her shoulder. "Find me tomorrow to say bye?"

"Of course. Happy New Year," she says, as the rest of the group coo goodbye.

I savour the walk back to my room, running my fingers along the bushes and palm trunks, as if trying to soak up their essence. I feel a pang of sadness, knowing this may be my last night here ever. Unless something happened with Daniel... or Gia? I shake my head, as if trying to make the very dilemma fall out of one of my ears onto the floor. I drown out my thoughts and focus on the sound of the crickets chirping, the soft crashing of the waves, the small eruptions of laughter behind me from the main building. I stop in my tracks to avoid stepping on a perfect frangipani flower, bending down to pick it up. I lift it to my nose and smell, the fragrance making my heart sing. Someone needs to bottle it. I tuck it behind my ear to carry on, just by my room and gasp.

A trail of frangipani leads from my door, further down the path towards... Daniels room? I feel my heart flutter as I follow them, and sure enough they scatter on down the secluded path, winding between the palm trees all the way to the steps up to his door. I laugh a little, I suppose it could be an accident? They just happened to fall like that? A very strong wind? Or did he really place them all for me to find? Only one way to find out I suppose. I gingerly make my way up his stairs, only lit by the moonlight and gently tap on the door. I can hear the TV on in the background pause, and footsteps towards the door. He opens it and smiles, my heart pounding.

"Hello, you."

"Hi." I gesture to the delicate trail of white petals behind me. "I may have misinterpreted–"

"You didn't."

"I didn't?"

"Would you like to come in?"

"Uh, sure." I say, as he holds open the door. He's still wearing his suit trousers and shirt from earlier, now fully unbuttoned. As I follow him his musky cologne lingers in his wake, making my skin prickle. He steps to the side revealing the coffee table. On it sits a pizza, a bottle of champagne, a bouquet of roses and a bowl of grapes.

"Party for one?"

"I thought, we've not had a chance to have a first date. And didn't want to wait a moment more to do it," he laughs, "I wasted enough of them last year." He sits down, patting the space next to him and I feel my breath catch. All this, for me. From Daniel. I sit next to him, and he pours us each a small glass of champagne.

"Everything is optional, I know it's late. I wasn't sure that you'd want any of it. You're very welcome to take the pizza and fuck off if you're too tired." He offers me the drink, and I accept.

"This is... very sweet. I can't promise I'll stay up long, but I'll do my best. I am flying tomorrow," I say, taking a sip.

"About that," he says, drumming his fingers against his glass. "My plans have changed slightly, and if you wanted to stay on a couple more nights, I'd love the company."

"Really?" I say, swirling the champagne around my mouth.

"Really. And you've got Gia to keep you company too!"

I nearly choke on the bubbles, quickly setting it on the table as I splutter. Daniel laughs and leans over to rub my back.

"You alright?"

"Oh, yeah, of course!" I panic, trying to think of how I can divert Gia from the conversation. "Grapes seem a random choice."

"You don't know the tradition?"

I shake my head, dabbing the corners of my mouth on the back of my hand.

"Technically you're meant to do it on the countdown, but eating twelve on New Year's is meant to bring you good luck, for the next twelve months. Do you fancy it?"

"Twelve in one go?"

"As quickly as you can."

"Ok!"

He places the bowl between us, and we start shovelling them in. On my sixth, we're both in stitches of laughter.

"This is certainly one of the weirder first dates I've been on!" I try say, my mouth full.

"You can't stop!" Daniel splutters as I laugh so I hard I can't possibly eat anymore. I hold my hands over my mouth, trying to swallow the sweet flesh between giggles.

"I can't!" I splutter, feeling some pulp land on my hand. I take a deep breath, trying to swallow both my laughter and the grapes. "Six will surely do?"

"Let's make it seven, just in case," says Daniel, picking up a last green grape and holding it to my lips.

"Lucky seven. Sounds good," I say, leaning forward, letting him feed it to me. My lips linger around is fingers for a second, and I sense his breath go ragged. As I chew, he gently grazes a thumb across my lips.

"It's worrying that if anything I find you more attractive shovelling in grapes on my sofa."

I feel my cheeks flush at his gaze, like he's staring into my soul. Really seeing me.

"That is a little worrying," I rasp, suddenly aware of how much I want him. I reach out, gripping his crisp shirt pulling him towards me. The bowl topples to the floor, the soft patter of grapes hitting the carpet. We ignore it as he leans in closer, our lips finally meeting. I'm timid at first, softly pressing mine against his. But once he flicks his tongue across mine hunger erupts in my core, and I kiss him faster, harder, gasping at the feeling. He tastes like dry wine and sweet grapes, I can't get enough.

I rip off his shirt, running my hands along the muscular ridges of his back, feeling them ripple as his arms run up and down my body. His kiss grazes down from my lips to my neck and I can barely breathe as he tears the straps of my dress off my shoulders, my dress down to my navel. Everything feels animalistic, like we're both aware that the months of building passion between us that have led us to here. To where neither of us can take it anymore. He kisses down and down, past my sensitive nipples which he halts at to suck, grazing his teeth against them making a shiver run down my back. Further down to where my dress now sits, which he pulls lower until I'm lying on his sofa in nothing but my panties. He almost growls at the sight of them, ripping them off in one fast motion before resuming his kisses. His lips glid further down, and he gently spreads my legs, hoisting my right one over his shoulder while the left dangles off the sofa. And then he devours me. He starts softly, his tongue as light as a feather, gently flicking up and down, making me ache for more.

"Please!" I beg again, barely able to make the words, desperate for more. He softly chuckles, and then slides his tongue up me, stopping at my clit and pressing down. I writhe at the sudden sensation, my whole body on fire, and he holds me in place as he continues, before letting out a moan.

"You taste exactly how I imagined."

I moan even harder, at the thought of him imaging me, us, this. I feel his fingers travel down from where they'd been firmly gripping my waist, until they meet his mouth. He slowly slips them inside me as his tongue circles my clit, and I can feel the eruption building. I'm sure he can sense it to, my squirming under him, panting and moaning at the feeling. Just as I feel the wave nearly crash over me, he recoils chuckling. I look up at him dazed and confused. He kisses his way up my body again, and as he presses his body against mine I can feel his bulge against his suit trousers.

"We're not nearly done yet." He says breathlessly, kissing my neck as he undoes his belt with his left hand. I hungrily help him, pulling his trousers down and gasp at the length of him. His fingers graze me again, as he positions himself to enter. It's driving me insane, having to wait to feel him.

"Please, Daniel." I pant.

"Say my name again." He purrs into my ear.

"Daniel." I gasp at the stretch as he plunges into me. I feel myself melt into him as he powerfully thrusts into me, every hair on my body prickling up at the sensation. I can't think, can't talk, can only feel me and him and what he's doing to me. He gently cups the back of my neck with his left hand, as his right grips my ass for leverage as he pushes in deeper, and I feel my eyes roll back in my skull in pleasure and pain. I feel the familiar wave crash over me, and shake at the release, feeling myself grip tighter around him as I climax, Daniel catching my moan with a deep kiss.

After we'd made love on the sofa for what felt like both an eternity and a millisecond, forever yet not long enough, Daniel scooped me up and carried me into bed. I'd fallen asleep just as the sky was turning a light lilac, the mesh white curtains billowing softly against the ocean breeze.

It's just gone 11am, and I'm wearily peeling myself away from the warmth of his body in our cocoon of sheets. He holds my hand, shielding his eyes from the light with his arm. "Stay!" Daniel groans, and I laugh, kissing his forehead.

"Let me go do my last edit. Send it off to Maria. And then we have the next two days, all to ourselves" And Gia. I bat the thought from my mind, trying to stay focused on the present.

I quietly pad through to the living area, mouth agape. I wasn't aware we'd caused such a mess. The carpet is strewn with green grapes, some smushed onto the sofa by I'm guessing our bodies. I quickly grab my dress and slip it on, scooping up as many grapes as I can and tipping them into the bowl. I grab our hardly touched champagne glasses and tip them down the sink, leaving them in there and whacking the bottle in the fridge. I see an old T shirt of Daniels splayed over one of the chairs and throw it on over my dress to try cover up the walk of shame from any staff or guests who may see me on my short walk back. Just as I reach the door, the pizza box catches my eye, and I decide to grab a slice for the journey. I shut the door behind me, high heels in my satchel, pizza in hand and make my way down the steps. I feel so giddy with glee I feel like I could float down them. The frangipani flowers must've been blown away by the morning breeze, as only a handful of little ivory petals remain in their place. I'm just making my way past the small wooden fence lined in shrubs, about a minute from my room when I hear my name.

"Maddie!"

Gia waves, from the other side of the fence. I nearly drop my pizza in shock and press my body against it, hoping she can't see the bottom of my dress peeking out below the t shirt. Thank God it's a plain white one so she can't tell it's his. "Hey!"

"Happy New Year!"

"You too!"

"You just been with Daniel?" she smiles, gesturing towards the remote path I've emerged from. Shit. I hope I don't smell like him. Or sex.

"Uh, yeah, just going over final notes before I'm off!"

"I was just gonna drop by to see him, but we could grab brunch first if you're hungry, Mrs. Workerbee."

"Oh, I'd love to, maybe dinner? Really gotta get this work done!" I scramble, edging myself further along the fence away from her while still trying to conceal my dress.

"Uh, Ok, text Brielle or Cassie and they'll keep me posted!" She says, making her way to the small gate at the corner towards Daniel's hut.

"Will do! Gotta dash!" I bolt out of Gia's view just as she exits the gate, dashing to my door and fumbling with the key. The door finally yields and I pour in, stumbling onto the bed. I can't help but feel laughter ripple through my belly and escape out my lips. I'm not sure if it's the adrenaline, or the attention, or the fact I've never really had anyone amazing like me before. And now I have two, at once. The laughter subsides as the guilt creeps through me, and I place a hand to my head feeling my heart race. I'm single, I'm not cheating on anyone. But maybe I'm not being fair to anyone either. I have to speak to someone, get another view before I go crazy. Mum would be the person, I know she wouldn't judge me. She'd listen, she'd laugh, she'd lecture. Mum's not here, but Anya is. And although my stomach drops about the idea of telling her about Gia, I've clutched onto this secret long enough. And if I don't talk to someone soon, I feel like it might consume me from the inside out.

CHAPTER 38

"I cannot fathom why you sat on this for so long – it's major!" Anya wails, cupping her forehead in her palm.

"I know, I'm sorry, I just… wasn't even sure if I was into women–"

"Mate! No! I mean she's like a major celebrity!"

"Oh. I guess that too. You don't think it's a big deal that… she's a girl?"

"God, Maddie, what do you think of me?! I've been to bloody pride! Multiple times!"

I laugh, maybe I'd overthought it. "That's true. I guess I was just scared it might change my whole identity to you. And everyone"

"Maddie, I love you, but you're loopy. It's 2024, no one cares who you fancy! I think you kept this to yourself for so long that you dug a massive hole and ended up getting stuck in it."

"That might be true. I just thought I was too old to… change orientation" I huff, fiddling with the zipper of my hoody.

"Jesus, you sound like you're straight out of the Women's Institute. I had an aunt who realised she liked fanny at 57." I wince, and Anya laughs. "I'm sorry, but you're a real muppet for not telling me."

"I know. I'm sorry. I got in my own head; you know what I'm like. And now I just don't know what to do. Or who to pick."

Anya bites her lip. "Well, Gia has always been lovely with you. Daniel was a bit of a prick but sounds like he's done a 180. Did he ever say why he acted how he did?"

"Vaguely... I think he assumed it wouldn't work and didn't want the pain of starting something that wouldn't last."

"Hmmm. It is very tricky. My advice, is refrain from doing anything physical with either of them until you know which one of them you want. And then kindly tell the other one at some point so there are no secrets."

"That sounds very smart, and very healthy."

"I do pride myself on being smart and healthy."

"So, nothing physical. Make my decision. Tell the other. All's well that ends well."

"Exactly, easy!"

"Right... easy..."

I spent the rest of the day holed up in my room, half editing photos, half wallowing in self-pity. I know Anya's right, I know I have to choose. And soon. But I genuinely don't know who I want. Gia is so ethereal, so warm, so caring. But this sudden thing with Daniel, something I never thought would even materialize... and now it's here, passionate, tempting. God, I get shivers just thinking back to last night. And this morning. I close my laptop, staring up to the ceiling fan, watching it spin lazily. I'd rescheduled both Daniel and Gia who'd both asked to see me today, telling them I was busy with work. But I know I can't avoid seeing them tomorrow, so that means I should really choose tonight.

My head pounds, and I rub it till I can feel it go red. I need to get out of this room. I've been holed up here all day surviving off room service fries and mini fridge cola and feel like a fat lard. I feel like all the garbage has got me in a daze, I need to clear my head. It's just gone 11, the pool's probably closed. But I do suppose I know the owner, and just imagining diving into the cool water under the stars already sends a chill through me. It's exactly what I need, somewhere quiet, to think and analyse everything. I slip through my mosquito net and put on my beige string bikini, one of my more revealing ones I've been too shy to wear so far. But luckily no one will see.

I quietly open the gate to the pool, careful not to make any noise. To avoid detection, I've refrained from using my phone torch, and thanks to the near full moon everything is lit with a faint silver sheen, helping guide my way. I pad across the cool stones by the pool and place my phone and towel down on one of the loungers. I spend a moment taking everything in, so still, so quiet. There's no breeze tonight, and the pool provides a perfect mirror to the sky above, almost milky with clusters of stars. The silhouettes of the palm trees stand tall and dark above me, and I can't help but imagine what it might be like living here. With Daniel. But then with that logic there was magical Carmel with Gia. And I can't pick who I want to be with based on what holiday destination I'd get. I stretch and run my fingers through my hair. I can't think about them anymore, I need a moments peace. I dive into the pool, the shock of the cold water waking up every cell in my body. I splutter to the surface shivering, sad to see the mirror now disrupted by a thousand ripples.

"It's pretty cold without the sun on it, huh!"

Her voice makes me jump, and I let out a little shriek before clamping my hand over my mouth. "Hello?"

"It's me, idiot!" I see her lazily wave from a lounger across the pool, and I kick myself for not instantly recognising that voice.

"Oh. Sorry, you scared me!" I say, treading water. Probably the last person I want to see now. Especially draped over a sun lounger, wearing a skimpy bikini, curls falling around her face, her whole body lit by puddles of moonlight. I gulp, and make my way to the edge, clinging on for leverage. Suddenly my muscles feel weak. She gently dog ears her book and sets it on the floor before rising.

"Finally done with work?"

"Uh, yeah," I stumble, "didn't wanna waste the pool and not use it."

"Even though it's closed." she laughs, striding towards me.

"Well, you're complicit." I tease, as she sits on the edge next to me, dangling her long legs in the water, letting out a gasp at the cold as she submerges them. My mind flicks back to the other times I've heard her gasp and electricity pounds through me. I quickly dunk myself underwater, trying to rid myself of the feeling, keep a clear head. Nothing. Physical. I come up panting and Gia laughs.

343

"You're such a water baby. You really oughtta live by the sea."

"Maybe one day."

She leans back, tilting her head up to the sky, the moon illuminating her bikini top, the line of her abs, her soft hair. I clear my throat. "How come you're here?"

"Wanted to look at the stars and have a dip, same as you."

She slides off the edge and plunges into the pool, a loud splash following her. She immediately emerges panting, "JESUS CHRIST! IT'S FUCKING COLD!" she shrieks, and we both roar with laughter.

"Hello?" A hotel guard calls from afar, flashing a torch towards the pool, scanning around the area.

"Shit!" Gia winces. I shush her and we huddle together, still as statues in the pool. The flashlight flicks around us, as if it's a spotlight and we're escaped convicts. I can feel my heart pounding, or maybe it's Gia's seeing as we're so close. After a moment of holding our breath, the guard grows bored, flicks off his light and saunters away.

"That was close!" I pant, finally letting out air. We both try muffle our laughter, causing little waves to ripple around us with the convulsions of our bellies. I feel a slight breeze pick up, biting at my bare skin. Gia rubs her shoulders next to me, and I can see little silver goosebumps rise on her arms.

"When did it get so cold?"

"I think the adrenaline from that fucked us. Race you to the other end to warm up?" she asks, her eyes flickering mischievously.

"A very. Quiet. Race."

"Agreed!"

"Three, two, one!" we both say before gingerly peeling off the wall trying to doggy paddle as fast and as silently as we can till the other end. We're nearly neck and neck, until Gia stretches out a long arm, fingers just grazing the edge of the pool.

"I– win–!" she splutters, trying not to sink. I finally join her at the edge, and we both cling to the cool stone for a moment, bodies panting.

"I can't remember the last time I raced someone." I giggle, rubbing water from my eyes with my right hand.

"Me neither. We should do it more often!" Gia says, hoisting herself over the side. I look up to her, her head framed by the palm leaves and stars above. It could be a painting. She holds out an arm, and my slippery fingers grab it. She pulls me over the edge and I land with a wet splat, which makes us giggle more.

"Ow!"

"Sorry! I thought you'd have a bit more upper body strength!" she laughs, chucking a towel at me as she plonks down on a lounger. I dab myself dry, hairs pricking against the breeze and sit on the lounger next to her's. "I think the stars here are nearly as good as the Mara, I saw a shooting one earlier," says Gia softly. I squint, looking up at the cloak of black above us. We lie still for a few moments, eyes on the sky, as the ripples of the pool settle.

"There, see!?" Gia jolts up, gripping my arm and pointing up with her other hand. I lean in and follow her fingers, and sure enough see a little fleck of light zip across the sky.

"Oh my God!" I breathe out, my eyes widening.

"Maybe you were meant to come down to the pool tonight. Meant to see it. Maybe it's her." Gia says quietly. I feel my eyes pool up, making all the constellations I can see double. One escapes me, rolling down my cheek, and Gia catches it with her finger. "Sorry, I didn't mean to…"

"You're so lovely." I say, tilting my head up to hers. I feel that pull between us, just like in Carmel, and just like the day we very first met. And I give in. I feel myself lean forward, our lips softly grazing, and then crashing together. My hands run through her wet hair, down her neck, across her breasts. She lets out a gasp as they creep further to her bottoms, running my fingers across the material. She kisses me back harder as I roll on top of her, legs straddling either side of her hips. My fingers slip inside the fabric, stroking her, savouring her warmth and her wetness. Gia lets out a loud groan which makes my spine tingle, and her hand reaches between my legs, pushing aside the small strip of fabric concealing me, her fingers circling my core. It sends shivers down my spine, and I can barely keep enough concentration to keep touching her as she slips her fingers inside, making me tremble on top of her.

Gia walked me back to my room, but I told her I needed the night alone in case Maria called in a crisis. A lie, but I felt I had to draw the line somewhere. I'd already failed the one rule I'd set myself, given in to my lust. On entering my room, I feel that familiar pang of guilt stab my stomach, seeing a blue glass vase overflowing with fresh frangipani on my bedside table.

No need to check the little letter this time to know who they're from. I'd practically raced to the shower, as if trying to rid myself of my sins. The water was far too hot, my skin dappled in pink streaks from the boiling stream, but I needed something to distract me. I'd slipped into my sheets naked, savouring the crisp feel against my skin and fallen into a fitful slumber made up of dreams of Daniel and Gia, pondering which fig to pluck from the tree. At 3am I bolted up, drenched in sweat, but somehow smiling. I think I know.

CHAPTER 39

I groggily rub my eyes, squinting from the bright puddles of morning light leaking in through the curtains. Ten more minutes, then I'll properly wake up. Face the day, and my decision. My phone buzzes on the nightstand, but I ignore it, burying my face in the soft pillow. Buzz. Ignore. Buzz. Ignore. Buzz, buzz, buzz. Jesus Christ. I flip over, fumbling for it, trying to wake up as little as possible. Maybe there really is a Maria crisis. My fingers finally meet its cool metal, and I slip it back through the mosquito net, the buzzing still relentless. I try focus my sleepy eyes on the bright screen, I've got over 50 notifications. What the fuck? Anya, Instagram, Daniel, girls from Uni and school I hardly ever speak to...

I storm through the lobby still in my pyjamas, seeing red. I'd tried Gia's room first, pounding on the door like a maniac. Cassie had answered half asleep, and told me she might be at breakfast. I didn't consider then that she could've been hiding her from me.

"Morning Ms. Wilson!" Rita beams at me from reception. She's talking to a glamorous Kenyan woman, wearing oversized tortoiseshell sunglasses and a white flowing kaftan. I muster the strength to smile back at them, before scouring the bar for Gia. Not here. I look through the arch to the dining area, no Gia. I'm sure I see a young couple look at me and then whisper something, and quickly turn on my heel out to the balcony. And there they fucking are. Those deceitful curls, blowing gracefully in the wind down by the sea. I race down the steps to the beach, tumbling down the last one, the sand catching my landing. I scrape the bottom of my hand on the railing, catching myself, but don't let it slow me down. Once I'm a few feet away from her, the waves crashing around us, I feel it all pour out of me.

"You fucking bitch!" I shriek at her. She turns slowly to face me, her eyes red and puffy. I don't care. She betrayed me.

"I'm guessing you saw." She croaks, defeated.

"Yes. I saw. And Anya saw, Maria saw, Daniel saw, about half the fucking world saw. I have 20 thousand new followers, and counting."

"I guess... maybe it could be good for your photography work?" She sniffles. I scoff, feeling the tears of anger start tumbling down my cheeks.

"I had to turn off my comments. Your little army were in there, talking about me as if I'm not really a person. Saying that I turned you gay, that I took you from them and ruined you, that I'm not pretty enough for you, too fat for you, too normal for you."

"What happened to your hand?"

"You had no right. I just don't understand. We didn't even know what we were, and you told the whole world? What, for good PR? Is that all I ever was? A PR move?"

"No, Maddie, no! I didn't want this to... I didn't choose this."

"Then who did, huh? How'd they get the photos? Break into your apartment?" I say, showing her the article on my phone. It's the front page of The Daily Mail, *"Hollywood Bombshell Gia Tucci Shocks the World with Lesbian Lover!"* The photos we'd taken the night after The Bureau plastered underneath the headline. "You had no right."

"I know. I'm sorry, I promise I didn't know!"

"How could you not know?"

"I sent my team a bunch of photos for potential posts, I shouldn't have included those ones. I just thought if we ended up... Anyway, they had access to them. And yesterday those stories about me and the new project were picking up traction, so they panicked. And they leaked them."

"You expect me to believe that?"

"I promise it's the truth, I really do!" She reaches a hand out to me, and I recoil.

"Fucking liar." I spit at her, turning back to the hotel.

"Maddie, please! I promise I didn't do this!" She begs after me. I can feel my blood boil, my heart pound. I've never felt so betrayed, so humiliated, so used.

Daniel sits before me on his small balcony, brow furrowed looking at his phone. After seeing Gia I'd called Anya, who luckily answered right away. I bawled to her for a good hour, wishing I could be home in London, instead of having to be here with her, with Daniel. Poor Daniel. I told him everything… well nearly everything. I told him about what happened with Gia, up to San Francisco. I know it might be wrong, hiding from him what me and her did here last night, but my heart can't take anymore stress right now. And he sat and listened. I could tell it hurt him, the way his jaw feathered, the way his smile sank. One of his childhood friends, and the girl he likes. Or maybe liked. I bite the loose skin around my thumb, a habit I grew out of in school which has suddenly reared its nasty head again. I'm snapped back to the present when he softly pushes my hand from my mouth, I hadn't realised I'd drawn blood.

"Here, let me get you a bandage."

"Oh, don't worry, it's only tiny!"

"For the other one…" he says, pointing at the dried cut along my right palm. Oh yes, the railing. I smile at him in thanks as he rises, looking out to the sea. How did such a small work trip to Kenya all those months ago turn into such a life altering event. I haven't checked my Instagram since this morning, but my face was splattered all over gossip magazines and fan pages. Anya assured me it will pass, some other celebrity gossip will happen and people will forget. I hope she's right. Daniel emerges with a roll of gauze and antiseptic wipes and kneels on the floor before me.

"I can do it, sorry, I'm sure you want to get me out your hair."

Daniel looks up at me, and gently pinches my chin between his thumb and forefinger. "I think you've already been through quite enough for one day. It's ok, I understand. You had every right to do whatever you wanted, with whoever you wanted. You didn't owe me anything, not after how I'd treated you."

I feel a lump grow in my throat, guilt pitting in my stomach thinking about being with Gia just last night. At least now I know, Daniel. I choose Daniel.

"Now, this is going to sting," he says, softly cupping my hand in his, grazing the antiseptic wipes over the cut. If anything I wish it'd sting more, a distraction from all the guilt and pain wringing my innards. He delicately wraps the gauze around it, and plants a kiss in my palm. I feel all my thoughts nearly melt away.

"So, here's what we're going to do, Wilson. You're going to go to your room and pack your bag. Then you're going to meet me at reception later, and we'll spend the night at one of the other hotels, before I take you to the airport tomorrow. And I'll see how my calendar's looking, and if I can spare a trip to London in the next couple weeks. Oh, and don't get that wet," he says, gently tapping my palm. I laugh, feeling my eyes well up.

"Thank you."

He kisses my forehead before taking my non-injured hand and guiding me to my feet towards the door. "Now get packing. Big night later!"

I walk back to my room feeling lighter, a weight lifted off me. I choose Daniel.

CHAPTER 40

I manically threw the contents of my closet into my suitcase, not bothering to fold anything. Gia had obviously given up on her detox as she'd tried to text me, but I'd blocked her as soon as I saw the first message this morning. She was relentless, having room service deliver pizza, champagne, and a note to my door. I'd snorted at the apology letter, barely reading it before I tore it up. It's now just approaching 6pm, and I've polished off the half the champagne and three quarters of the pizza. I'm now floating around my room, trying to figure out which dress to wear tonight. Something sexy? Classy? I'm not sure of the vibe of the new hotel. All I know is that Gia won't be there, and that's good enough for me. I flop on the bed, trying to ignore the pain in my chest and be happy. I am happy, right?

I decided on a flowy white dress, inspired by the glamorous woman I saw at the front desk earlier. Just as I manage to get my case zipped up, I hear my phone buzz. It can't be anymore articles as I blocked notifications for everything but close friends. I pounce on my bed to read it, feeling slightly giddy from the champagne. It's from Daniel.

"Sorry, work came up, rain check. Will make it up to you. Get tucked up in bed and order everything you want from room service."

I scowl at my phone, heart thumping. How important could his work be? He bloody runs the place? He's seriously going to bail on my last night? No. I won't take it. I'd rather sit next to him and watch him work than be alone. I try call him, no answer. I make my way up the little path, Bird of Paradise flowers swishing in the twilight around me, but when I reach his room all the lights are off. I knock on the door, still hopeful, my golden bangles jangling down my arm. No answer. I huff out a puff of air, running my hand through my hair. Am I being crazy, looking for him this hard?

My last shot is reception to see if they know anything. I'm too scared of running into Gia to check the pool or the beach. Gia. I feel that same stab of betrayal and longing in my gut and try push her out my mind. Gia is done. She used me. I make my way to reception and spy Rita tapping away at the computer.

"Hey! Still working?"

"Just for one more hour," she says, smiling.

"That's nice! I was just wondering, have you seen Daniel this evening? Or know where he is?"

"Mr. Kimani?" she asks raising an eyebrow.

"Yes!"

"Ma'am, I believe he's having dinner with his wife." she says, gesturing to the restaurant.

"Wife?" I laugh. She's funny!

"Yes, she arrived this morning, earlier than expected."

I feel a lump form in my throat. She's surely just joking. Or there'll be an explanation. "Would you like me to leave a message?"

"Um, no it's fine. I'll find him," I say, barely nodding goodbye at her before I'm up the stairs approaching the restaurant arch. I stand behind it concealed, scanning the room. And there they are, nestled at the back. Daniel, and the glamorous woman I saw at the front desk earlier. That doesn't prove anything. It could still be a joke. A misunderstanding. I smooth out my dress and casually make my way over. As soon as Daniel sees me his smile sinks, and so does my heart.

"Hi." I say dryly as I reach the table. Daniel looks like he's seen a ghost.

"Hi." he says hoarsely.

358

"Hello!" the woman turns to me, smiling. My heart cracks seeing how beautiful she is. There's an awkward silence, and she looks between Daniel and I expectantly. Daniel clears his throat.

"This is Maddie Wilson, she's been taking photos for the new website."

"Oh lovely!" the woman smiles sweetly. Almost sickly sweet.

"And this is Nuru, my uh, wife."

"Your wife. Lovely to meet you." I say, sticking my hand out to shake hers. I can feel my palms sweat, and if I thought my blood was boiling earlier it's absolutely molten now. Daniel watches, his eyes sullen, barely able to look at me. "Well, I just wanted to find you to come say goodbye, I'm off tonight and wanted to wish you the best. I hope you're pleased with the website."

"I'm sure I will be. Are you sure you don't want to stay and enjoy one more night–"

"No thank you, Mr. Kimani. That's very kind, but I think I've seen quite enough of Utulivu for a lifetime."

Nuru laughs awkwardly, taken aback by the statement. I don't care. I turn and stride back to reception as quick as I can, ignoring the curdling champagne and pizza in my gut. I brace my hands on the cool counter and look up to Rita. "Can you organise me a cab. To take me to one of the other hotels on the beach." I say through gritted teeth.

"Uh, yes ma'am. For when, and which hotel?"

"For now. And any of them."

I spent my last night in Kenya alone, in an unfamiliar hotel with unfamiliar people. I ate at the restaurant, the glowing orange dot of Utulivu glimmering just above the shore in the distance. I thought of the two people inside it I thought I knew, who turned out to be bigger strangers than the family on the table next to me. I barely ate my ravioli, pushing it around the plate, ghosts of what could have been plaguing me, erasing my appetite. When I turned in for the night, I didn't even bother unpacking my pyjamas, feeling too numb or too tired. Maybe both. I lay awake under the mosquito net, watching the ceiling fan whirl and whirl, waiting for it to be morning. My eyes were still open as the sun started seeping through the gaps in the curtain. And then I gathered up my bags, and I left.

CHAPTER 41

I've been back for three weeks, and London has never felt colder. Maybe because of all those months in the sun, or maybe because of that sliver of warmth in me that died when the two people who I thought I might love betrayed me. But life goes on, and I'm happy to be back. At least there aren't any ghosts of them in London to haunt me, places we went together, or memories made. It's a clean slate. Aside from Gia's face, which happens to be plastered on every other bus it seems.

I deleted all my dating apps on my second day back and decided to choose me. And a new bunny, I thought even though I'm to stay single forever I needn't curse Sprout to the same fate. And it's peaceful. So peaceful, so quiet. Work with Maria. Dinners with Anya and friends. Takeaways for one. I can't help but sometimes think it's too peaceful, wonder if maybe I wasn't built for peace. There was something so electrifying about it all, I suppose until the lighting struck and demolished everything in its path. Perhaps including me. So now I'm enjoying– or trying to enjoy my peaceful lunch at work. I can hear Maria cackling in her office, on the phone to her daughter, as I shovel down Fortnum and Mason's

Caesar salad. We finished off Daniel's site on the first week back, luckily as I'd done a good chunk of it while I was there. Maria was proud, and said she'll think if there are any upcoming jobs abroad she'd feel comfortable sending me on. To be honest I don't know if that would help, or just tear off the scab before the wound has properly healed. But I suppose that isn't up to me. I set my salad aside, picking up the rogue leaf that fell on my leg and tossing it in the bin. Cracking my neck, I swivel my desk chair round and head back to the never-ending inbox and spreadsheets.

It's just gone seven, and I finally decide to head home. Maria left two hours ago, trying to usher me out with her to no avail. I shut my laptop and slip it into my crisp tote. I decided to replace my satchel as it held too many memories of everything. It now sits banished in a drawer, among the clothes I bought in America and my fleece from Nairobi.

I flick off my desk lamp, chuck the rest of my salad in the bin and bundle up in my trusty leopard coat. Just as I'm locking the door my phone buzzes, and I scramble to keep my tote from slipping down my arm as I dig for it. Exactly why I was a satchel girl. It's Anya.

"Hello?"

"Hey!" she sounds frantic, unlike her.

"Hey… you ok?" I say as I make my way down the long flight of stairs.

"Yeah, yeah, good, you?"

"Yep, all good."

"So, what are you doing now?"

"I was gonna head home and veg out, you wanna join? We could get Chinese?"

"Yeah, maybe! I'm actually in town right now, do you fancy meeting me by Piccadilly Circus?"

"Uh, sure, it's right by the office… Why?"

"Haven't been in ages and just fancy it!"

I'm finally at the bottom and jump down the last step towards the large iron door. "Strange. But ok. I'll be there in 10."

"Ok, love you, bye!"

"Bye!" I tuck the phone in my pocket just as I burst through the door, a billow of cold making my ears chill.

I walk through the streets approaching Piccadilly Circus, one in a sea of people. I'll never understand why they don't leave the Christmas lights up in January, it feels like such a stark contrast to merry December, almost like it's a totally different city. In January everyone's either sober, or fatter, or poorer. A lot of the time, all three. We could use what little joy we can get, even if it's from dinky LED lights. As I approach Piccadilly Circus the crowd seems larger than normal, packed with tourists taking photos of the billboards. My cold fingers fumble around my pocket for my phone, so numb I can barely feel its icy screen. I scoop it out and call Anya, who answers after the first ring.

"Hey, I'm here, where are you?"

"Look up."

"What?"

"Look up!" Anya squeals and hangs up. What is she on about? I look up to the grey blanket of cloud, nothing out of the ordinary. But as my eyes scan down I see it. And my heart stops. On the biggest panel of the Piccadilly Circus billboard, the one usually occupied by Coca Cola is a message. I cling onto the pole of scaffolding next to me to steady myself. It reads:

"M – I'm sorry. I really didn't know, but I should've done more. I think I love you. Pls hear me out – G x"

My phone pings, a message from Anya. I can barely read it, my left hand still firmly gripping the scaffolding, my knuckles going white. *"She's at mine. Brian and I are going out for dinner. She's cooking something that smells good, at least come and see what she has to say. Or what she's cooking. I really like her."* I squeeze my eyes firmly, fighting the tears that want to pour out of them. An American family push past, "I hope M forgives G momma! It's so romantic!" Their little girl squeals.

I can't help but feel something turn in my belly, relief... or excitement? Another message from Anya. *"I seriously cannot believe Gia Tucci is in my living room!"* I laugh, releasing my grip from the cool metal pole to dab my eyes. I text Anya back as I walk, *"I'll be there at 8.30."*

I increase my pace, dodging and weaving through the tourists, anxious to get home. I need a shower.

CHAPTER 42

I pant up the stairs, sweaty palm clutching the smooth wooden banister. I'm practically running to get in, just because I'm mad at her doesn't mean I don't want to look good. And maybe I was harsh on her at the beach, she looked just as upset as I did. And I'd blocked her straight away, not letting her fight her case. But she did still betray my trust, and I mustn't let one outrageously romantic gesture outweigh that. I'm one floor below mine and I slow down to catch my breath, surprised my perfume still smells this good. As I climb higher, the floral scent grows stronger, and stronger, until I reach my landing, and my eyes boggle at the sight. Clustered around my door are nearly 30 flower arrangements, all beautiful and detailed, some containing orchids, peonies, roses... but all containing frangipanis. This couldn't be Gia too, could it? I gently move the flowers, creating a path for me to unlock my door.

It took about ten minutes to delicately carry each bouquet in, and ten more to figure out where to put them all. As I'd carried in the last one, I spotted a letter tucked amongst the petals. I'd needed a moment before opening it, and here it now sits, on my kitchen counter. And here I sit, all dressed up, not knowing where to go.

Dear Maddie,

I hope you don't find this offensive or tacky. It felt more offensive and more tacky to just send you one bouquet, so I settled for thirty.

I can't apologise enough for how we left things, or how I handled our whole relationship - or you'd call what we shared.

Like I said, I knew from the moment we met that I wanted you. Needed you. The reason I stopped myself and was so distant from the get-go was my marriage. Nuru and I wed three years ago, it was my father's dying wish. Her family own a lot of land and country clubs, and our business wasn't bringing in enough to stay afloat the way it was. I should've told you from the beginning, but I was so utterly embarrassed. I tried to fight my feelings for you every moment, but they just kept growing stronger and my willpower weaker.

I want to assure you, Nuru and I are both fully aware that it is a marriage of convenience, I would never do anything to hurt her. She is a dear friend, and I know she will understand. If you'll let me explain properly, I've flown into London today and am staying in Chelsea. I've booked us a table at Roka at 9. I'd love it if you'd join me. But you also deserve to stand me up a few times, so no worries if you don't.

I have the upmost respect and love for you and hope maybe one day you could say the same about me.

Yours entirely,

Daniel

So here I am once again, a girl with two paths, two options, two lives. And not a clue which one to choose.

Acknowledgements

Firstly, thank you to you, the reader, for getting this far. This novel is, at its heart, a love letter to Kenya, the country where I grew up. *Seventy Six Sunsets* is my way of sharing my favourite corners of it with the world. The concept for the story came to me while I was back in Kenya on holiday in 2022 - a tiny spark of an idea that, two years later, has grown into a full novel. I can hardly believe that the seed of inspiration I found on Watamu Beach has blossomed into something I can now share with you all. I hope the landscapes, the people, and the spirit of Kenya come alive through these pages, just as they have lived in my heart.

I would like to express my deepest gratitude to my mum, Katie, and my dad, Adam. Your unwavering love, encouragement, and belief in me have been the foundation upon which this book was built. Thank you for always pushing me to be the best version of myself, both as a writer and as a person.

I am also incredibly grateful to the *National Film and Television School (NFTS)* for providing me with the tools and guidance to grow as a writer.

To my fellow writer friends, thank you for your constant support, encouragement, and for reading through the countless drafts I sent you at ungodly hours. Court, Izzy, Liv, Lyndon, Niky. Your feedback has been crucial in shaping the story into what it is today.

A special thank you to my long-time friends, Georgia, Sophie, Lea, Jamie, whose friendship and support have been an endless source of inspiration. You've been a constant in my life, always there to lift me up, offer advice, or simply listen. This book is as much yours as it is mine.

A massive thank you to Lyam for creating such a beautiful cover, and dealing with me being constantly indecisive.

This book also carries a reminder to never be afraid of who you are or what you want, even when the path ahead seems uncertain. I hope this story encourages anyone who reads it to step into their truth, to love who they love, and to pursue their dreams without hesitation.

Lastly, to everyone who has believed in me, cheered me on, and shared this journey in any way - thank you. Your love and support mean the world.

I look forward to starting the sequel, and continuing Maddie's journey.

Printed in Great Britain
by Amazon

50698014R00207